There Ain't
No Justice

There Ain't
No Justice
James Curtis

With an introduction by Martin Knight

LONDON BOOKS CLASSICS

LONDON BOOKS
39 Lavender Gardens
London SW11 1DJ
www.london-books.co.uk

First published 1937 by Jonathan Cape
This edition published by London Books 2014

A catalogue record for this book
is available from the British Library

ISBN 978-0-9568155-3-8

Printed and bound by CPI Group (UK) Ltd
Croydon, CR0 4YY

Typeset by Octavo Smith Publishing Services in Plantin 10.5/13.5
www.octavosmith.com

INTRODUCTION

There Ain't No Justice was the third novel by James Curtis, hitting the bookstalls in 1937 and following on from the commercial and critical success of his debut and second novels *The Gilt Kid* and *You're In The Racket Too*. The next year (1938) *They Drive By Night*, Curtis' most famous work, would be released and that, along with *There Ain't No Justice*, was committed to celluloid within a matter of months. James Curtis was on an extraordinary roll – his momentum only to be interrupted by and eventually lost after the Second World War.

The book and the film were pigeonholed as sports or boxing titles but, as with all Curtis' work, the pugilistic plot and backdrop is mainly a device to illuminate the meagre conditions endured by the London working-class and the poverty of choice facing them. (My Ace Books paperback edition from the early 1960s declares the book to be a 'vivid and racy story of London's boxing world'.) The criminal 'heroes' of *The Gilt Kid* and *They Drive By Night* are fundamentally decent men – products of their environment, drawn to crime by necessity, not choice.

Tommy Mutch, the central character of *There Ain't No Justice*, is not a criminal. He is a young working-class boy from Notting Dale, street-wise but innocent, still living with his parents and siblings, who has displayed a talent for boxing and as the story unfolds will be stripped of that innocence as he is manipulated and mauled by crooked promoters, hucksters, prostitutes and small-time gangsters. Curtis' main point is that boxing represented a way out for young working-class men – or at least they thought it did – but it was an illusory goal. Many would end up penniless, physically and mentally damaged, taking some small comfort from peer admiration in the caffs and pubs of their manor, where old fighters were always held in some misty-eyed esteem. Tommy's morality triumphs in the end, and his inherent decency runs through the narrative, but the reader is left with the lasting feeling that poor Tommy Mutch will never emerge from the ranks of London's downtrodden.

Literary history has it that in the modern-era the gritty, realist depiction of the working classes was first broken into the mainstream by the so-called Angry Young Men in the late 1950s. These authors included John Braine, Alan Sillitoe and John Osborne with such works as *Room At The Top*, *Saturday Night And Sunday Morning* and *Look Back In Anger*. However, it is clear that Curtis, along with Gerald Kersh, Robert Westerby and Patrick Hamilton, was producing literature twenty years earlier that celebrated and dissected the working classes, the deprived and the depraved, and the generally seedy. Curtis, perhaps, nursed the deepest ire of this first crop of angry young men. A sub-plot of the book highlights the misery and horror of back-street abortion.

There Ain't No Justice pulls no punches and it is astonishing that the book got past the censors given the 'public morals' strictures of the time and the raging controversy over the abortion theme in the film *The L-Shaped Room* nearly thirty years later. Take this following extract:

'Blimey, Tom,' Fred was saying. 'We di'nt half have a laugh tonight. Me and Reg takes a ball of chalk up to Notting Hill Gate and we picks up a couple of janes outside Woolworth's. Neither Reg nor me's got no lob to spare so we lumbers 'em into the Park. Laugh? You should of seen us. Reg says to his tart, right pusher she was and all, "Do you take it?" he says. Gawd, she di'nt half carry on. Thought she was going to jump straight down his throat.

'"That's all right," says Reg, straightening his tie, you know the way he does, "I meant sugar in your tea." Caw, laugh?'

Fred roared heartily. Tommy smiled. Somehow he felt above such boyish pleasures as taking girls out.

'Have it off wi'em?' he said.

One can only assume that the censors, and possibly the publishers, were so far removed from everyday cockney vernacular that they had no clue as to what was actually being indicated here. The language feels real, if dated, with cowsons, milkys, blimeys, bleedin's and caws galore – words and phrases that today have dropped from everyday street banter. Harry Dunn, one of the more sympathetic characters in the book, boasts about 'clouting' his wife. It was a different time, but none the less real for that.

Curtis is almost psychogeographical about places, detailing streets and routes, caffs and pubs, buildings and houses as the characters move around West London, adding to the overall authenticity of the novel. Ironically, Wilsham Street, where the Mutch family toiled, brothers slept two to a bed and racing pigeons were nurtured in a coop next door to the outside toilet, has now been redesignated as Notting Hill and the average property fetches £1.5m. The latest temple of consumerism, the Westfield Centre, overlooks Wilsham Street. Notting Dale no longer exists as an area. The name and its associated slum connotations airbrushed out of history to disguise another land-grab by the affluent. Today, one is more likely to bump into Stella McCartney and Robbie Williams crisscrossing the local streets than Tommy Mutch with his latest jane on his arm.

The author's grasp of the real world and how real lives were being lived is no more evident than in the boxing scenes. One can almost smell the iodine during the fight passages, his boxing knowledge technical. There can be no doubt that Curtis immersed himself in this world one way or another, even though his own early background was middle class and public school. Boxing was in its heyday. Across the Atlantic the heavyweight class had been dominated by Jack Dempsey and Gene Tunney and, in the year *There Ain't No Justice* was published, Joe Louis, the Brown Bomber, had just become the new World Heavyweight Champion, marking the beginning of black dominance of the sport that has endured until recently. In Britain, Cornishman Len Harvey was a national hero. Boxing was practised routinely in schools and in the armed forces and its bills attracted crowds up and down the country. It was second only to football as *the* national sport.

As with football there was a well-worn route from the backstreet slum to fame (but not necessarily fortune in those days) as talented boys could and did break through. However, in boxing the opportunities were fewer as there was only room for a handful of fighters at the top at any one time, whereas the world of football could accommodate hundreds of household names. Also, unlike football, the sheer physical attrition endured by a boxer climbing that greasy pole was off the scale in comparison. However, there were enough rags-to-riches stories to encourage the likes of Tommy Mutch and his real-life equivalents.

When I co-operated with golfer Gypsy Joe Smith on his book a couple of years back we established that his grandfather Rymer Smith had boxed professionally on the circuit under the name of Jack Daly in the 1930s. Rymer/Jack was exactly the sort of boxer on exactly the sort of bill that Tommy Mutch was being matched against. Further research revealed that Rymer had beaten a man who later went the distance with Don Cockell, who himself lasted nine rounds with the legendary Rocky Marciano. Proof, therefore, that it was a few steps, on paper at least, from the gypsy fairground boxing-booth to Madison Square Gardens and sporting immortality, and an explanation of the lure to the poor and underprivileged able-bodied men of the world, past and present.

Sport it may have been, but there was no escaping the element of voyeuristic violence that was (and remains) part of boxing's attraction. Curtis recognises this and is uncomfortable. A fighter with the fitting name of Johnny Basham is namechecked in the book. Basham had knocked an opponent named Harry Price down and he subsequently died, and Basham was charged with manslaughter before eventually being acquitted. Few would acknowledge the fact, but it is the risk and prospect of such extreme consequences that can excite crowds the most. My own uncle – ninety years old and still living in his Battersea birthplace – recalls attending a fair near Dog's Home Bridge where he was roped into 'blindfold boxing', he and another thirteen-year-old lad masked and put into a ring to flail widely at each other until one was knocked over for the amusement of a paying crowd. The only rule my uncle remembers was 'no peeping'.

There Ain't No Justice, the film, was well-received when released in 1939, although it did not enjoy the critical acclaim of *They Drive By Night* or, indeed, the British commercial success of *The Arsenal Stadium Mystery*, Will Hay's *Ask A Policeman* or George Formby's *Come On George*. All of these would have been overshadowed enormously by the Hollywood blockbusters of the year – *Gone With The Wind* and *The Wizard Of Oz*. Jimmy Hanley as Tommy Mutch is, perhaps, an unconvincing boxer, but he does capture the decent innocence of Curtis' character. (He is not as unconvincing, however, as the John Le Mesurier/Sergeant Wilson lookalike on the cover of my 1960s paperback.) Despite the abortion sub-plot being erased and the language toned down it is nevertheless, for its time, a convincing and daring exposé of the corruption and criminality surrounding a much-loved sport. Curtis himself worked on the screenplay and would have fought against the undoubted attempts to over-sanitise the story.

The talent associated with the film have tentacles stretching backwards and forwards into British culture. The first-time director Pen Tennyson had worked as an assistant director to Alfred Hitchcock and was the great-grandson of the poet Alfred Lord Tennyson. A promising career lay ahead, but his life was cut short following a plane crash in 1941. Jimmy Hanley became part of the much-loved Huggett family on film, appearing with Jack Warner and Kathleen Harrison. In real life he married Dinah Sheridan, star of *Genevieve* and *The Railway Children*, who also married John Davis, one time chairman of The Rank Organisation, whose gong-banger at the beginning of all their films of the era was former boxer Bombardier Billy Wells, who appears in *There Ain't No Justice* as an extra. Edward Chapman is delicious as the bent boxing promoter Sammy Sanders. He would wait twenty or more years before becoming indelibly imprinted in the British consciousness as the long-suffering Mr Grimsdale, foil to Norman Wisdom in several of his once hugely-popular knock-about comedies. Michael Wilding, playing the villainous Len Charteris, came to prominence in this film. He enjoyed a career as a handsome matinee idol but his filmic achievements would be overshadowed in the public memory by a short marriage to Elizabeth Taylor.

Nineteen thirty-nine was a momentous year for James Curtis, as well as the world in general. By the end of it he had five books in print and two successful films under his belt. There would have been money in the bank and he was still only thirty-two years old. He was a literary star. The war and the breakdown of his marriage followed. He did not have another novel published until *Look Long Upon A Monkey* in 1956, and this proved to be his last. His daughter recalls him spending a great deal of time in libraries researching books but never wanting or being able to produce a finished product. He spent the latter part of his life in North London, frequenting the pubs and befriending the Irish community.

He converted to Roman Catholicism and died in 1977 at the age of seventy. His fame had long ago died although celebrity and the acquisition of wealth were never on his agenda. Indeed, the following comment by his sister Ruth may go a long way to explain Curtis' premature literary decline: 'He was the brightest and most gifted of all my siblings and had every opportunity to succeed in all areas of life. His personality meant he couldn't cope with success and he seemed intent on destroying everything good that happened to him.'

There Ain't No Justice is the third Curtis title to be republished by London Books. They have sold again respectably and there has been a trickle of enquiries from film and TV production companies, perhaps with one eye on the renewed interest in Curtis' contemporary Patrick Hamilton. Hopefully, one day the author and his work will similarly recapture the imagination of the reading public. If his catalogue remains buried under the weight of long-forgotten, now irrelevant, shifts in taste, there certainly ain't no justice.

Martin Knight, 2014

CHAPTER I

It was half-past five in the evening. The pubs were open. Harry Dunn was walking down the Prince's Road, Notting Dale. He wore an old suit, a grey high-necked sweater and a check cap. His nose had been nicely flattened by a neat right cross that had put him to sleep at the old National Sporting Club. His lower lip was swollen and wore the marks of three of his teeth. This scar he had won in a street fight in Bangor Street just after the war. Harry had always been a fighter. He could just remember the old boys who had fought with the raw 'uns on Wormwood Scrubs Common, for whatever the crowd liked to give.

He turned into Wilsham Street.

It was getting dark. Blokes were coming home from work. Their wives had left the laundries at Acton some time ago.

He pulled the latch-string at number 137 and walked into the hall.

Mrs Mutch put her head out of the kitchen.

'Watchew want?'

'Tommy in?'

'Who's that?'

'Harry Dunn.'

'Yus. He's in the front room having a bit of a lay-down.'

Harry pushed open the door and walked into the front room. Tommy Mutch was lying on the chair-bed: he had pulled an old blanket over his shoulders.

'Hullo, Harry.'

'What ho me old Tom.'

Harry sat down on a windsor chair. Tommy did not get up.

'Well, Tommy boy, how goes it?'

'Mustn't grumble. Knocked off early and came and had a bit of a lay-down same as you said.'

'That's right. Feeling like fighting tonight?'

'You bet.'

'Well, just take it easy a bit. I'll go into the kitchen and see your mum about your tea.'

'All right.'

Tommy closed his eyes. He was eighteen. Tonight he was having his third fight as a professional. All day he had been standing outside an Underground station selling papers.

In the kitchen Mrs Mutch was busy with the eternal business of a slum housewife. Young Lily was crying. Young Lily was always crying. She looked at Harry with disapproval.

'Well?'

'All right, ma. Got Tommy's tea yet?'

'Blimey, watchew expect, I only got one pair of hands, ain't I?'

'No need to jump down my throat.'

'It's all right for you men. You can lay about all day like lords. We got work to do.'

'I know, I know. But Tommy's got to fight tonight.'

'He don't have to.'

'This is a chance for him. You don't want him to lose it.'

'A chance? I wouldn't give a thank you for a chance like that.'

Mrs Mutch turned round from the stove and walked into the middle of the room. Although she was three inches shorter than Harry Dunn, he retreated apprehensively.

'Listen,' she said. 'I know chances like that. I was born round here. Everybody round this way knows me. You ask anybody about Mrs Mutch. They'll tell you. I seen boxers before. Stone me blind. There ain't a turning round this way that hasn't got a boxer living in it, what hasn't always had one boxer at any rate, and what do they amount to? Not a row a pins.

16

'I know 'em. Lay-arounds, that's all they are. Laying in bed, laying about all day long in the caffs. Caw. None of 'em get a regular job. Selling papers, pushing barrows, totting, thieving. That's all they're good for. Why can't Tommy get a good job like my Ernie?'

'Your Ernie!' Harry tried to stop the flow.

'Yes, my Ernie. Yes, everyone round here takes the mike outa him just because he wears glasses and can't talk without stammering, but my Ernie's worth ten of your tupenny ha'penny boxers. Only fifteen, going to school a year ago and he's got a good job, a regular job, clerking for a pawnbroker. You! What are you worth? Be surprised if you got more'n a couple of shilling in your pocket now. Married man you are with five kiddies and all you can do is a few days' market work every now and again and then signing on at the labour. And if you do get hold of some money you're like all the others round this way. Do it all in at the dogs or buy pigeons. Pigeon-racing! Caw. There's something for you.'

'All right, all right. There's no need to carry on that way. I ain't done you no harm.'

'No, and you ain't done me no good, neither. You're just like all the lazy bastards round here. Good for nothing. That's what you are.'

'If my old woman was to talk to me this way …'

'Pity your old woman don't never talk to you this way. Might make you show some sense.'

'… I'd clout her just where it would hurt her most.'

'That's about your mark. Clouting women. Why you bin up at the West London for that before now. Stop it, Lil.'

She turned round and smacked young Lily who immediately started howling louder than ever. Harry Dunn retreated farther.

'Well, if you won't give your own son no tea, I'll take him round my house and see what I can do meself.'

'Who said I wouldn't give him no tea? I'd have brought

it into him long ago if you hadn't of come into here argy-bargying about the place and keeping me from my work.'

Harry shrugged his shoulders despairingly and went back into the front room.

'Tea won't be long now, son,' he said.

'You been a hell of a time in the kitchen. What's up?'

'Nothing. Just chatting your mum.'

'You ain't been falling out with the old lady, have you?'

'No. Watchew expect me to fall out with her over?'

'Oh, nothing. Only, I guess she don't like me boxing.'

'Blimey, hark at him! Why she's proud of you.'

Someone came in the front door. Tommy sat up on the chair-bed, swinging his legs on the floor.

'That'll be the old chap.'

'Ah.'

Fred Mutch came into the front room. He was still in his working clothes. He had been doing a bit of navvying for a sand-and-ballast company up Paddington way. Bits of clay were still clinging to his boots and corduroys.

'Watcher, Harry boy, how you going on? That's the idea. How you feeling, Tom?'

'OK.'

Tommy was always vaguely embarrassed in his father's presence. Besides his stockinged feet felt cold on the oilcloth. Fred Mutch pulled out a packet of cigarettes.

'Smoke?'

Harry lighted up and blew the smoke out. The two men watched each other closely. Both were still wearing their caps.

'Coming to watch the boy fight tonight?' asked Harry.

'Can't, it's club night.'

Mrs Mutch came in.

'You and your old pigeons. Caw. Get a sub today?'

'Yus.'

Fred Mutch put his hand in his trousers pocket and brought out a handful of silver.

'How much?'

'Eight and a tanner. I spent tuppence on a packet of Weights and tuppence on me fare home. Here's six og for you. I'll keep the rest. I got to have some to go to work with.'

Mrs Mutch put down the tray. She took the three florins that her husband held in the palm of his horny hand and, walking over to the mantelpiece, put them inside a teapot. Three pairs of eyes followed her.

'Here's your tea, Tommy,' she said.

'OK.'

Fred Mutch looked at the tray.

'Blimey, steak,' he said. 'Watchew got for me?'

'Tin o' salmon. Go and get washed and you can have it in the back room soon as Else comes in. Want a cup of tea, Harry?'

'Well, I wouldn't say "no".'

'All right, I'll get another cup.'

She hurried out of the room. Fred Mutch still stood around vaguely, puffing at his cigarette.

'Give us my shoes, Harry, will you,' said Tommy standing up.

'Here you are.'

Tommy sat down again on the edge of the bed and put on his shoes. His father still stood around.

'Ah well,' he said at last. 'Good night, Harry. Got to get washed and have my tea before I go down to The Norland. Good night, Tommy. Hope you win.'

'Thanks.'

Tommy stood up again. His shoes were on.

'Light the gas, Harry. There's matches on the mantelpiece.'

'All right. I got some.'

Mrs Mutch came in again while Harry was lighting the gas.

'Here's your cup.'

'Thanks.'

'Got your fare for tonight, Tom?'

'Yes.'

'I hopes you win.'

'Thanks.'

Mrs Mutch went out again. The gas spluttered, flared up and then settled down to a steady flame. The sudden light showed up the little slum room in all its cheap shoddiness. Here slept Ernie, who was clerking for a pawnbroker, and Tommy. Still, the heavily-ornamented overmantel which, unlike most of those in the district, has not been broken up for firewood, and the cheap pictures and hangings which were everywhere, gave it the air of a parlour for which it had originally been intended.

Tommy poured out two cups of tea and began to eat his steak in silence. He felt little waves of nervousness coming over him. Until that moment he had not really comprehended the fact that he was supposed to be fighting that night.

Suddenly he spoke:

'Whatsa time, Harry?'

'Quarter-past six.'

'What time I got to be there?'

'Half-seven.'

'Better start getting dressed as soon as I finished this.'

'No hurry. Take your time. No sense in getting yourself all flustered over nothing.'

'Ah.'

Harry Dunn looked at Tommy with professional interest. He was not interested in his good-natured rather heavily-featured face with its as yet unbroken nose: he was not interested in his collarless shirt, or his heavy square hands. What mattered to Harry were the breadth of Tommy's shoulders, the way the muscles bulged on his back each time he moved his arms, the way in which his body tapered away below his waist. He was a natural-born lightweight. A few more years, a lot more experience, and eight to ten pounds more weight, then, given the chances, Tommy Mutch ought to be in the money among the top-liners. And with Tommy Mutch in the money, why a few pounds, shillings and pence ought to stick to the fingers of old Harry Dunn, who knew how to use them.

Tommy pushed away his plate, and emptied his cup. He had finished.

'How's chances for a fag?'

'No chance.'

'Ah well, suppose I'd better be getting dressed.'

He got up from the table and picked up his collar and tie from a chair.

Harry Dunn looked on disapprovingly. In his day real men, fighters from Notting Dale, had never worn collars. No, a smart blue-and-white dotted silk handkerchief that had, maybe, cost him as much as a guinea, was part of the uniform of a real wide boy.

Tommy went over to the mantelpiece and tied his collar and tie. He picked up his broadly-tailored, loudly-striped brown jacket from the back of the chair and put it on. He had just taken up his silk scarf, when he heard the front door opening.

'That'll be Else.'

Elsie walked straight in. She had just come from work. Her fair curls clustered out from under her little black hat and her pink face was shiny. When she went out tonight with the girls to walk about Shepherds Bush and giggle and run when the boys chased them she would be dressed up to the nines. For four or possibly five more years she would be pretty. But children, hard work, a lazy husband and a slum home were certain to beat her in the end.

'Hallo Tom, how you feeling?'

Tommy turned round in a sudden burst of irritation.

'Blimey, why must everybody say that? Don't none of you know anything else to say? Caw. It's enough to send a bloke bleeding crackers.'

Elsie tossed her head.

'All right, Mr Badtemper,' she said, 'if you can't answer a civil question, I s'pose you got to do the other thing.'

She flounced out of the room.

'Girls,' said Tommy and started tying his scarf.

Harry Dunn lit a new Weight.

'Here, Tommy,' he said, 'I may as well give you my orders now. This geezer what you're fighting tonight, he's good, see, but he ain't very good, but you got to watch him. He's had a lot of experience, see, and he's met some real good boys in his time, but he's on the downward track at the moment. He never was anything better than a good preliminary boy, but he was one of the best preliminary boys in the smoke, see? Now, he's got a lovely left-hand which you'll have to watch, but don't let that make you milky. He'll expect you to be scared at him and not take any liberties, so whip into it and belt him every now and then. That left'll tell, but he ain't got a real wallop there so it can't put you out. Don't box him or he'll win. Make a fight of it, see?'

'Yes.'

Tommy had put on his overcoat and was now adjusting his black hat.

'Always watch me while you're boxing towards your corner and I'll give you the office, see?'

'Yes.'

'Packed your bag?'

'Yes.'

'What you got in it?'

'Trunks, iodine pencil, towel, hand bandages, sponge, boots, gumshield.'

'That's right. Let's go.'

They went out of the front door together and started walking up through the back streets towards Notting Hill Gate where they would catch their bus to Mornington Crescent.

CHAPTER II

The little boxing hall was packed. The main event of the evening was to be a twelve-round contest between a Camden Town welterweight and an Islington lad. A fortnight previously the local boy had won on points after a gruelling bout. Perhaps if he had been fighting off his own manor he would not have been given the verdict. The Islington contingent, at least, thought so and had turned up strongly to see their own boy win. The floor was littered with newspapers and peanut shells.

A cone of smoke-filled light descended from the arc-lamps on to the raised ring.

The first contest had been dull and the boys who expected to see six murders committed for their eighteen-pence were howling.

Tommy walked out from his dressing-room. He was fighting in the second preliminary bout. Harry followed him. The crowd looked at him without much interest. These little six-rounders were never much bottle. Sometimes they put up a good show, but that was usually by mistake.

This kid could hardly be much cop. He couldn't even rise to a dressing-gown and had a towel draped round his shoulders.

Tommy ducked under the ropes. He was pale about the gills. It was all a bit scaring, particularly as nobody seemed to give a monkey's for him. He looked at Harry and smiled weakly. Harry, with his fist-scarred face, was not very reassuring.

The other boy climbed into the ring. His hair was neatly parted: he wore a dressing-gown. His left ear had taken a nice one some time. The crowd gave him quite a hand. They knew him as a competent workman. Tommy decided to buy himself a dressing-gown just as soon as he could find the money.

The Master of Ceremonies climbed into the ring. He had the personality of a successful travelling salesman and the local fight-fans liked him. He advanced into the centre of the ring and extended both his arms as though he were crucified.

'Lad-ies and gentle-men,' he intoned, 'the next event will be a contest of six two-minute rounds between Smiler Hogan of Kilburn and Tommy Mutch of Notting Dale. On my left –' he pointed – 'Hogan. On my right' – he pointed again – 'Mutch.'

The onlookers clapped perfunctorily; the MC climbed down into the ringside seat. The referee went into the ring. He was an old-timer in a shiny blue-serge suit. Once he had been a right 'un and had boxed with Johnny Basham, Jim Driscoll, Johnny Summers and Freddie Welsh. Today he refereed six contests once a week for an all-in fee of £4 and what he could make out of the gamblers. He called the boys to the centre of the ring and laid a podgy paw on each of them.

'Now, boys,' he said, 'put up a good scrap. I don't want you to do too much holding. You know all the rules about fouls. I shan't be hard on you, but remember the boys have all paid to watch you and if you want another fight at this hall you've got to give them action. Fight hard and clean and nobody'll argue. That's all.'

He gave them each a final pat and went back to his seat. He only remained in the ring when the main event was on or when a fight became either too raw or too slow for the liking of the fans. He was supposed to explain the rules to the fighters, but nobody bothered about that, so long as he went through the motions.

Tommy went to his corner and sat down. His mouth was

dry. Harry pushed aside the second whom the hall provided and whispered to him.

'Don't forget what I told you, kid. Mix it, but watch his left-hand. When I talk to you don't waste breath by answering. Jes nod for "yes" and shake for "no".'

'Ting.'

The first gong sounded. Seconds out.

'Go to it, Tom boy, and good luck.'

Harry dived under the ropes as he spoke.

'Ting.'

The second gong. The boys moved gracefully to the centre of the ring and touched gloves in token of a handshake. Smiler Hogan stepped back and Tommy tried to draw him to a lead. Hogan waited his time, sparring nicely. Suddenly his chin was unguarded. Tommy flashed out a straight left, but he was too slow. Hogan caught him a nice one downstairs in the kitchen and had stepped back. Tommy followed him, saw an opening and led again with his left, keeping his right down this time. Hogan countered with his right and caught Tommy flush on the jaw. His teeth rattled. He stepped back.

He did not know it, but his opponent had carefully manoeuvred him against the ropes. Hogan feinted. Tommy dropped his left and Hogan jumped in. Left, right, left. He was out again. There was, he knew, no sense in fighting too hard. He was paid to box six rounds. So long as he showed enough action to satisfy the fans and did not get hurt or over-exert himself he was happy. As far as boxing was concerned, he was a tradesman, not a would-be champion.

Tommy followed him to the centre of the ring. He was getting bewildered. This was not what he had thought about. An opening appeared, he darted out his left hand; Hogan swayed inside it, hit him in the ribs with a right and left, and went into a clinch, his left fist caught somehow up in Tommy's armpit.

Tommy remembered what the referee had said about

holding. He tried to push Hogan away. The left fist under his armpit dragged him forward off his balance and Hogan hooked him hard on the jaw with his right hand. This stung Tommy into action. He jumped forward, and Hogan, seeing that he had hurt his opponent and not wishing to goad him into making a real fight of it, retreated into safety. Tommy came after him.

The gong rang. The round was over. Tommy went back to his corner. The regular second worked over him casually: Harry whispered hoarsely to him.

'He's making a monkey out of you, Tom boy. You haven't landed one yet. Remember what I said. Don't try to box. Carry the fight to him. Show him you ain't scared. Has he hurt you?'

Tommy shook his head. It was against his rule to admit that any Kilburn Irishman could hurt him.

When the gong went for the second round he jumped out from his corner like a madman and dived into Hogan with a two-fisted attack.

Hogan retreated and Tommy's fists beat the air rather than his opponent's body. He was expending a lot of energy and was quite off his balance when Hogan jumped in with a right and left that sent Tommy right back on to his heels. Hogan followed up with a left and Tommy managed to counter with a right cross which connected with the other boy's mouth.

He was wildly excited and jumped in. Left, left, left, he caught Hogan in the ribs. He swung with his right, but Hogan beat him with an uppercut and stepped back out of danger. Tommy's mouth was bleeding, but he followed up.

Hogan stuck out his left. This fight was getting too tough and fast for his liking. Tommy knocked it aside with his right forearm and hit Hogan hard on the cheek. Hogan dropped into a clinch. Again, his fist was caught up in Tommy's armpit, but the kid was learning fast. Instead of trying to push the other away he hit him hard three times in the ribs.

Hogan broke of his own accord, at the same time bringing up his head into Tommy's already bleeding mouth.

The gong went.

Tommy was more satisfied as he went back to his corner this time. He was making a fight of it instead of a boxing lesson. The crowd were beginning to take notice. At any minute this bout might develop into a real slug-fest.

He sat down on his stool. The second took out Tommy's gumshield and rinsed his mouth with warm salt-water. He sprayed his lips and nostrils and stopped the bleeding.

Harry was talking.

'That's better, son. Nasty one in the mouth. Was it his head?'

Nod.

'Hurt?'

Shake.

'You want to remember what I told you. Always try to box towards this corner. You don't know how to use the ring proper. Sidestep when he leads and you can work round that way. He's got you messed up nice on ringcraft. Give him what you got now.'

The gong went. The second put back Tommy's gumshield. A hawker was walking about the hall shouting:

'Who says a nice juicy apple?'

The smell of tobacco smoke was terrific.

The second gong went.

Tommy dashed out again, hit Hogan twice and sidestepped a swing. Hogan jumped at him. Tommy sidestepped again. Out of the corner of his eye he saw Harry's hand hit the canvas twice. He knew what that meant. He gave Hogan a right and left in the stomach. Hogan caught him over the eye with a nice left-hander, but that did not check Tommy who kept on boring in.

Hogan sidestepped twice, feinted with his left and as Tommy led drove him back with a right cross. Tommy found himself in a neutral corner. He tried to cover up. Hogan hit him hard three times about the body and stepped back. Tommy uncovered. Hogan hit him twice in the face. His mouth was bleeding freely now. He swung desperately at Hogan's face which was bobbing darkly before his eyes. He missed. Hogan drove him back against the rope with a vicious right-hander to the stomach.

The ropes carried him back. His left hand hit Hogan's ribs with all the force of the rebound. Hogan dropped his guard and grunted.

The crowd yelled. This kid, what was his name? Tommy Mutch, from Notting Dale. Mightn't be much cop, but he was dead game.

Tommy swung at Hogan's unguarded chin, missed and stumbled forward. Hogan hit him with a left uppercut. Tommy sidestepped. His head was clearing. He could see Hogan quite plainly now. He jumped in, hit him three times to the body. Hogan stepped back. Tommy followed up. The gong sounded.

'You've got to watch what you're doing,' said Harry in the interval. 'You started off real good and then he drove you into that corner twice. I thought you was done. I was just getting ready to sling in the towel. That's three rounds you gone now. Feeling all right?'

Nod.

'You're going to have a nice kisser tomorrow. He keeps on opening it up. Hit him about the body all you know this round. His slats are getting proper red. Roast him there. He don't like it. When you're getting into a corner, don't go back. However much he hurts you, don't give no ground. It don't pay. Jump in, get into a clinch and try to push yourself clear, see?'

Nod.

Gong.

Harry was right. When Hogan came up for the next round

his ribs were covered with nasty red blotches. This was not his idea of fun. He saw no point in taking a preliminary bout so seriously. This kid was certainly a glutton for punishment.

Tommy jumped in again as hard as he could. With his head down and his fists swinging he flailed the other boy's ribs. Hogan jabbed down twice with his left then tried a right uppercut which sent Tommy's head back. Tommy broke. Hogan followed him and led with his left. Tommy sidestepped. Hogan turned round to face him. Tommy hit him hard with his left to the stomach. Hogan grunted.

The crowd cheered. This was really a fight.

Hogan drew Tommy to a left lead and swayed inside it, hit Tommy twice and was out again.

Tommy jumped after him. He could see Harry signalling. He obeyed instructions. He feinted with his left at Hogan's ribs, and as the other's hands moved, drove his right with all his force to the solar plexus. Hogan's guard dropped.

Tommy whipped over a left swing that hit Hogan's uncovered jaw and drove his head back. Hogan retreated and sidestepped. Tommy swung with his right. Hogan pushed aside the punch with his left forearm. Tommy led with his left. Hogan countered feebly with his right. Tommy rode the punch and led again. Hogan ducked. As his head came down Tommy brought up his right fist. Hogan straightened up. His knees seemed to be made of rubber.

Tommy jumped in. He hit Hogan four times to the body. Hogan tried to cover up.

Tommy flailed him. Hogan uncovered and in uncovering carefully drove one of his elbows into Tommy's ribs. This foul blow stung Tommy to action. He knew Hogan was weakening. He knew the round was nearly over, so he crowded on all-sail he could and jumped in again.

Four times he pasted Hogan's body. Each time Hogan's head wagged, each time he grunted. Hogan tried to go into a clinch, but Tommy hooked him to the head with a left and right over the outstretched, wrestling arms. Hogan tottered back.

Tommy feinted with his left at Hogan's head and his right at his body. Hogan brought up his right glove and dropped his left. There was a gap between them, a route straight to his unguarded chin.

Quicker than thought Tommy drove a straight, right-handed punch through the gap. It caught Hogan flush on the whiskers. He dropped like a log.

He was not really hurt, but this fight was too tough for him. It was safer on the floor. He hoped he would not be saved by the gong. He wasn't. The timekeeper counted him out.

CHAPTER III

Tommy dressed slowly. As he dressed he smoked. It was nice to have a cigarette in his mouth, even though his lips were puffed and swollen.

Harry had given him a good massage. Harry knew the way to massage a fighter, how to take all the tired knots out of a stomach and how to make leaden legs feel nimble again. But Harry didn't know the way to make sore ribs stop hurting every time a bloke breathed and Harry didn't know how to take away a punch-sore head.

Tommy bent down to tie his shoelaces and then regretted it. Bending made his head swim. Another boxer lying on the slab laughed at him.

'Took a good hiding, didn'tcha, mate?'

'Good hiding nothing. I was on a KO in the fourth.'

'Who were you fighting?'

'Smiler Hogan.'

Tommy threw away the cigarette. Its taste was no longer so good and it made his lips smart.

'Tried to mix it a bit, didn'tcha?'

'Yes.'

Tommy tied his tie and put on his hat. He was standing with his scarf in his hand.

'Take my tip, kid,' said the other. 'Don't do too much for your wages, or you'll go the same way as all the others. Punch-drunk or blind. How many professional fights you had?'

'This is the third. But I done a bit of amateur at the boy's club.'

Tommy put on his overcoat.

'Thought as much. Three fights, eh? Take my tip, mate.

Go easy. Give the customers a good show, but don't give them too much. Then you'll be able to talk about three hundred fights. No sense in taking hidings.'

Another boxer and his trainer came in. Tommy looked at them. The boy who was lying down sat up.

'You was the semi-wind-up, wasn't you mate?'

'Yes.'

'How'd you get on?'

'Won on points.'

'Blimey. Bleeding lot of champions we got in this dressing-room. Ah well, I s'pose we better get dressed and see the guv'nor and draw our dough.'

The swing-door of the dressing-room opened again. In came the promoter followed by Harry Dunn. The promoter wore a dinner-jacket which failed to conceal his bulging shoulders. His face was red and his features coarse.

He pointed to Tommy.

'This the kid, ain't it?' he asked Harry.

'Yes, guv'nor.'

'All right, son. Come out into the corridor a minute, I want to talk to you.'

Tommy went out with Harry and the promoter. The latter turned to him.

'You're a game kid,' he said. 'Here's your wages.'

He gave Tommy a crumpled ten-shilling note and four half-crowns.

'But,' stammered Tommy, looking appealing at Harry who shook his head.

'But what?' bullied the promoter.

'You promised me thirty og if I had it off.'

'Yeah? Remember what I said? I said a dollar if you got put out, a once if you went the distance and lost, and thirty bob if you won, didn't I?'

'Yes, that's right.'

'Well, you didn't go the distance, see? You was scheduled

to box six rounds and you only went four, messing up my programme. You're lucky to get a oncer if you ask me. Take it or leave it.'

'All right, guv'nor. I'll take it.'

Tommy put the money in his pocket.

'Want to fight here again next Thursday?'

'Sure.'

'All right, same terms. Be here the usual time and go the distance this time. And don't forget to drop your second half-a-dollar. Go into the hall now and see him before the main bout comes on.'

Tommy went back into the hall. The Master of Ceremonies was in the ring reading out next week's bills. Everybody was laughing. He was a wise-cracker.

He caught sight of Tommy and looked towards the promoter who was lounging in the doorway. The promoter nodded.

'Also, ladies and gentlemen,' declaimed the Master of Ceremonies, 'I am authorised and privileged to announce this added special attraction to our next week's programme. At considerable expense the management has decided to add a further contest to a bumper bill. Tommy Mutch whom you have seen tonight and whom all sportsmen will agree is a game boy and a clean fighter will fight six two-minute rounds with a contestant to be selected later. I am sure that with this extra piece of spice to an already splendid programme you will all show up. As the farmer's daughter said …'

He told a mildly obscene story. The crowd roared.

Tommy made his way to the corner of the ring. The smoke-laden air made his tired eyes smart. He went up to the second.

'Here you are, mate.'

The old man took the half-crown and nodded.

'Thanks, kid. That was a nice little scrap you had, but you don't want to show the public too much for their money. Be seeing you next week. So long.'

'So long.'

Tommy threaded his way back through the ringside seats. The contestants for the main bout were just coming into the ring. Both wore very brilliant dressing-gowns and plastered hair. Bandages showed white on their hands. A box of new gloves lay in the centre of the ring. The crowd were clapping and cheering. Possibly the Islington contingent were making the most noise.

'You're Tommy Mutch, aren't you?'

Tommy turned round. A man was talking to him. He was flashily dressed with a check overcoat and a diamond in his tie. He wore a little thin moustache and his eyes were close together. Over them his dark eyebrows nearly met. A girl with platinum hair sat beside him.

'Yes, guv'nor. That's right.'

'Nice fight. I'm glad you won. I'll be here to watch you next week. I hope you have it off again.'

Tommy smiled. The girl smiled back at him. She wore three expensive-looking rings and a fur coat.

'Me, too,' she said.

Tommy felt himself going red. He was glad when the man went on speaking, for he did not know how to make a departure.

'You come from the Bush, don't you?'

'Wilsham Street, Notting Dale, but I get round the Bush a bit.'

'Know The Star?'

'Sure.'

'I drop in there sometimes. Maybe we'll see you there some night. Sundays we're often here. Good night.'

'Good night, sir. Good night, lady.'

He stumbled away, his cheeks red with embarrassment. Harry was standing by the door leading to the dressing-rooms. He turned on Tommy fiercely.

'What'd that geezer want?'

'Just spoke to me about the fight and wished me luck. That's all.'

'Didn't like the look of him,' grumbled Harry. 'Crooked looking bastard if you ask me.'

'Oh, he's all right. Didn't mean no harm.'

'Yes? Didn't like his looks all the same. Feeling tired?'

'Kind of.'

'Want to watch this fight?'

'No. Don't know as I do.'

'Let's go home. I got your bag here.'

'All right.'

The fresh air of the street was pleasant after the smell of sweat and smoke and cloth that the hall had held. They walked down to the bus stop together. Both were contented.

'That was a nice little bundle, Tommy. It didn't do you no harm. Once you get a name for gameness, you're made, see?'

'That's right. But everyone's bin at me telling me not to go too hard. They reckon you don't want to give the public too much for their money.'

They paused by the bus stop. In the light of a street lamp Harry turned on his pupil. His battered face glared.

'Yeah? They been telling you that? Well, ferget it, Tommy boy. If you don't you won't do yourself no good. You're a fighter, see? Well a fighter's got to fight, ain't he? That's what they pay him for. If you're going to the top of the tree you got to be good and you got to do your best all the time. I don't hold with this new stuff. None of the old-timers used to talk that way. I don't know what's come over boxing, straight I don't. For Christ's sake, Tom, try to be a good 'un.'

'Yeah, but what about getting punch-drunk.'

'If you're a good 'un you won't get punch-drunk. I reckon you ought to have a good enough defence soon to stop that and anyway what's a bloke want to be a fighter for, if he can't take a bit of punishment? Soft. That's what they all are today. Proper soft.'

A number 27 bus came along and they boarded it, climbing the stairs to the top. Tommy sat on an empty front seat. Harry behind him.

'You want to polish up your ringcraft a bit, Tommy. I don't know how we're going to do it. That's the worst of sparring on the street corners, you can't get learnt ringcraft. Best thing'll be to stick to defence and clinches for a bit. You're weak on clinches. Then as soon as we get some dough we'll pay your subs to a gymnasium.'

'Fares, please.'

'Two fourpennies, please.'

Tommy bought the tickets. Putting away the change he turned to Harry.

'I never give you your whack, did I?'

He handed the old man a couple of half-crowns.

'Proper carve-up over the pay-off, wasn't it?'

'Dunno,' said Harry. 'It don't do to argue with the promoter. It's a bastard if they take a dislike to you. You can't get nowhere.'

The bus jolted on its cross-town journey. Down Hampstead Road, turn right, Marylebone Road, across Edgware Road, Praed Street. It was in Westbourne Grove that Harry spoke again.

'You better take it easy tonight, Tom. Go straight to kip as soon as you get in. I'll see you tomorrow evening on the corner of Prince's Road at about half-six and we'll do a bit o' sparring.'

'I ain't going to kip so soon.'

'You better, Tom boy.'

'No. I'm going to the caff.'

'Don't you go to the caff tonight. You want to start early hours. Standing around caffs, scratching yourself all night won't do you no good.'

'Oh no?'

'No.'

'Well, I'm going there.'

'Have it your own way.'

Harry shrugged. There was no sense in arguing with the kid. At Notting Hill Gate they got off the bus. Harry gave Tommy the bag.

'Good night, son,' he cried. 'Don't suppose you'll be coming my way. See you tomorrow.'

'OK. I'm copping a bus down to the Bush.'

Tommy crossed the road. Outside the Coronet Cinema he boarded a bus and gave the conductor the penny for his ride before mounting to the top deck.

His head was hurting. It would be silly not to go to the caff and chat with the boys.

CHAPTER IV

At Shepherds Bush Tommy got off the bus, crossed over by the tramlines and walked along to the café-bar he used. There were a lot of cafés round the district, but there was only one which the Notting Dale boys frequented. All the boys were there tonight.

As he walked in, they all turned to him. The bag in his hand and the stiff way he was carrying his head reminded them of his trade.

'What ho, me old Tom,' said Fred. 'How'd you get on?'

'All right.'

'What'd you do … go the distance?'

'Put him to sleep in the fourth.'

'Cushty, eh?'

Tom set down his bag and puffed out his chest, ready to receive his meed of praise. Stan came over to him. Tommy looked up at Stan's broken nose and cauliflower ear with grateful recognition that they were both craftsmen working in the same material.

'That Smiler Hogan's a good boy, ain't he?'

'Yerce. He's all right. Ain't got no wallop, though. I kayoed him easy. I'm having another fight at the same joint next week.'

'Yeah? Give you a bit of a north an' south didn't he?'

Tommy felt his lips gingerly. They were good and swollen now.

'Yerce. The dirty cowson headed me in the kisser.'

'The bastard.'

Stan threw his cigarette on the floor and ground it under his heel.

'What you going to have, Tom?' asked Reg.

'Well, I don't mind having a tea with you, Reg, me old pal.'

'Two teas, Charlie.'

Stan was looking at Tommy critically. Three years previously he had been thought of as a coming young cruiser-weight. Today he was just another boxer.

'Third fight, ain't it, Tom boy?'

'Yes.'

'Two verdicts and a kayo?'

'That's right.'

Stan lit another cigarette and breathed heavily. It was no fun for him breathing. Noses cannot be indefinitely punched.

'That'll look nice on your record, but keep it up for Christ sake. Don't mess about. You'll be all right s'long as you go straight. Take my tip, mate.'

Reg brought over Tommy's cup of tea. Tommy breathed at the top, stirred it and drank a sip. It was too hot. His lips stung. He set the cup down on a ledge. Stan spoke again.

'I made a bleeding mug outa meself, Tom. I might of done all right. I didn't that's all. It's bleedin' awful boxing is. Don't let it get you down. Soon as it gets you down you're done, see? Got a fag?'

'No, I ain't got a bastard.'

'Here.'

Fred butted in. He gave a cigarette to Tommy and another to Stan. Fighters were the heroes of Notting Dale. They lit up.

'No, mate,' said Stan. 'It gets you down and you don't want to let it. Take me. I was doing nicely. I'd built meself a nice little record and I'd had a couple of twelve-rounders. Top of the bill I was. Headliner at one of the bills at the Paddington Baths, headliner at another in Lowestoft. I thought I was set, see?'

He took a puff from his cigarette.

'But I wasn't in the money. I was getting bleedin' impatient. Blokes of me own class was frightened of me and the good boys wouldn't meet me. It's easier for a bloke your stamp, but for anything over a middleweight it can be a bastard getting a fight.'

Tommy drank a little of his tea. It was cooler now, but his lips still stung.

'Geezer came and propositioned me,' Stan was still talking, 'put it to me to take a dive. He was backing a boy he was trying to build up. That boy's at the top o' the tree now. No names, no pack drill, but he's a big name. Well, this geezer puts it to me that I fight this boy of his. I don't get paid if I win. I get fifty nicker if I take the dive. What do I do? I has two pound bet on the other boy and takes the dive.

'Blimey, you want to 've seen it. Proper carve-up. It's in the fifth of a ten-rounder. Crash, out I go from a hell of a right-hander on my biceps what wouldn't of knocked the skin off of a rice-pudding. Best bloody actor in the fight game I am. Fifty nicker for the dive I cops and a fiver for the gambling. Sounds easy money. Hardest earned money in the world.'

Tommy drank a little more of his tea.

'Yerce. Don't take no dives. I take half a dozen after that, make meself some lovely money,' went on Stan, 'but the scream was in. They was all after me for carve-ups. "What kind of bloke's that Stan?" they've asked. "All right, best bleedin' actor in the boxing ring." That ain't good enough. The news gets round all my fights are in the bag. I get finally so I can't have a fight nowhere. Yes. Everyone's wideoh to me. If I'd 've gone straight I'd 've been maybe at the top of the tree earning lovely money.'

Tommy drank a little more tea. Stan's bellyache had depressed him. He wished that he had not come to the caff that night. He felt with his foot to see if his bag was all right or whether one of the boys had lifted it. It was still there. Jimmy came in. He was cursing. The brim of his black hat was snapped down right over his eyes.

'Been to Harringay, Jimmy?' asked Reg.

'Na, Wimbledon.'

'Do any good?'

'Do any good? Don't make me laugh. Caw, in the first race I has a forecast. Three and five, four times. What happens? Five and three turns up and pays forty og. Then in the fourth I takes Armed Bandit with the field on the forecast. Blimey, bleedin' dog's beat be a short head.'

'What won?'

'Here's the card. Look at it yourself. I can't stand it.'

'Grecian Romance'll win at the City tomorrow.'

'Get on wiv yer.'

'Well, it's good enough for my money anyhow.'

'Might do it on a forecast.'

'Blimey, you blokes with your forecasts make me sick. Can't see it myself. No sense in it.'

'Think of the odds the bastard pays.'

'Think of the diabolical risks you got to take. Blimey, look at yourself tonight, doing three and five and five and three turning up. Back the bloody first and second and you still don't cop. That don't make sense to me ...'

Tommy's attention began to wander. The dogs did not interest him much. He was tired. If only he knew how to do it he would slip off home to bed.

Fred spoke to him. Tommy collected his wandering thoughts with a jerk.

'Blimey, Tom,' Fred was saying. 'We di'nt half have a laugh tonight. Me and Reg takes a ball of chalk up to Notting Hill Gate and we picks up a couple of janes outside Woolworth's. Neither Reg nor me's got no lob to spare so we lumbers 'em into the Park. Laugh? You should of seen us. Reg says to his tart, right pusher she was and all, "Do you take it?" he says.

Gawd, she di'nt half carry on. Thought she was going to jump straight down his throat.

'"That's all right," says Reg, straightening his tie, you know the way he does, "I meant sugar in your tea." Caw, laugh?'

Fred roared heartily. Tommy smiled. Somehow he felt above such boyish pleasures as taking girls out.

'Have it off wi'em?' he said.

'No,' answered Fred a little shamefacedly, 'weren't that sort I guess. But talking about tarts, you want to watch that Else of yours.'

'Why, what's up?'

'Nothing much. Only I seen her walking along the Avenue tonight with a leary-looking geezer.'

'The bastard. I'll knock his head off. Who was he, d'you know?'

'No, never seen the cowson before as I knows of. Here, Reg.'

Reg left Jimmy and came over to the boys.

'Didja ever see that geezer before?'

'Which geezer?'

'The geezer what we saw walking up the Avenue with Tommy's Elsie.'

'No. Never seen him before.'

'What kind of bloke was he?'

'Toff, I guess. Di'nt look like one of the local herbs.'

'I'll do the bastard if I lay me hands on him.'

'No need to get so bleeding airyated, Tom boy. Don't expect there's any harm done.'

'Better bleeding well not be.'

Jimmy joined them.

'Hear you had it off at Camden Town tonight, Tom boy.'

'That's right.'

'Fighting there again next week, ain't you?'

'That's right.'

'Goin' to have it off again?'

''Spect so. Can't say for certain though till I know who I'm fighting.'

'That's right. Have a cigarette?'

Tommy and Jimmy lighted up. Jimmy leant forward and caught Tommy by the arm.

'Here, Tom, I want to talk to you. Come outside a minute.'

Tommy picked up his bag and followed Jimmy out on to the pavement. Jimmy puffed on his cigarette for a couple of seconds and then looked round to see that nobody was listening. When he spoke he hardly moved his lips.

'Listen, Tommy,' he said. 'Let me know when you're going to win, see? I'll have a bit of money on you and I'll see you all right. Stick to me and you won't come to no harm.'

'Yes, but you can't always tell in the fight game. Outsiders turn up.'

'You're telling me? But there are such things as carve-ups, you know.'

'Maybe. But I don't want to fight in them.'

Tommy turned to go back into the café, Jimmy caught him by the arm.

'Listen, Tommy, get wise to yourself. I know big blokes, real gamblers. Blokes what'll speculate a thousand pound on a good chance and you can meet 'em, see. Just so long as you bring home the bacon. You don't want to fight in six-rounders all your life, do you?'

'Course not.'

Jimmy dropped Tommy's arm. He threw away his cigarette butt.

'If you want to get into the real money you got to have backing. A boy can be all right and never do no good, because he never had a bastard interested in him. You know that? Am I right?'

'That's right enough.'

'Well, I can introduce you to the boys what'll give you that backing. Don't forget. Think it over.'

They stepped back into the café-bar. Tommy decided to go home.

'Good night all,' he said.

'Going home, Tom?' said Fred.

'Yes.'

'Half a mo'. I'll come with you. Coming, Reg?'

'Yes. Come on, Stan.'

The four boys walked up through Norland Market together. Reg and Stan were on the outside of the pavement, Tommy walked next to Stan, and Fred was on the inside. Fred suddenly caught sight of Tommy's bag.

'Watchew got in there?'

'Me fighting clobber.'

'Christ, I thought you'd done a job. You don't want to let a copper see you carrying that, he'll lift you.'

'You ought to of bin in kip hours ago,' said Stan. 'Bleeding silly standing around caffs all night if you want to do anything in the boxing racket.'

''Ere, Stan,' said Tommy, 'd'you ever come acrost this trick? You get your left fist caught up in the other bloke's armpit in a clinch, give a little tug and while he's off his balance hook him with your right.'

'Yerce. That's a good 'un. It ain't quite in the book of rules, but you can gamble on having it off.'

'Old Harry's never showed it me.'

'Harry who?'

'Harry Dunn. He's bin training me.'

'Old Dunny ain't no bleeding good,' said Stan contemptuously. 'He useter be all right in his time, but he's old-fashioned and too bleedin' clean and straight be a long sight.'

'Well he's been a good pal to me. He's taught me all I know and he's got me three fights.'

'Yerce? And if you don't watch your step you'll have him round your bleeding neck like a millstone all the while you're in the boxing game.'

The boys paused on the corner of St Anne's Road. This was where they separated. They said good night.

Alone, Tommy walked rapidly through the back streets to his home. He pulled the latch-string and let himself in. The house was in darkness. As he stood in the narrow hallway he could hear his family snoring. He went into the front room. Ernie sat up in bed.

'Th-that you, Tommy?'

'Yerce.'

'How'd you get on?'

'Knocked him out in the fourth.'

'G-good.'

Tommy lighted the gas. He put a ten-shilling note in the teapot for his mother. Of his fight winnings, now he had paid his bus fares, all that was left was 1s 11d. He undressed rapidly, turned out the gas and jumped into bed. His body was cold. It made Ernie shiver.

'Move over, Ern,' he said, 'and give a bloke a bit of room.'

Ernie complied. Tommy laid his head on the pillow. A sudden thought struck him.

'Here, Ern,' he said. 'Else ain't going with a feller, is she?'

'N-not as I knows of. Why?'

'A couple of the boys seen her in the Avenue tonight with a flash-looking bloke, looked like a toff, he did. Know who it is?'

'N-no.'

'Go'night.'

'Go'night.'

CHAPTER V

Sunday afternoons were dull. Tommy was sitting in front of the kitchen stove reading the *News Of The World*; Elsie was reading *Peg's Paper*; Ernie was trying to get Radio Luxembourg; Mrs Mutch was darning socks; Lily was playing on the floor; Fred Mutch was out with his pigeons. He had a race on that afternoon and might pick up twenty-five bob.

Tommy threw down the newspaper, crumpling it on the floor. From behind his ear he took half a Woodbine and lighted it from a coal that had fallen from the range. He looked about the room, hoping to find something interesting. His eyes rested on the battered alarm clock, which stood on the mantelpiece. The hands pointed to a quarter to eight. It was always necessary to do some complicated mental arithmetic about that alarm clock. Somehow or another the alarm pointer had got stuck and, in order to set the alarm for the time when they wanted it to sound, they had to put the ordinary hands at a most improbable hour and subtract till they arrived at an approximately correct estimate. It had started a lot of arguments.

It was boring.

Tommy had got up early. On Sunday mornings he had an early paper round. Then he always picked up a couple of shillings helping out at Rag Fair. Now that they had stopped Sunday afternoon boxing he was always at a loose end.

Ernie left the wireless.

'Can't you get nothing?'

'Only London. Something's gone wrong.'

'Strikes me something's always going wrong with that bleedin' set.'

'Your language,' said Elsie, looking up.

'Getting too good for us, are you, Miss Pound-Note?'

Tommy stretched himself.

Maybe the best thing to do would be to find himself a girl. If he had a tart of his own there'd always be something to do. Funny how some blokes always ran round with girls instead of with mates.

He got up to walk to the window. In getting up he knocked over his chair. Elsie looked up again.

'There's a Mr Clumsy for you.'

'Shut yer bleeding row.'

'Don't you swear at me. Who'd you think you're talking to?'

'Hark at her!'

Tommy looked through the lace curtains. They were the pride of Mrs Mutch's heart. In the yard was the lavatory, an old pram and the pigeon-loft. Soon the judges of the pigeon race would be arriving.

Blimey, he didn't half feel browned off.

He turned round again.

'Else,' he said.

'What you want?'

'What come of that girl you used to go with?'

'Which girl?'

'The girl as you useter know at work. You know, what lives in Penzance Place. Phyllis, wasn't it?'

'That's right. Why, I dunno. She's still around.'

'Don't you go with her no more?'

'No, why?'

'Just wondered. What happened? Have you fell out?'

'There's a Mr Inquisitive for you!'

'Gor blimey, you can't even arst a question. Nice thing that is I must say.'

'Now then,' put in Mrs Mutch.

'Whyn't you sit down? You give me the c-creeps fi-fidgeting about,' said Ernie.

'You hush,' said Tommy.

He was proper fed up now and no mistake. He had a good mind to go out without his tea and all.

He went into the front room and started to dress himself. He had three and sixpence. Mrs Mutch heard him moving about, and called out:

'Watchew doing, Tom?'

'Getting ready.'

'Whaffor.'

'Goin' out. I'm proper browned off. Gives me the horrors laying around.'

'Have your tea before you go. I'm going to have a nice tea. There's them two judges coming.'

'Don't want no tea.'

Tommy went out. The street was not empty. Kids were playing about. Mothers sat on doorsteps. At the corner a knot of youths were standing. Tommy went up to them.

'Whatcher Tom.'

'What ho mate. What's on?'

'Nothin' much. We thought of getting up a little spieling party. Like to take a hand?'

'Watchew going to play. Nap?'

'Na. Pontoon.'

'Well, it's got to be low stakes then, mate. I only got a couple of bob to lose.'

'Oh you'll be all right. We won't none of us go heavy. Come on. The more the bleedin' merrier.'

'All right. Don't mind if I do. Where you going to play?'

'In the cellar of that empty gaff in Penzance Place. We got the duracs and a couple o' candles. But look, we don't all want to go round there together. Makes it too bleedin' obvious. Come round in two and threes and keep your peepers open so as no one don't rumble you.'

Ten minutes later six boys were sitting uncomfortably in the cellar of an empty house playing cards by candlelight.

Reg had the first bank and cleaned up nicely for a bit. The cards passed to Stan who could not hold quite such a nice bank. Finally it broke him.

He dealt Tom an ace. Tom wagered threepence. Stan glanced at his card. It was the ace of hearts. The other four boys had ha'pennies and pennies for their stakes. He doubled. Tom put down his last sixpence and picked up the coppers which he had originally staked. Stan dealt again.

With trembling fingers Tom picked up his second card and then with a cry of triumph flicked it over. It was the queen of hearts. Stan looked at his card. It was the six. Seven or seventeen. All the other boys stood. He had the table against him. He dealt himself another card. It was a five. Twelve. He dealt again.

All the boys craned forward to see what luck he was going to have.

'Blimey!'

'Gawd stone me dead!'

'Bleeding hell.'

'A bit o' paint.'

Stan's fourth card was the king of spades.

'Over the top,' he said philosophically and paid out.

Tommy picked up eighteen-pence. It was his bank. Before the first candle had burnt itself out all the boys were skint. He had made over ten shillings.

They all stood up and dusted each other down.

'Blimey, Tom boy, you ain't half lucky.'

'Must be a bleeding Yid.'

'If it wasn't that I knew you hadn't got enough sense I'd say that bleeding game was crooked, Tommy.'

'You'd be surprised, mate.'

Tommy went back home. It was quite dark now and rather cold. When he got in there was quite a crowd in the kitchen. Most of them were pigeon-fanciers whom Fred Mutch had brought home to tea.

Tommy called his mother into the hall.

'Here, Mum,' he said. 'Here's a dollar for you.'

'Wherever'd you get that?'

He poured an assortment of ha'pennies, pennies and sixpences into her hands.

'Been in a bit of a gambling school.'

'Now, Tom,' she said anxiously. 'Mind you don't land yourself into no trouble. Boxing, gambling. Gawd knows where you'll end up.'

'In bleedin' Park Lane I shouldn't be surprised. Don't you worry, Mum. I won't come to no harm. I got enough sense to keep out of trouble.'

'I hope you have, Tom. Had your tea?'

'No. Got any left?'

'Yes, there's plenty in the kitchen.'

Tommy followed his mother into the kitchen. His father looked up. He had lost the race that afternoon and was in a bad temper.

'So you got back then?'

'Seems like it.'

'Don't want any of your bleedin' lip.'

'You want to be careful of that boy of yours, Fred mate,' put in one of his cronies. 'I hear he can handle his dukes all right. Turning into a regular terror, ain'tcha Tom?'

Tommy grinned and sat down at the table. He cut himself a thick slice of bread and spread it with margarine and sardines. The teapot had been stewing on the range. His mother brought him over a cup of strong tea made with condensed milk.

Tommy was hungry. By the time he had eaten three slices of bread and sardines, a plate of stewed apples-and-custard and a slice of cake, he felt better. He poured out his fourth cup of tea and lighted a Woodbine.

One of his father's friends glanced up at the clock.

'Gawd blimey all bloody hurray. That ain't the time fer Christ's sake.'

'No. Clock's a good three hours fast. It's round about quarter-past seven.'

'Well, they're open then. How about stepping round to The Norland and having one?'

'That ain't a bad idea.'

The pigeon-fanciers got up and went out. Tommy was left alone with Ernie, Lily and his mother.

'Where's Else?' he asked.

'Gone out with her feller.'

'What feller?'

'The feller she goes with.'

'Yes, I know that, but who is he?'

'He's a new feller she's just taken up with.'

'Flash-looking kind of geezer is he?'

'I dunno, she don't tell me nothing.'

Mrs Mutch began to collect the tea things. She had a lot of washing-up to do and some ironing. She wanted to get it all done so that she would have time to go out to the local and have a glass of stout before they closed. Tommy got up.

'Just going for a bit of a stroll round,' he said.

'Don't you get up to no more gambling.'

'Trust me.'

Tommy walked quickly through Notting Dale in the direction of Shepherds Bush. In Rag Fair there were just a few people about, but Uxbridge Road wore the usual Sunday evening air. The Bush itself was crowded with promenaders. He looked in at the caff. It was too early for any of the boys.

Charlie was not behind the counter. There was the Sunday night relief man instead. Tommy stood for a few moments outside, jingling the coins in his trousers pocket.

With the money which he had won gambling he could go to the pictures: he could try to pick up a jane and take her for a walk across Wormwood Scrubs.

He watched, for a few minutes, the passers-by.

There was not much chance of picking up a girl while he

was on his own. Most of them went about in couples. He lighted a Woodbine.

There were a hell of a lot of girls about. Some of them looked all right. A couple of real snappy pieces – right flash bramahs – came past.

'What ho sweetheart,' he called out. 'Where you goin'?'

'Somewhere you can't go!'

They crossed the road and went into the public lavatory.

He whistled after several couples. None of them as much as turned their heads. He felt a bit disheartened.

Perhaps it would be an idea to go and have half a pint somewhere. Perhaps it would not.

Blimey, he thought, Sunday was a proper bastard and no mistake. Here he was with about seven and a tanner to spend and nobody to spend it with.

The best thing would be to have half a pint. The Bush Hotel – or The Star?

Caw, there was that geezer he had met at the boxing. He used to get in The Star. Got in the saloon bar too, he'd lay a pound. And there was usually a crowd there.

Tommy crossed the road and went in the saloon bar of The Star. Somebody was playing a piano. There did not seem to be anybody interesting about although there was a good crowd there.

He went up to the bar to order himself a drink. Somebody hit him on the back. It was the man who had spoken to him at Camden Town.

'Tommy Mutch, isn't it?'

'Yes, guv'nor.'

'Remember me?'

'Yes, you're the bloke what chatted me after I'd been fighting at Camden Town.'

'Have a drink?'

'I don't mind having a brown ale with you, guv'nor.'

'Good. And one brown ale,' called out the man.

The barmaid brought him two Scotches, a gin-and-lime and a brown ale. He threw a ten-shilling note on to the beer-slopped counter.

'Help us carry these drinks across, will you?' he said collecting his change.

Tommy picked up the two Scotches. Somehow he felt it would have been bad manners to have carried his own drink. He followed the man across to where a woman and another man were sitting at a wicker table beside a palm tree. The woman was the same one that the man had had with him the other night.

They set the glasses down. Tommy stood shyly in the background.

'You remember Tommy Mutch, don't you, darling?' he said. 'This is Tommy Mutch, the boxer. Tommy, this is a friend of mine, Mr Sanders.'

With limp ceremony Tommy shook hands all round. Everybody sat down. There was an awkward pause. Tommy looked at his new companions and tried to figure them out.

The girl was a good-looker and well-dressed. A slightly oversexed air hung about her. Mr Sanders was red-faced. He looked about forty-five. Below his closely-cropped hair his red neck bulged out over a tightly-fitting and very clean stiff white collar. Across the waistcoat of his dark suit was draped a thick gold watch-chain from which dangled several tokens and emblems. He wore a ring on the little finger of his podgy left hand. He might have been a bookmaker.

Tommy's friend broke the silence. He squirted a little soda water into Mr Sanders' glass and his own.

'Well, all the best,' he said, picking up his glass.

'Here's how,' said the girl.

'Good luck,' said Mr Sanders.

'Best of luck,' said Tommy.

Mr Sanders set down his glass of Scotch and soda. All

his movements, mental and physical, seemed to be conditioned by his podginess. He turned to Tommy.

'So you're a boxer?'

'So they tell me.'

'Where you fighting next?'

'At the Marlington Hall, Camden Town, on Thursday.'

'Six-rounder?'

'That's right.'

'Going to win?'

'Hope so.'

'Not certain then?'

'No. Other contestant ain't settled yet.'

'I see.' Mr Sanders picked up his glass again and took another drink. 'Got a manager?'

'Well, no. Not exactly, that is, I got a geezer what's bringing me on. Old-timer, name of Harry Dunn, he is. He kind of trains me and helps me to get fights. Lot of blokes know him.'

'I see. You're not under contract to him?'

'No. But I wouldn't like to carve him up. He's been good to me.'

'H'm. You'll never get anywhere, you know, without a manager. You don't want to spend all your time fighting six-round preliminaries, do you? Whyn't you join the stable of someone good?'

'Don't see no sense in giving all my winnings to some cunning bastard. Why should I take all the bashings and have him poncing on me, just because he can fix me up with a fight or two?'

'Well, if you look at it that way,' Mr Sanders shrugged his heavy shoulders. The charms on his watch-chain danced. 'All boxers' managers aren't cunning bastards, you know.'

Tommy winced. He realised that he had been guilty of using obscene language in front of a lady. And a right flash one too. Anyhow, thank God, she probably wouldn't understand the meaning of such a low word as ponce.

'Sorry, miss,' he mumbled. 'Forgot meself.'

She flashed a smile at him, which made his flush deepen. 'That's all right.'

'Is the boy any good, Arthur?' asked Mr Sanders.

The flash-looking man set down his glass.

'Is he any good? He's a damned good little six-rounder if that's what you mean. He put Smiler Hogan to sleep with as nice a right-hander as you've ever seen. And he's got what it takes. Down here.'

He tapped his stomach significantly.

'Sounds all right. How many fights you had, son?'

'Be my fourth professional on Thursday.'

'Well you got a lot to learn yet. I'll be along on Thursday and see how you shape. If you got the right stuff in you I might be able to do you a bit of good. Mightn't I, Arthur?'

'That's right. If you want anybody to help you, you can't have anyone better than Sammy Sanders. Am I right, Dot?'

The girl again flashed her smile. Tommy was captivated. She was the goods and no error.

'Well, give it a name,' said Sammy Sanders. 'Give it a name. As for you, son, after your next drink you'd better lay off of it. It won't do no good to you. Not a ha'porth. Take my advice. Your best place is kip. Eat, sleep, work, that's the ticket for you. Skip the beer – and the janes. Neither done a bloke any good. All they do is waste his money, eh Dot?'

'Go on with you, Sammy. Giving the boy ideas about me.'

CHAPTER VI

Tommy was in his dressing-room at the Marlington Hall. He had changed into his boxing clothes and lay on the slab while Harry Dunn kneaded his stomach muscles. Other boxers sat or lay round in various stages of undress.

The door swung open. The promoter came in. Arthur and Sammy Sanders were with him. Sammy looked more opulently ponderous than ever. A smell of bay-rum, whisky and cigar smoke hung around him.

'Tommy Mutch here?' called out the promoter.

'Yes, guv'nor.'

'Me and these other gentlemen want to talk to you for a minute. Get outside you other blokes.'

The other blokes complied. Tommy struggled into a sitting position. Harry stood aside. Sammy Sanders sat down.

'Listen, Tommy,' said the promoter, 'I want to see what you can do tonight. I picked out a bloke that'll test you out. Frank Franks of Dagenham. Yiddisher boy he is. Now these gentlemen here are interested in what you can do. Show them. You was on a KO last week. Do the same again tonight and I'm not lying when I say you'll be hearing some good news. See what I mean? Am I right, gentlemen?'

'Ar,' said Mr Sanders.

'Yes,' said Tommy, 'but, look here, guv'nor. Last week you reckoned I spoilt your show by putting Smiler Hogan to sleep.'

'What I said last week and what I say this week's a couple of different things. Besides, last week there wasn't anybody interested in you. Don't forget, kiddo. Go to it and show these gentlemen what you can do.'

'Yerce,' said Mr Sanders. 'Watchew getting for this fight, Tommy?'

'Well, the guv'nor promised me thirty holes last week, but he only give me a quid because I put the other geezer out in the fourth. Didn't go the distance he reckoned.'

The promoter expanded his hands in deprecation.

'You know how it is, gentlemen,' he explained, 'I got me show to think of. He gets thirty shillings tonight – win, lose or draw.'

'Yerce,' said Sammy Sanders. 'You got friends now, Tommy. You got someone behind you. Don't forget it, see? Well, if you put this Frank Franks to sleep, I'll give you another pound on top of what you earn, see? I can't speak fairer than that, can I? You Harry Dunn, ain't you?'

'That's right.'

Harry dropped into the defensive. He had met people like Sammy Sanders before.

'I see, well, good luck Tom boy. Don't forget what I said.'

Arthur spoke:

'I got a message for you, Tommy. Dot'll be watching you and she hopes you win. Good luck.'

'OK.'

The three men went out. The other boxers came in. They had been standing shivering in the passage trying to overhear the conversation.

'What'd he say?'

'What's up? Wanted you to take the dive?'

'Throwing the fight, eh?'

'Just a little chat,' said Harry, fluttering round like a broody hen. 'Couple of sporting gentlemen interested in the lad. That's all.'

'Sporting gentlemen? That's a good 'un. I met their sort. The bastards.'

'Come on, Tom, lay down,' said Harry ignoring their remarks. 'I got to get busy on that kitchen of yours.'

Tommy settled back on the slab. Harry got busy. As he worked he whispered with his mouth close to the lad's ear.

'Don't like the bastards,' he said, 'slimy cowsons if you asks me. Still they may do you a bit of good, you never know. Hope so anyway. Wouldn't trust the bleeders, though. Hell of a lot they understand about handling fighters, coming in and flustering and flummoxing you about just before you got to go into the ring...'

The first preliminary was over. Tommy walked through the spectators and climbed through the ropes. The introductions bored him. He looked around for Dot, Arthur and Sammy. Dot waved her hand, her diamonds sparkling. Tommy mitted them.

He went to his corner. Sitting down he glanced at Frank Franks for the first time. He was a slim-built young Jew with a lithe figure. He had the narrow eyes and thin lips of a fighter. He was, Tommy knew, building himself a nice little reputation. Well, here was where Frank Franks lost it.

Harry was talking.

'Give him all you got, Tom. Make a fight of it from the first gong and if he tries to box clever, smother him. This may be your chance of a lifetime.'

The gong rang. The stools were whisked out of the ring. The gong sounded again. The contestants touched gloves. Franks stepped back hoping to work his way for an opening, but Tommy jumped in. He hit the Dagenham boy three times on the ribs. Franks countered with a light left to Tommy's head. Tommy kept boring in. Franks gave ground. He saw no sense in standing up under such a hail of blows. He sidestepped. Tommy, off his balance, slipped. He was up again. Franks uppercut him and Tommy checked his rush. The Jew followed up his advantage. He tried to crowd Tommy back to the ropes, but Tommy was having none of that. He stood his ground and swapped punches. The crowd roared. This was action.

Franks yielded ground again and Tommy came in. He caught Tommy in the mouth with a stinging left, but Tommy hit him twice on the ribs. Franks began to show red patches about his body. The gong sounded.

Harry flapped at him with a towel, while the other second sponged his mouth.

'Don't go mad, Tommy boy. This ain't a street fight, you know. Fight fast, but use your nut and don't keep on walking into his left hand.'

The gong went again.

Tommy rushed across the ring, ignoring Harry's advice. Franks, who was hardly out of his corner, stopped him with another left-hander to the mouth. Tommy caught Franks a nice right-hand swing. It was a little too high, but drove his head back. That was Tommy's opening. He ducked in under the guard and punished his opponent severely about the body. Franks backed and Tommy paused breathless. His mad rush had spent his energy.

Noting this, Franks hastened to press home his advantage. He aimed a vicious left at Tommy's face. Tommy, however, blocked it with his right glove and countered with his left to Franks' body. The punishment the Dagenham boy had taken downstairs began to tell. His head sagged forward. Quick as a flash, Tommy knocked it up again with a right uppercut and, while Franks was still off his balance, hooked him hard with his left hand.

Franks dropped to the floor.

At a count of seven he was up again, steadying himself with one hand on the ropes. Mercilessly, Tommy jumped in and drove Franks back into a corner. Franks covered up beneath Tommy's flailing fists. He slipped to the floor again. Angry red weals showed all over his body.

Gamely he struggled to his feet and tottered forward. His guard was low and weak. Tommy hit him at will five times about the head. He crossed his hands in front of his face.

With all his force Tommy's right hand hit him in the solar plexus. He dropped.

He was out this time.

Tommy skipped blithely to his corner, mitting his hands high above his head in acknowledgement to the applause he was getting. Franks got a good hand, too, for being such a game loser.

'Good work, son,' said the regular second, 'you put him to sleep in jig-time.'

Harry was not so laudatory.

'Don't want to lose your head like that, Tom,' he said. 'Blimey, you had him wide open that time he come out of the first count and you let him cover up. When you got your man like that measure him with your left and whip over your right hand as hard as you can. Don't mess about hitting him all over the shop, see? Still, there's no harm done, I suppose. I wonder what these bastards of got to say to us now.'

Tommy waved a hand at the second.

'Be seeing you,' he said.

'OK, kid.'

In the dressing-room Tommy took a shower and then let Harry get to work on him. Sammy Sanders and Arthur came in.

'Nice work, kid,' said Arthur.

'Well done, me old Tom,' said Sammy. 'I got a nice little oncer for you. Now, listen, you done well. I'm interested in you and I'm going to help you. Get done quick and we'll all go and have some supper together. You could do with a good feed, I reckon, after that. You'll come, Harry me old cock-sparrow, won't you?'

'Don't mind,' said Harry not looking up from his work.

'Now, Tom,' went on Sammy, ignoring the other fighters who were gawping. 'You don't want to make mistakes. Boxing's a business, same as anything else, and you need a business head to guide you. I'll give you some advice free, gratis and for nothing, and what could be fairer than that? That crook of a guv'nor will be here in a minute, breaking his neck to sign you up for a series of fights in his hall. Tell him it's ixnay, see? Take your wages and don't do nothing else. I'll get you more and better fights than that schlemihl. See you in the car park in a few minutes.'

Arthur and he were out of the door again.

'To hell with him,' growled Harry. 'Who's he think he is, telling you to hurry? Take your time. Fighters got to be treated right. Ordering everyone about like a lot of slaves. Thinks he's Hitler, I s'pose.'

He massaged more slowly than ever.

'Bit o' sense, though, what he said about the guv'nor. It's not every preliminary boy with a record like yours. Not out of the novice class yet and you got two KOs to your credit. Caw, your kisser ain't half coming up. He's landed twice on the same place as Hogan did. You want to watch left-handers, son.'

The promoter came in. He was all smiles.

'Seen Mr Sanders,' he said. 'Good.'

'Going to have a bite to eat with him.'

'That's right. Well, here's thirty bob for you. I don't grudge it. It was nice work. Now listen Tommy, you just step into my office after the show and we'll talk things over. I can see you doing big things.'

'Not interested,' said Harry.

'Don't be silly,' said the promoter. 'You'll harm the boy's chances.'

'You heard,' said Harry. 'We're not interested. Don't you understand English?'

CHAPTER VII

Tommy sat at the back of the car. Arthur was driving with Dot beside him. Mr Sanders' bulk overlapped Tommy's slim, hard body. Harry was crushed into a corner.

Tommy's mind was busy on financial details. He had given his second half-a-crown and Harry ten shillings. If he gave his mother a pound he would still have seventeen and six. He would keep the seven and sixpence and put ten shillings away towards buying himself a dressing-gown.

A boy who was coming on as fast as he was needed to study his public. They'd always think him just a punk unless he managed to flash himself up a bit. A bloke who climbed into the ring with a towel on his shoulders didn't look worth a handful of coppers.

It was a bit of all right getting two-pound-ten just for one fight. Very handy. Like to see his mother's face when she got handed a oncer.

The car was going down Tottenham Court Road. Sammy Sanders leant forward. His movement disturbed all his fellow occupants of the back seat.

'Where are we going, Arthur?' he asked.

'Well, I was thinking of the Corner House. Thought that would be best for all of us.'

'Ar,' said Sammy Sanders, struggling back.

They parked the car in Hanway Place and went into the Corner House. The other customers looked up at them. They made a strange party even for that locale of queer parties. First, there was Dot, with her blonde hair, her fur coat and her diamonds; then there was Arthur, in a smart suit, but with a general air of shiftiness; then came Sammy Sanders' loudly-clothed bulk; Tommy in his square-shouldered belted overcoat, with his cropped head and swollen lips; Harry with his fist-ravaged face, an old check cap and a high-necked sweater.

The bright lights made Tommy's eyes, still tired from the glare of the ring, smart.

They found a table and sat down.

'What we going to have?' asked Sammy Sanders. 'Steak suit everybody? Good. Five steaks, chipped potatoes and cabbage,' he told the waiter. 'And drinks? Beer for you Tom? And Harry? Right. Two pints of beer. Dot, you'll have a gin-and-lime I suppose, and Arthur a Scotch? A gin-and-lime, two pints of draught beer and two double Scotches with a small soda.'

He passed round his cigarette case and settled himself more comfortably until his chair creaked. When they had lighted up he spoke, clearing his throat first with a loud rattle.

'Well,' he beamed. 'I don't know if you know who I am. I'm Sammy Sanders the bookmaker, well-known on the turf, on the dog-tracks and for my football pools. Honesty and civility, that's been my business motto. You've heard of me. Everybody's heard of me. Now, I taken a night off from the dogs specially to see you fight, Tommy lad, and I'm glad I done it, because whatever anyone may say nobody can deny that Sammy Sanders knows a good thing when he sees one, and I think we're one and all agreed that young Tommy here's a good thing. If we're sensible we'll all make a lot of money out of it, besides helping on the good old English manly art of self-defence. Am I right, Arthur?'

'That's right, Sammy.'

'Good. Well, Tommy, I'm prepared to give you a chance and I don't think we'll fall out. Anyone'll tell you that Sammy Sanders'll always give a chance to a likely lad. If he won't tell you that, he's a liar. Now, Harry, you don't like me, I know ...'

Harry stirred uneasily and cleared his throat. He wished that they had not come to this place, all bright lights and so on scaring a bloke out of his mind. He would have been a whole lot happier having a pie and beans at a coffee stall.

Sammy Sanders held up his hand.

'That's all right. Harry, me old cock. Don't tell no lies. You don't like me. That don't harm me. There's plenty of blokes don't like me and I don't lose a night's rest over it. Jealous of me, that's what they are, jealous of me and my success. But there's no need for us to fall out, Harry, no need at all. You do me no harm and I won't do you no harm. That's fair enough.'

The waiter brought the drinks.

Sammy paused long enough in his speech to pour some soda into his glass and take a mouthful of liquor.

'Good health, all,' he said. 'Now Tommy, the first time he met me, told me about you and said you'd treated him right and he was going to treat you right. All the more credit to the lad, that's what I say. Now this is what I suggest. Take it or leave it. Tommy comes under my management – we'll talk the details over later, and with Tommy comes Harry. Harry's not a businessman or else Tommy wouldn't of bin wanting a manager: Harry's a fighting man and Tommy wants a trainer. What's more sensible than Tommy having Harry for his trainer?'

The waiter brought the steaks. Sammy Sanders paused while the man busied himself around the table. When he had gone, he spoke again.

'Right, well, that's the general idea. Let's think it over while we get stuck into this grub.'

Tommy hesitated. He watched how the others ate, not wishing to make a fool of himself. Dot spoke to him.

'I thought you were wonderful tonight,' she said. 'I was ever so thrilled.'

Tommy choked with embarrassment.

'Aw, that was nothing. He wasn't any good. He couldn't take it.'

'He would have to have been a pretty tough guy to have taken what you were dishing out,' said Arthur. 'What did you think of the fight, Harry?'

'It was all right,' said Harry, showing all the food that was in his mouth while he spoke.

'You know,' said Arthur, 'I think Tommy's going to be a title holder. He's going to be a popular boy with the crowds anyhow. He's got what it takes. Colour, fire. He's got a lovely wallop, he's game enough to stand up to punishment and he's quick as lightning. And with his good looks he'll have all the girls wild about him. Won't he, Dot?'

'I expect they're all nuts about him already,' said Dot smiling at Tommy.

Tommy was red and choking with shyness. He wished that they would lay off a fellow.

Arthur raised his glass.

'Here's to the new lightweight champion,' he said.

All except Tommy drank. Harry was frowning with fury. He did not think it was good for the boy cracking him up this way. Sammy Sanders pushed his empty plate away and took a mouthful of whisky and soda.

'Ah,' he said with satisfaction. 'Now let's get to business.'

'What you do for a living, Tommy boy?' he asked.

'Paper boy,' said Tommy.

'There's not a lot of money in that, is there? Now, if you'll come under my management I'll guarantee you three pound a week. Whenever you fight you get an extra pound. If you win it's thirty bob. I'll be losing money on you at first. Is that fair enough?'

'Yerce,' put in Harry, 'what abaht this. Tommy's on the upgrade. He wins a fight say and there's a purse of twenty-five quid in it, all he pulls in for hisself is four-pound-ten. Call that fair?'

'What you don't understand, Harry me old pal,' countered Sammy, 'is this. Here's Tommy getting three pound a week all the year round. That's hundred and fifty-six pound. Suppose for the sake of argument he has thirty fights, there's another thirty pound, one hundred and eighty-six. Right. Of them thirty fights he wins twenty. There's an extra tenner. One hundred and ninety-six pound. Bleedin' near four nicker a week. Excuse me language, Dot.'

'Yerce, but suppose he gets in the big money class?'

'Suppose he don't. Think of what I'm gambling on losing. Close on two hundred pound in a year.'

Tommy looked from one to the other. This was beyond him.

'You can do anything messing figures about that way,' said Harry.

'Figures never lie,' said Sammy. 'Live at home, Tommy? Well, think of the extra money you'll be able to bring home to the old lady. Don't that make any difference?'

'Yerce,' said Tommy, 'but how about Harry. Don't he get nothing? You said as you was going to cut him in.'

'What you work at, Harry?' asked Sammy.

'Market work,' said Harry.

'Well, what you mean? Porter at Covent Garden or something?'

'Nah. I puts in a day's work Saturday helping out a mate of mine what's got a stall in Portobello Road and on Sunday mornings I helps round at Rag Fair. Sometimes I gets an afternoon at Shepherds Bush market.'

'Don't do very well at that, I'll bet. Can't be much in for you.'

'Me old lady goes to work charing,' said Harry defensively, 'and me eldest gel's got a job in a factory on the Great West Road. Thirty-five bob a week she's drawing. And what with me broken time money from the labour and the allowance I get on me two youngest what are still going to school I can manage all right. Of course I can't run to this.'

He waved a hand round, taking in the room compre-
hensively.

'How'd a pound a week look to you acting as trainer to
Tom? You wouldn't have to give up your market work and
the extra money would be all bunce.'

'Wouldn't be worth it to me.'

'Why not?'

'I'd lose me labour money if I was working for you.'

Sammy gave a sigh of despair. This was not being so easy
as he had thought. He had hoped to have picked up Tommy
at bargain rates.

He signalled to the waiter.

'Let's have another drink all round,' he said.

'Very sorry, sir. You can't, it's too late. You'll have to have
something to eat with it.'

'All right, all right. Bring us ham sandwiches and the same
drinks all round again.'

'Very good sir.'

'Now, listen, Harry,' he said, 'you're spoiling Tom's chances.
Have a bit of sense for the love of Mike. Look, how'd you
like to work for me?'

'Doing what?'

'Well, I got street blokes collecting for me. How about
being a runner? I'll pay your fines and give you a couple o'
quid a week. It's a light job and it won't take all day and in
your spare time you can train Tommy.'

'Sounds all right.'

'It is all right, blast it.'

Sammy was pleased at his new suggestion. His business
would have to carry the burden of Harry instead of him
having to pay personally.

'I'll have to think it over.'

'Why can't you answer now?'

'Well, I don't know exactly what me old lady's going to
say.'

'She's going to be pleased, ain't she? Gawd almighty. Two pounds is more than you'll be drawing from the labour for half a week, I'll lay.'

'Yerce, but then there's me market work.'

'Oh, my good Gawd. You and your market work. Carry on with that and all.'

'Yerce. But how long's this job of yours going to last?'

'As long as Tommy's under my management and you train him.'

'Yerce, I see. And how long's Tommy going to be under your management?'

'As long as me and him agrees. We'll have a contract, of course.'

'Yerce, I see. And s'posing Tommy climbs to the top of the tree he's still drawing three pound a week from you? No, it ain't good enough. Not near.'

He took a healthy pull out of his new pint of beer.

Sammy sighed again. Arthur was listening intently, but Dot was bored and powdering her nose. Tommy was watching her.

'We'll have a time clause on the contract and if Tommy makes good he gets a raise. That fair enough?'

'S'pose so,' grudged Harry. 'But listen, you give Tommy twenty pound down and me ten pound and the deal's on.'

'What, in advance wages?'

'No. Nothing like that. Just a sweetener.'

'All right. Have it your own way. It's a bargain. Come to my office tomorrow morning and we'll sign it up.'

'You got a licence, ain't you?'

'Watchew mean, licence? I'm running boxers not boozers.'

'A Board of Control licence. That's what I mean. If Tommy boxes not under the management of a bloke with a BBBC licence he'll lose his own.'

'Listen. You trying to teach me my business or have you gone just plain screwy? I got a BBBC manager's licence. I got six boys I handle already. My name's Sammy Sanders. Never heard of me?'

'Can't say I have. I'm a fighting man. In my day a bloke could be a fighter without a lot of lice trying to suck the blood off of him.'

'Garn. Shut up. You make me sick. Straight you do. Here'm I trying to help you and all you do is make trouble. Now listen, Tommy, I told you I got other blokes I handle. Well, I want you to box with them. That's part of what I pay you for, see?'

'Watchew mean? You want me to throw fights?'

Sammy Sanders sighed and frowned.

'Gor blimey. I never met a pair o' blokes like you. Take me up on every bleeding thing I say. No, I wanchew to act as a sparring partner. Is that clear? Don't I talk plain English?'

CHAPTER VIII

Tommy left the gymnasium. It was about half-past four. A December dusk filled the streets. He walked through the crowds in Hammersmith Broadway. There was a terrible noise going on. He was feeling fine. That last rubdown he had been given made him grand. He was wearing a new suit which he had got at Shepherds Bush. In his pocket was eight and sixpence.

He stood for a minute on the corner. There were not many girls about. The girls would be coming out later. A lot of married women were out shopping. Tommy would have liked to have had a girl of his own.

There was not much to do at half-past four. It was both too late and too early to go to the pictures. Tea would not be ready at home until about six. His body was glowing with health. He would have liked to have had a cigarette, but the geezer at the gym had made him knock off smoking.

It was a whole lot better training in a gym than on a street corner in Notting Dale. It was all right in the gym. A bloke learnt a lot. He kept on learning. That was the way to do it, to keep on learning. There was plenty to learn in the fight game.

A bloke could not be training all day. He needed something to do to fill in his time. It was best to have a tart and go straight. Then he didn't lay around caffs all the time. If a bloke got a tart and started going with her regular all the boys gave him the bird. Unless you put her in the family way and had to marry her, there did not seem to be any way of going with her regular.

Ernie hadn't never looked at a tart twice in his life and

he never seemed to want to. Some blokes were funny that way.

What the hell was there to do?

Oh yes, he could go and see Arthur and Dot. They had a flat in those buildings near the Olympia. They had asked him to come up and see them some time, just like Mae West. If they weren't out this would be a good time to go and see them.

He crossed the road and caught a bus. It was only a short ride, but what the hell.

At Blythe Road he got down, and looked at Olympia. They had championship fights at Olympia. Had there been any fights there since the Empire Pool had been opened at Wembley? He did not think so. He strolled along to the buildings the flat was in.

He walked up the stairs. His feet echoed. The flat was, so they had told him, on the third floor. He reached the third floor. There were two flats. Two equally blank front-doors facing each other. He rang the bell on the left-hand door. There was a smell of metal polish. He waited a long time for an answer. He rang again. There was no answer.

A feeling of despair gripped him. They must be out.

He crossed the landing and rang the bell of the right-hand flat. After the left lead, the right-hander. He waited. There was the sound of woman's footsteps. Tap, tap, tap. Slither. She had stepped on a mat. That mat had slipped. Thirty-three to one against it being Dot. The door opened. It was Dot. She was wearing a wrapper.

A grateful warmth rang through him.

Dot peered at him. It was dark in the hallway. The light was behind her. She could not make out who was there.

'Hallo, me old Dot. How you going on?'

The words cost him a pang to shoot out. He felt tongue-tied. Dot was right flash. He was only a six-round fighter out of Notting Dale.

'Tommy! Come on in.'

Tommy came on in. He carried his hat in his hand.

'Thought I'd look you up,' he explained. 'I'd nothing better to do.'

Dot laughed.

'That's not very complimentary of you, Tommy.'

He flushed again. She smiled. It was great to hit a man on the raw, even if he were only a cheap fighter. He twisted his hat in his hands.

'Well, you see, Dot. I was round this way and …'

'And what?'

'And … well, I came along.'

'Sure, Tommy, you came along. Well, drop your hat and come into the sitting-room.'

Tommy followed Dot into the sitting-room. She snapped on the electric light. The room looked right to him. Arthur must be pulling in something like real money.

'Like it?'

'Ever so. 'Tain't half nice.'

'All right, isn't it. Sit down and take it easy. Arthur's out. Come on, take this chair by the fire.'

Tommy sat down on the edge of an easy chair. Dot sat opposite him. Her wrapper gaped open. He could see the whiteness of her knee.

'Cigarette?'

She picked up a packet of twenty Craven 'A' that lay on a small table beside her.

'Well, I ain't s'posed to. I'm in training, you know.'

'Come on, one cigarette won't bust you. Light it up even if you don't smoke it. Makes it more homelike to see a man smoking.'

She tossed him over a cigarette. He caught it with his left hand and put it in his mouth, twisting it awkwardly in his lips. He had no match. Dot lighted up, her red lips curving round the tip of her cigarette as she drew in the first puff of smoke. She noticed that Tommy had not lighted his own cigarette.

'Match?'

She threw him a packet of book-matches. He lighted his cigarette and inhaled. The cigarette tasted good. She looked at him. Clearly, she had to put him at his ease. Two things put a man at his ease. Smoking and talking about himself. Tommy was already smoking.

'Well, Tommy, how're you getting on? How's the fighting game going?'

'All right. I won another fight at the Marlington Hall on Monday. The guv'nor wasn't half wild.'

'Why?'

'Why? 'Cause I signed up with Sammy instead of with him. Caw, he carried on something chronic. Still, Sammy'll get me fights there all the time and I'm building up my reputation. I've had six fights there and I ain't lost a bastard – sorry – I ain't lost one yet. The public's getting to like me.'

'You'll go a long way, Tommy.'

'Think so?' He threw his cigarette into the fire. He had not taken more than four pulls out of it.

'Why not. You got what it takes. Once your name is known, you'll be all right. You'll find all the girls after you. They like a good-looking fellow.'

She drew on her cigarette, watching Tommy's face all the while. It was fun.

'Yeah?'

'Yeah.'

He fidgeted uneasily. He lay back in the chair and then sat on the edge again. Dot got up.

'That light bothering you. There's quite enough light from the fire.'

She got up. As she moved she showed her limbs through her wrapper. Tommy's eyes followed her. She switched off the lights. Instead of sitting where she had before, she flopped down on a sofa that fronted the fire. The glow from the flames illumined the white of her knees.

'You comfortable there, Tommy?'

'Yes, sure.'

'Why don't you come and sit on the sofa next to me. You'll find it a whole lot nicer.'

Tommy rose. He did not understand. Dot was a right bramah. A bloke had to be polite. Unless a bloke did what a tart asked, particularly one like Dot who was a real rye mort, he was showing himself up as an ignorant bastard.

It took him a long time to make the three steps to the sofa. Some guys would have made it in jig-time. It was easy to take three quick steps in the ring. A thousand pairs of eyes were on you. Shuffle on the canvas. Wallop. You had taken three steps, quick dancing steps forward, you had buried your left in the other feller's kitchen, you had danced back again. It was one hundred per cent different when you walked across a room with a tart's eyes on you.

He sat down on the edge of the sofa. Shyly, he looked to his left. Dot was sitting there. What did a fellow do next? Maybe she was short of a bit. It was on the cards that Arthur could not serve her good. He looked like a weakling sort of a bastard.

Dot looked up at him with amusement.

'Relax, Tommy, sit back. You've been in the gym this afternoon?'

'That's right.'

'Well, sit back and take it easy.'

He sank back on to the cushions and crossed his legs. This was a slice of cake. It was all right. The sofa was fine. There were no springs broken. Caw, it must of cost a bit to furnish this flat.

Dot leant over.

'Put your head back,' she commanded.

Tommy put his head back. She thrust a cushion underneath

74

it. As she leant over Tommy caught the whiff of some scent. He was conscious of a pleasant glow of health. His stomach muscles contracted.

'That better?' her arm was still behind his head.

'Ever so. That's swell.'

His head dented the cushion. He made no further move. He dared make no further move.

'Another cigarette?'

'No thanks.'

'Come on. Be sociable.'

She leant forward to the little table. He could catch a glimpse of her firm, small breasts. His stomach muscles had yet had no chance to relax.

'Here you are.'

Saucily she stuck a cigarette into his mouth, struck the match and lit it for him. Still Tommy made no move. Dot was despairing. She put a cigarette in her own mouth – and waited.

'Aren't you going to give me a light?'

He took the matches, struck a match. The flame flickered out in his trembling fingers. He struck another, held it to the tip of Dot's cigarette. With a gentle pressure of her fingers she guided his hand. The flame licked its way like an angry cat round her cigarette. Still her fingers lingered. Their sensuous touch made Tommy's curiosity outrun his fears.

Greatly daring he took her hand in his. Her fingers were limp, lifeless. Maybe she was mad at him. After all, he was taking a liberty. He held her hand a trifle more firmly, she answered his pressure. Now, he was making progress. He let their linked hands drop to his lap. Dot's smile danced at him in the fire-glow.

'Arthur's out,' she said. 'It'll be simply ages before he's back.'

Maybe it was an invitation. Tommy did not know. Still, in for a penny in for a pound. After all, every woman, ribby or rye, was the same. He ran his fingers up her arm. She drew closer to him. He put his disengaged arm around her shoulders. Cleverly, she made no move, either of encouragement or reproach.

The fingers of his right arm lingered on her right shoulder. He could feel the flesh beneath the silk of her wrapper. Gently he released his right hand. First, he took the cigarette from his own lips and tossed it, a sparkling arc, into the fire. Then softly, he took the cigarette from Dot's lips. Softly she acquiesced. Her cigarette followed his.

He put three fingers of his hand underneath the smoothness of her chin, tilting it towards him. Again he paused, waiting for the smack on the chops to which he felt he should be entitled. No smack came.

He leaned forward and kissed her on the lips. At first, she was merely coldly complacent. Let the kid kiss her. Her lips did not move. Of a sudden the full vigour of his healthy young manhood smote her. She threw her arms round him, drawing him close to her. He felt the warmth of her body. Her lips were moving over his face, savouring its muscular tautness.

Tommy lost control. He had wanted a girl. Now he had one.

He kissed her all over her face, pushing back her blonde hair and exploring the roots of her nose, her eyes, her ears.

Beneath the weight that Tommy thrust upon her and the unexpected fervour of his passion, Dot recoiled.

On a sofa this was not comfortable.

'Tommy, dear,' she said, twining her fingers in the hair of his eager head, 'don't you think we'd be more comfortable if we went into the bedroom?'

CHAPTER IX

They lay outstretched in bed together. It was nice; both Dot and Tommy were enjoying it. If she stretched down her foot so far that she could touch his toes she got a feeling of cramp in the calf of her leg. It was a nice cramp. She liked it. Both were smoking cigarettes.

Tommy had forgotten that he was supposed to be fighting at the Lancaster Baths, Shoreditch, on Thursday. Anyhow, he had already smoked two cigarettes before going to bed and had later sampled that strange touch of a woman's flesh that is supposed to drain all the strength out of a man's body. Dot's fingers were drumming playfully on his thighs.

'You in love with Arthur?' he was impelled to ask.

'Why?'

'Just wondered. I mean, you and me, and I thought how could you be the same with Arthur.'

Dot stopped drumming her fingers. Her hand caught hold of his thigh instead. He was so sweet – and so young and strong.

'Why should I be in love with Arthur?'

'Well you wouldn't do this. I mean properly like you and me if you was, would you?'

There was the plaintive fierceness of a street beggar in Tommy's tone.

'Why not?'

'Well you know. I mean. You done this with me as if you liked it. Caw. It makes me curl up to think of you and Arthur.'

She leant over and kissed him. This was unbelievable.

'Silly kid,' she said.

'Why?'

'Well, haven't you thought? P'raps I stick with Arthur because he's a good provider, because he brings home the bacon. Never thought of that?'

Tommy squirmed.

'That's what a man's for,' she pursued relentlessly.

'I'm not much cop to you then,' he said heavily. 'I ain't got no real money.'

'No, but you'll have it. You'll have oodles of dough when you've made good as a boxer. With your money and your body you'll be able to get yourself most any girl in London.'

'That's all women want then, is it?'

'Of course, you darling. Whatever else did you think?'

Tommy was silent. After his great happiness, a weight lay on his heart. Other girls he'd had, on doorsteps, against railings or lying out on the grass of Wormwood Scrubs, had not chatted like this. A thought came to him.

'What's Arthur do to get his money?'

'What's Arthur do? There's a Mr Inquisitive for you.'

'Sorry. I didn't mean to take a liberty.'

'That's all right, darling. Forget it and kiss me.'

Tommy obeyed. Their bodies clung together for a minute. She ran her hands over his strong back.

He was so sweet, so young, so strong. She determined to hurt him all she could.

'What d'you think Arthur does?'

'Don't know. Something that brings in the money.'

'Something that brings in the money. There's a laugh. D'you know what Arthur's good at? I'll tell you. He's good at laying around doing nothing. I bring in the money.'

'You bring in the money. What d'you mean?'

Tommy turned over in bed and lay propped on his right elbow. He was uneasy.

'How does any girl bring in the money for her man? On the bash of course. Tommy darling, you're sweet, but you're a mug. Practically every night I walk Clifford Street and Bond

Street. I'm a brass, a cow, an old bag. D'you understand what I mean?'

For the space of a minute Tommy was silent. Then he spoke.

'You mean Arthur's poncing on you?'

'What else?'

'The dirty bastard. I'll kill him stone dead. I'll break every bleeding bone in his body. The cowson. I always thought he was a dirty looking son of a bitch.'

Dot laughed out loud.

'Really, Tommy, you're too funny. Supposing I don't want him killed? Supposing I like working for him? Arthur's all right. You forget about this. Forget about him, forget about me. There's nothing you can do about it, Tommy. Nothing at all.'

Tommy sprang out of the bed. His naked white figure gleamed in the darkness of the room. As he moved his muscles rippled.

'Blimey, Dot,' he said, 'you don't mean that. You can't mean that. Come along home with me. There's plenty of room for you. I'll fight meself punch-drunk to earn dough for you. Straight up I will. No kidding.'

'Don't be silly, Tommy,' said Dot wearily. 'You're a nice kid, but you're an awful mug. Get back into bed again and lay down.'

Tommy walked about the room with short, springy steps. His mind was working furiously, trying to face up to this new problem. Suddenly, he came over to the bed again and sat down on its edge. Words dribbled slowly out of his mouth. He was having a hard fight with his own inarticulateness.

''Ere, Dot,' he said, 'I got idea. Look. I'm fighting at Shoreditch Thursday against Young Donnelly. It's reckoned to be a set-up for me, see? The word's gone round I'm OK, see? They'll be laying odds against Donnelly.'

He paused.

'Two-to-one most like. I can get a bet on, see? A bet on

Donnelly, I mean. Maybe the book'll wear up to a fiver's worth of my dough. Well, if I lose, there's a tenner in it for me. That'd be handy. We could tally up together.'

'Supposing you don't lose?'

'But I will, that's easy.'

'But that'll spoil the reputation you're getting for yourself.'

'Oh no. I won't do anything'll harm me, see? Look, if I hit him low, kind of accidental done on purpose, the fight's given to Donnelly on a foul. I'm laughing. It's not as if I take a dive. I can still fanny that I ain't been kayoed or outpointed in seven contests. Won't do me ha'porth of harm.'

'And what are we going to do when that tenner's spent? Sammy's pay-off to you's only three pound a week.'

'Oh, I'll get it somehow. We'll manage, don't you worry.'

Dot mocked the serious boy with a laugh.

'It looks to me that the only difference is going to be that I'll have you poncing on me instead of Arthur. That the idea?'

Tommy flushed up. Dot laughed happily. He was easy game.

'Caw, you don't mean that. Blimey I wouldn't do that to a jane, course I wouldn't.'

Dot caught hold of Tommy's arm in a caress. After the powder, the jam.

'Now, listen to me a minute, Tommy. You're awfully sweet, but you've got a terrible lot of growing up to do. You stick to your fighting, I'll stick to Arthur. Remember that every fight you win is a fight for me. That's something, isn't it? Then, maybe, one day, when you're successful, when you're a champion, I'll leave Arthur and come to you. That's fair enough, isn't it? You haven't got much to offer a girl right now, you know.'

'S'pose I haven't. Blimey, Dot. I hope you don't reckon I've been taking a liberty do you, talking to you like I done. But I don't like to think of what you told me.'

'Well that's simple then, Tommy, you silly kid. Don't think

of it, skip it, forget it. Just think that perhaps one day we'll be together for good and all.'

'Blimey that wouldn't half be wonderful. Caw.'

Dot ran her fingers up and down Tommy's arm. Beneath its satin, almost hairless skin she could feel the hard knots of muscle. The inside of his forearm was almost as smooth as her own. He really was ever such a nice boy. Her fingers travelled down from the softness of his sinewy wrist to the sudden harshness of his palm.

She glimpsed the pulse beating in his forehead, the tenseness of his jaw. It was a shame to take the money.

His fingers tightened on hers. He was hurting her hand. It was nice.

'Dot,' he called hoarsely.

'Yes?'

'Dot,' he called again taking no notice of her amused inquiry.

'Silly Tommy.'

She pulled him down to her. The smooth muscles of his chest quivered like those of a racehorse as their skins touched. Her lips sought his mouth.

CHAPTER X

Tommy left Dot's flat and walked quickly along the back streets northwards. Up past Olympia, Sinclair Road, turn right over the bridge, Holland Road, across the Avenue, and into Notting Dale. His jaw was set and purposeful. His strides were short and quick.

He had broken training badly and he knew it.

In Sirdar Road one of the boys called out to him.

'Watcher, me old Tom!'

'What ho.'

He did not turn his head. He walked steadily on.

'Snotty bastard.'

The boy forgot all about him.

Tommy turned down the squalid little back streets and elbowed his way through the kids playing in the gutter. He swung round in to Wilsham Street. His father was standing on the corner talking to a couple of men.

'That's your Tommy, ain't it, mate?'

'Yus.'

'Hell of a hurry he's in.'

'Yus.'

'Doing all right, ain't he? Boxing.'

'That's right.'

Tommy pulled the latch-string, went into the hallway and stood there for a couple of seconds. It was nice to have the old familiar sour smell of home in his nostrils again. Why he had come home he did not know.

He went into the front room, throwing his hat down on the bed. He stood around. It was cold. He could hear his mother moving about in the kitchen. She called out to him.

'That you, Tom?'

'Yerce.'

'Tea ain't ready yet.'

He sat down on the table swinging his legs. What did he care if tea were ready or not! Still it was warmer in the kitchen. He got up and went there. His mother was, as usual, working at the stove. Washing hung from ropes festooned all over the room. He sat down on a chair. This was home.

'What ho, Mum.'

She turned round and smiled at him. Something, she could see, was wrong. If it was important Tommy would tell her about it.

'Seen your dad?'

'No.'

'He said he was going to the corner to chat a couple of blokes.'

'I never seen him.'

Mrs Mutch started to lay the table for tea.

'Just laying up,' she explained.

'Aw.'

The front door opened and closed.

'That'll be Ernie.'

'Aw.'

Ernie went into the front room. Tommy could hear him. His was hanging up his clothes. Ernie was a careful bloke with his clobber. Maybe it was working in a pawnshop that made him so.

Ernie came into the kitchen.

'Hello, Mum.'

He kissed his mother on the cheek.

'What ho, T-Tom. You b-back?'

'No. I took a header off of Hammersmith Bridge and drowned meself.'

'Yerce. You look like it.' Mrs Mutch rounded on Tommy. 'There's no call to take up Ernie sharply just 'cause he arst a question. I don't know what's a matter with you nowadays I'm sure.'

'All right, all right. Why can't you let me alone?'

Fred Mutch walked in. He was still wearing his cap. He rubbed his hands.

'Blimey, what's a matter? Bit of a barney going on, ain't there? Nice thing I must say. Ain't tea ready? Caw. Here'm I, come in fer me tea and all I hear's a bleeding argy-bargy. Like a lot of old women. Strike a light.'

'Yar. Don't you start too,' said Mrs Mutch.

'Caw. Ain't there no peace around here?'

Tommy got up disgustedly.

'Sit down Tommy and show a bit of sense. Tea'll be ready in a minute.'

Mrs Mutch laid the teapot on the table. Fred Mutch began to cut the bread.

'Where's Else?' he asked.

'I dunno,' said Mrs Mutch. 'She never tells me when she's coming in, I don't know what she's getting up to.'

'Not since she's been gallivanting around with that flash feller of hers, I s'pose,' said Tommy with a bitterness that made him surprised himself.

Ernie shot him a look. Mrs Mutch laid four plates of sausages on the table.

'Tea's ready,' she said.

The three men pulled up their chairs and fell to. Tommy was extremely hungry and made a good meal. At last, finished, he pushed his empty plate forward on to the table with his hands, at the same time shoving back his chair with the lower part of his spine. His father was blowing on a saucer of tea. Ernie was reflectively sucking his teeth.

'W-what you d-doin' tonight, Tom?' asked Ernie.

'Dunno. Might go up to the corner and chat the boys, I s'pose.'

'Have a b-bit of a walk round wi' me?'

84

'All right,' said Tommy. 'Might as well, I s'pose.'

The two boys went into the front room and got their hats and overcoats. They went out into the street together and stood hesitantly on the kerb.

'Which way we goin', Ern?' asked Tommy.

'Anywhere,' said Ernie. 'L-let's go up the back way to the Gate.'

They set off together up a back street towards Notting Hill Gate. At first they were silent, with that shy silence that only brothers can achieve. Ernie was struggling to get the courage to speak.

'L-look here, T-Tom,' he blurted out, at last, 'I g-got to speak to you. It's about Elsie. You g-got to do something. She's in trouble.'

'You mean, whatsaname,' said Tommy, 'she ain't in the way?'

'That's just what it is,' said Ernie.

They were passing the police station that stands at the corner of Ladbroke Grove and Ladbroke Road.

'It's that flash-looking feller of hers, I s'pose.'

'The-the-that's right.'

'The lousy cowson. I'll break his bleeding neck.'

The road was a steep gradient. It led from Notting Dale to Notting Hill Gate.

'Listen, T-Tom. There's no n-need for you to get tough about it. D-don't lose your t-temper and we ought to straighten th-things out.'

'How?'

'I d-dunno, b-but there m-must be a way.'

'You tell it to me and I'll do it. Where's she now, out with the bastard, I s'pose?'

'Yerce. I s'pose so.'

'How'd you come to find this out?'

'She told me.'

'Mum know?'

'No.'

They had climbed up to Notting Hill Gate and stood under the lights watching the traffic.

'Where we going now?' asked Tommy.

'How about going into the p-park?'

'No, let's go and have half a pint and think things over.'

'B-but you're in t-training.'

'I broke training already this afternoon.'

'W-why?'

'Blimey, now you're asking me something. I don't know I'm sure. I went round to a tart's flat and before I knew where I was, there I was. Couple of half-pints won't harm me after that. Besides, it ain't good to stay in training too long. A bloke gets stale.'

'All right, then. Let's go and have a quiet one.'

They went into the public bar of a Meux's house. Tommy ordered two half-pints of ale. He paid for them.

'Good luck, Ern,' he said.

'Good health.'

They drank. Ernie pulled out a packet of cigarettes.

'S'pose you won't have a W-Woodbine?' he said.

'Might as well,' said Tommy.

He took a cigarette and lit it from the match which Ernie held for him.

'Well,' he said. 'What we goin' to do?'

'I d-dunno.'

'Look, Ern,' Tommy said. 'You might as well give me the strength of this. Tell me what you know and I'll tell you what I think you ought to do.'

Ernie sucked his hollow tooth.

'Y-yerce. T-that might be best. W-well, it's like this. Elsie's b-bin g-going with this feller …'

'What's his name?'

'Leonard Watts, so she says. W-well, she's bin going with this Leonard Watts for some t-time now and h-he's got a bit of m-money to spend and he's spent it with her, see?'

'Yerce. What's he by trade that he's got this dough?'

'Well now you're arsting something. I don't exactly know. Why?'

'Well. It's like this. I thought if we was to find out where the bastard was working we could put the black on him and make him do something.'

'Yerce. There-there's s-something in that.'

'Well, go on.'

'W-where was I? Oh yus. Well, this feller's spent a b-bit of money with her, see, and I s'pose he's arst her what about it and she's thought to herself well he's entitled to a b-bit, see, and anyhow he's had his way with her, s-see?'

'Um. How many times did she say he done it?'

'She di-didn't say nothing about that.'

'No? Was he the first?'

'R-reckon so. Though she-she's always bin one fer a bit of a lark with the boys. W-well anyhow the j-job's done and n-now she's carrying. That's all I kn-know.'

'That's not a hell of a lot to go on. Don't you know no more? She didn't tell you how long she'd bin missing?'

'It's well over a month now. Maybe mo-more.'

'That's not a hell of a bleeding lot. We ought to be able to fix that up all right. I'll get hold of one of the boys and he'll be able to tell me the name of one of them old women what'll get rid of the load she's carrying fer her.'

Tommy emptied his glass. Ernie hastened to follow his example. He was not really fond of beer, but it was unusual for him to be out with Tommy and to be treated on equal terms. He had to play his part.

'Goin' to have another?'

'I don't mind.'

'T-two halves of ale.'

The barman served them. Ernie paid. The bar was beginning to fill up. When the two boys had first come in

87

they had been the only customers except for an old man in a dusty bowler hat, who was sitting by himself on a bench and was doing the crossword puzzle in the *Evening News*. By the bar-counter it was getting too crowded to be comfortable. They carried their glasses over to a corner and set them on a narrow wooden shelf. Tommy took a mouthful of beer.

'Here,' he said. 'What I don't understand is how she come to tell you.'

'N-no more d-do I. I g-guess she f-felt s-she had to t-tell someone. I was in. I was the only g-geezer in the h-house and s-she was alone so I s'pose she had to t-tell me 'cause ther-there wasn't nobody else to tell.'

'Yerce. I reckon that's about it. Well, there's three things we can do. All we got to decide is which one's the best. I can get hold of an old dear who'll manage things, it won't cost much, see? Else we can make the bastard marry her and the other one's to let her have the kid and make the bloke pay her half-a-quid a week. What d'you reckon's the best?'

Ernie assumed a ponderous air. He liked to have Tommy consulting him and he was out to give Tommy value for money. Besides, he was genuinely fond of his sister and really wondered what was the best policy.

'Here,' he said, after thought, 'I d-don't see as how th-this is fer us to say. After all s-said and d-done, it's Else what's g-got herself into trouble and s-she's entitled to choose which w-way out she likes, ain't she?'

Tommy ran his hand over his chin.

'Yerce, I s'pose so. Well, we'd best arst her that's all. Let's wait for her at the corner tonight and arst her before she gets home. I'd like to get hold of that bastard though and give him a right bashing. He's entitled to get done, messing up decent girls that way. That's what I think.'

He took another mouthful of beer.

'W-what's a time?' asked Ernie.

'There's a clock over there,' said Tommy. 'Quarter to nine, it says.'

'W-well, I kn-know w-where she is now. At least I think so.'

'Where?'

'Just about coming out of the Bush Empire.'

'How'd you make that out?'

'Th-this way. If that there c-clock says quarter to n-nine, it m-must be about twenty to, eh? And the B-Bush Empire chucks out rou-round about that time, don't it?'

'Yerce. But how'd you know she's gone there?'

'W-well, she didn't come b-back fer her tea and she's told me last night that she was g-going with this geezer to the Bush Empire tonight so she's gone to the first house. That's about it.'

'Yerce. You're right.'

Tommy swallowed the rest of his beer. He went up to the counter.

'How fast's your clock, china?' he asked the barman.

'Just over five minutes, mate.'

Tommy turned round. Ernie was struggling to down his glass of beer rapidly.

'Come on, Ern,' he commanded. 'Make it a bit lively. We just about got time to catch them if we puts a jerk into it. I'd like to catch her with the cowson. I'd give him what for.'

Ernie, gasping, finished his beer. The two boys went outside, ran across Notting Hill High Street in the teeth of the oncoming traffic and just caught a westbound bus outside the Coronet. They went up the stairs. The exhilaration of the chase was in both their hearts.

CHAPTER XI

The first house at the Shepherds Bush Empire was just over. A laughing crowd was coming out on to the pavements. Another was going in; respectable people, disreputable people, a cross-section of the community of West London.

Elsie's hand was tucked under Leonard's arm. They were both smiling. Neither would have admitted it to the other, but each of them was worried.

Elsie was wondering what Leonard was going to do about what she had told him: Leonard was wondering what he ought to do. Elsie had told him that her brother was a professional boxer. Even apart from that he wanted to play straight with her. Still, it was a bit unfair, he felt, to have to marry her as the payment for a few evenings of fun. After all, she only came from Notting Dale.

'Well, dear,' he said, as charmingly as he could, 'what are we going to do? Shall we go and have some supper and a chat about you know what.'

'S'pose we'd better.'

'Where'd you like to go? We could go to the Bush Hotel, or we could go to that place in Goldhawk Road.'

'Which'd you like to go to?'

'Whichever you'd prefer.'

They had halted and stood facing each other on the broad pavement under the lights. Suddenly they turned their heads, they had heard a shout.

'Elsie.'

Two boys, dressed in cockney style, with tightly fitting overcoats and black hats snapped down over their eyes, were running towards them. Elsie's heart gave a jump. It was Tommy and Ernie. Trust brothers to come butting in where nobody wanted them.

Tommy and Ernie came up. Ernie was panting. Tommy's mouth was set in a straight line. His shoulders were squared. All four of them knew that for three ha'pence he would crown Leonard.

'Hallo,' gasped Elsie. 'What do you want?'

'You'd be surprised.'

Leonard felt that he had to step in. He would use all his suavity and, perhaps, he might be able to smooth over what promised to be a very ugly situation.

'Aren't you going to introduce me to your friends, Elsie?' he said.

'This is a gentleman friend of mine, Mr Watts. These are my brothers, Tommy and Ernie.'

'Pleased to meet you,' said Leonard, extending his hand.

Without realising what he was doing Tommy found himself shaking hands with the flash-looking fellow.

'We were going to have some supper, won't you join us?' said Leonard.

Tommy looked him up and down. He was a weedy-looking bastard for all his flashiness.

'Don't know as I'd care to,' he said. 'I've got one or two things to say to you if you'll step round the corner.'

'Well, have supper with us. We can all talk as we eat. Or perhaps you don't want Elsie to hear. Perhaps it doesn't concern her?'

'It concerns her all right,' said Tommy grimly.

'Well, in that case, don't you think she's got a right to hear what's said?'

'All right,' said Tommy, 'have it your own way. You got her into trouble. How're you going to get her out?'

Leonard Watts stepped back a pace. This was far too brusque for him. He would have preferred negotiations to have opened up a little more diplomatically. Tommy stepped forward a pace. If a geezer gave ground, follow him up. That was Tommy's motto.

'Well?' he inquired, menacingly. 'You ain't answered my question.'

Watts tried to play for time.

'I think that's something between Elsie and myself.'

'Oh, you think, do you? Well, you know what thought done. Don't you?'

'I don't see how you come into this,' said Watts, edging still farther back. After all, the chap could hardly set about one in such a public place as this.

'Oh, you don't, eh? Well, I'm her eldest brother, see, and if I don't look after her, I don't know who else will, I'm sure. I'm still waiting on you to answer what I arst you.'

'All right, all right, don't talk so loud. You'll have the whole of Shepherds Bush listening to you in a minute. You don't want to give a free show, do you?'

'I'll be giving them a free show in a minute of something they usually has to pay good money to see. Free, gratis and fer nothing I'll let them watch me give a bloke a bleeding good hiding.'

'Your language,' put in Elsie.

'You shut up,' said Tommy. 'This ain't nothing to do with you.'

'Well, I'd like to know who it is to do with then.'

'All the more shame you.'

'Look here, can't we talk this over? Let's go into a pub and be reasonable.'

Leonard Watts was becoming not quite so certain that he would not be getting a right bashing, although he was in a public place.

Ernie put in his first words of the encounter.

'Y-yes, th-that's right. Why d-don't you, Tommy? You won't get anywhere j-jest shouting in the street.'

'All right, let's go,' said Tommy sullenly.

The four of them went into a pub nearby, Leonard Watts pushing open the door of the saloon-bar.

'Saloon? This is going to cost a bit,' thought Tommy.

With Elsie leading the way and Leonard following her, the party moved through the saloon, across the passage, and into the lounge bar.

Ernie glanced up at the clock. It was twenty-past nine.

They sat down at a table in the lounge. A waiter came up to them.

'What are you going to have?' asked Leonard Watts.

'Thank you,' said Tommy, feeling the coins in his pockets, 'I'll buy the drinks for me and Ernie. Elsie can suit 'erself.'

'I'll have a Guinness, Len,' said Elsie hastily.

'All right,' said Leonard, 'have it your own way. One Guinness and a brown ale.'

The waiter stood by patiently.

'Bring me two more brown ales,' said Tommy.

The waiter went away to get the order. Leonard offered Tommy his cigarette case. It was made of silver and had a monogram, consisting of an intertwined L and W in one corner.

Tommy shook his head.

'In training,' he said.

Leonard offered the case to Ernie who, dumbly following Tommy's lead, shook his head also. One display of initiative had been quite enough for the time being.

'Don't you have a cigarette, Else,' said Tommy. ''Tain't respectable for girls to go smoking in public.'

'If I had thought that Elsie wanted to smoke I would have offered her a cigarette first of all,' said Leonard lighting up.

'All right, Mr Poundnoteish.'

The waiter brought the drinks. Tommy and Leonard paid for their respective orders. The waiter went away.

'Well?' said Tommy.

'Well, what?' asked Leonard, truculently, knowing now that he was on safe ground. If Tommy were to try a fast one here he would get thrown out quick.

'What you going to do?'

'About what?'

Tommy made a gesture of impatience.

'You know. You got Else here into trouble. You going to do the decent thing or hev I got to make you?'

'What do you call the decent thing?'

'You going to marry her?'

'I don't know. I haven't asked her yet. Maybe she won't want to marry me.'

'I wouldn't blame her at that,' said Tommy. 'Want to marry him, Else?'

'He ain't arst me yet,' said Elsie.

'Well he better,' said Tommy, 'and a bit sharpish too, if he knows what's good for him. Can you keep a wife?'

'What d'you mean, can I keep a wife?'

Leonard moved about uneasily with the result that his chair creaked. Events were moving too fast to be really comfortable. He had better stall for time.

'You earning enough money?'

'Yes and no.'

'What the bleeding hell do you mean? Yes and no. That's talking silly. Can't you give a straight answer to a straight question, Mr Clever?'

Angrily, Leonard stubbed out his cigarette.

'What I said's plain enough for anyone who understands English. I'm earning enough money right now to support a wife. I can't promise that I'll go on earning enough.'

'How's that?'

'Here,' put in Elsie angrily, 'what you think I am, shouting about me like this without a sa'much as by your leave.'

'You shut up,' said Tommy. 'If you'd 've thought of what you was doing of before you let this 'erbified cowson here

94

take advantage of you I wouldn't 've had no call to go shouting about you.'

Elsie began to sob dismally.

'L-leave the k-kid alone,' said Ernie.

'Well, she don't want to come poking her nose in. I'm handling this affair. Stop snivelling fer Christ's sake.'

Leonard patted Elsie's hand tenderly. He fancied himself as a consoler.

'Stop pawing her about,' commanded Tommy, 'or I'll hit you right on the nose.'

Hurriedly Leonard ceased his caresses, at the same time shooting Elsie a glance full of meaning. It conveyed sympathy and asked what was one to do in the face of such barbarians. It built a bridge between them. It helped to restore his prestige which had been badly shattered. It was, in short, the best move he had yet made that evening.

'Where'd we got to?' asked Tommy. 'Oh yerce. You was explaining what money you was earning. What are you be trade fer Christ's sake?'

'I work for my father,' said Leonard, still stalling.

'Well that tells me the hell of a lot. Who's your old man fer the love of Gawd? The Dook o' Wapping or something?' A sudden spasm of irritation shook him. 'Look here, if you don't come clean I'll set about you. I'm a boxer be trade meself and I'll show you I'm a tradesman. Come on. Skip all the argy-bargy and get down to cases.'

'My father's got a gent's outfitters, and I work in the shop,' answered Leonard reading the signs. 'I don't know exactly as he wants me to get married. He might throw me out and then where'd I be?'

'You want to think of things like that before you go taking liberties with decent girls. Here you, Elsie, stop snivelling fer a minute and answer a question. If I can get you out o' this trouble do you want to marry this bleeder? Take a good look at him. He ain't got the strenf to knock the skin off of a rice pudding. How you come to let a bastard like him mess you about beats me. S'posing I get you out o' trouble, how about marrying a decent feller instead?'

Leonard and Elsie exchanged a rapid glance. Both tried to read each other's thoughts and failed.

There was silence. Tommy glared at the pair of them. Elsie gave a convulsive sob.

'Go on, answer, can't you?' said Tommy impatiently.

'He ain't asked me yet,' reiterated Elsie plaintively.

Tommy rounded on Leonard fiercely. Leonard quailed.

'Yes, you dirty, poncefied cowson,' he stormed. 'You ain't got enough bloody manliness to arst her. You just sit there yammering about your old man like an egg-bound old hen. Arst her. Go on. Arst her. I'll make you bleeding arst her if it's the last bleeding thing I do.'

He swung back his right fist in a wide arc.

'Will you marry me, Elsie?' Leonard asked in a small voice.

'No,' said Elsie. 'Not if there's another way out.'

After all, a girl had her feelings. A feller who had to be forced into asking you to marry him and hadn't got the guts to stand up for himself couldn't be much cop.

'Well there is,' said Tommy bluntly, 'and I'm bleeding glad you're not going to marry this berk. I seen better things than him down the pans of public carsies. How much money you got, poncy?'

'What you mean, ready cash?'

'You heard.'

'Well, I ain't got much ready.'

'Got enough to pay fer an operation?'

'Operation?'

'Yerce, an operation. I can find out the name of some old dear what can get Elsie out of her trouble, but you got to pay for it, see?'

Leonard sat with drumming fingers. He was thinking fast. Probably a tenner would square this. It would cost a whole

96

lot more to have to keep Elsie for the rest of his life. A tenner ought to be easy enough to raise. Plenty of people would like to do him a good turn, travellers and so on, knowing that he had his father's ear. Yes, he could probably do it.

'How much'd the operation cost?' he asked.

'About twenty pound,' said Tommy. After all there was nothing like being on the safe side. They might make a profit of five or ten pound out of the deal.

'That's a lot of money,' said Leonard.

'Cost you a lot more if you had to marry her or pay half-a-quid a week for sixteen years.'

'Those operations are illegal, aren't they?'

'You're a nice one to talk about what's right and what's wrong after what you done, I must say. You going to pay up?'

'Yes, of course, oh yes. But I haven't got the money right now. You'll have to give me about a week to raise it.'

'How can I trust a dirty cowson like you?'

'You got my name. You'll find my father's address in the telephone book. That's genuine enough, ain't it?'

'Yerce, but how'm I to know it's genuine?' There was no defeating Tommy's native cockney shrewdness. 'Got anything on you? Letters or anything to prove you're what you say you are? I wouldn't wonder if you're the biggest bloody liar in the smoke.'

'Yes,' said Leonard, fishing in his inside pocket.

He brought out a tumbled mass of letters, football pool forms, photographs and papers.

'Here you are,' he said triumphantly. 'Here's three letters addressed to me.'

Tommy took the envelopes and glanced at them. Sure enough, they bore the name Leonard Watts and carried the address he had given. He handed them to Ernie.

'Here y'are, Ern,' he said. 'You freeze on to these here. And listen, Mr Bloody Wattsy, if you don't send a letter round to 137 Wilsham Street, addressed to me, inside a week, Ern and I'll be round at your old man's shop and knock the eternal daylight out of the both of you and kick up such a bleeding row that we'll show you up in front of all the neighbours, see?'

'You'll get your money all right,' assured Leonard.

'And here's one thing to be getting on with. I bin wanting to do this all night.'

While its owner was still sitting down, Tommy's fist travelled about eighteen inches. There was a sharp click as it connected with the side of Leonard's mouth. Over went Leonard, chair and all. He lay gazing up stupidly. There was a trickle of blood down his chin.

CHAPTER XII

Waiters started rushing to the spot, drinkers got up ready to join in any free for all that might start, girls screamed. It seemed to them to be the thing to do to scream.

In the middle of all the din Tommy walked out. Ernie and Elsie gaped after him. Things had suddenly moved too fast for them to fathom.

A waiter helped Leonard to his feet. The manager, who had come rushing in, gripped him by the arm.

'What's a matter. Don't you start anything here or I'll call a policeman and have you arrested. What happened?'

'Bloke hit me.'

Leonard shook his head and wiped the blood from his mouth with the back of his hand. A crowd surrounded the manager and him. Faces were open-mouthed, eager, but a little disappointed. It was quite clear now that there was not going to be any fight. Instead of listening to what was being said they were all asking each other questions.

'What bloke?' asked the manager.

'Her brother.'

Leonard pointed to Elsie. There was a smudge of blood along the back of his hand. His mouth was rapidly swelling. Two of his front teeth ached terribly.

'Outside,' said the manager.

'But I never done nothing,' protested Elsie. She was crying.

'Never mind. Outside. That goes for you, too.' He stared rather fiercely at Ernie, who caught his sister by the arm.

'C-come on, Else,' he said, obediently.

They slowly made their way out, followed by pairs of disappointed, but still staring eyes. Something *might* happen yet. The manager let go of Leonard's arm. There was no sense in holding it any longer. It was obvious there was no fight in a bloke like this.

'You all right?' he asked curtly.

'Yes, I s'pose so.'

'All right, then. Get outside too.'

'But I haven't done nothing.'

'Never mind. Get on.'

Leonard reluctantly left. The spectators still hung around.

'All right,' said the manager. 'That's all. Show's over now.'

Hesitantly they went back to their tables, still babbling about what had happened.

When Leonard finally got outside, he felt a bit better. Elsie and Ernie were there. He looked around furtively. Elsie was watching him.

'All right,' she said. 'Tom's not here.'

'He shouldn't have done that,' Leonard stated.

'No?' countered Elsie. 'Well, there's lots of things you shouldn't have done and all.'

'Meaning?' said Leonard, belligerently.

'D-don't you try and g-get tough,' put in Ernie, 'j-just because To-Tom's not here. D-don't forget I'm Elsie's b-brother and all.'

Leonard stepped back a pace.

'Well, what you want?' he asked.

'N-nothing,' said Ernie, 'except to t-tell you that if you d-don't keep your b-bargain there'll be m-more of th-that waiting for you. Tom'n me'll be down at your old m-man's gaff round about s-six tomorrow n-night, and we hopes to collect, see?'

Ernie wished that Tommy were there to see how well he was doing.

Leonard thrust his hands deeply into his overcoat pockets. He would have enjoyed a cigarette, but did not have the energy to take one out and light it.

'Don't do that,' he protested. 'You'll gum up the works altogether. If my old chap gets to hear what's bin going on I won't be able to raise a penny. Tell you what, I'll meet you outside the Shepherds Bush tube round about half-seven and I'll have the dough. That be OK?'

'S-sure. B-but you better b-be there. Or T-Tom and me'll b-be round kicking up hell, s-see?'

'All right, all right. I'll be there.'

'R-right. C-come on, Else.'

Ernie caught Elsie by the arm.

'Aren't you going to say good night to me, Elsie?' said Leonard.

Elsie's answer was the high-pitched laugh of the slum girl.

In the meanwhile Tommy had walked across to the coffee-bar. Of course, it was still a bit early. Probably none of the boys would be there yet. But it was not a dog night at the White City so there was a chance that some of them might be around. That had been a lovely wallop he had caught poncy Wattsy. Smack on the kisser. He'd have a nice north and south.

He looked at his hand. The skin had broken between the knuckles. There was no swelling.

That was the worst of sloshing a geezer with your bare fists. You were stone-ginger on hurting your hand. A boxer couldn't afford to go hurting his hands. A boxer's hands was his stock-in-trade, like a plumber's tools or a coster's fruit. It was nice to hit a bloke like that. Click.

At the caff there was nobody about yet. Only an old bum who sold matches in the street. All the boys called him Kreuger. The boys never talked to Kreuger: Kreuger never talked to the boys. He had complained that they used bad language. Kreuger always seemed to have plenty of money. He never smoked hard-ups like most bums, or Woodbines. Players were his smoke. He never slept in a bed, but went a round of all the coffee stalls. There were some stalls where they got offended at Kreuger if he did not put in his nightly appearance. Sometimes he had a shave and then his skin looked pink. Usually he had about three or four days' growth of curly black whiskers. His glasses had black metal rims and had been mended in two places with pieces of white string.

Tommy ordered himself a tea, set the cup on the ledge and went and stood in the street outside the caff. The wind made the trees on Shepherds Bush Green rustle and sigh.

Ernie and Elsie came past on their way home.

Tommy smiled at them, a little shamefacedly. They stopped to talk to him. He stepped further away from the entrance to the coffee-bar so that Kreuger would not overhear them.

'Did you see that one I give him?' he asked.

'Yerce.' Elsie's face was pale with anger as she answered. 'I did'nall. You're too handy with your dukes. You didn't want to have done it. He was agreeing to everything. You might have spoilt it all if it hadn't of bin for Ern.'

'The bastard's going to pay or I'll give him what for. 'Sides I had to slosh him, putting you in the family way the dirty cowson.'

'He'll b-be at the B-Bush t-tube at half s-seven tomorrow night,' said Ernie.

'What's he want to be there for?'

'So's we c-can collect.'

'Yerce? I thought he said he wanted time to raise the lob. Well, you be there Ern and see what he's got. If I get my minces on the bastard again I'll break him in half, straight I will. I'm not a-kidding to you.'

'R-right.'

'Going to have a cup o' tea, Ern?' asked Tommy magnanimously.

'No. I'll b-be seeing Elsie home.'

'All right. Be seeing you.'

'That's right.'

Tommy watched them until they had mounted the hill by the Uxbridge Road station. Somehow, Ernie seemed to have come out of it better than he had. Strange.

He went back inside the café and drank his tea.

Fred and Reg came in. They were laughing. Fred took a cigarette end out of his pocket and lighted it.

'How's the game, Tom?' asked Reg.

'What game?' asked Tommy gloomily.

'Hustling,' said Reg.

'On the ribs,' said Tommy.

'Going to have a tea, Reg?' said Fred.

'Yerce, mate. Don't mind if I do seeing as how you arst me.'

Fred went up to the counter.

'Two cups of smashing ackermaracker, Charlie, and see there ain't no flies in it, neither.'

Tommy felt annoyed at their cheerfulness.

'Here, Reg,' he said, 'come outside.'

'If you want to have a fight,' said Reg, laughing, 'I'm on. I'm no chicken, but I'm game.'

'Don't talk silly. I want to talk to you.'

'Whyn't you say so?'

They went outside. Tommy cleared his throat. He was finding it harder than he thought to ask this question.

'Here,' he said. 'Reg. You put a tart in the family way once didn't you?'

'Too bloody true I did, mate.'

Reg was serious now. He realised that Tommy wanted to talk business and appreciated his motives.

'How'd you get out of it?'

'Operation.'

'One of them old women, wasn't it?'

'Yerce, mate, that's right. Old tart what lived up the top end o' Clarendon Road. That's who it was.'

'What she charge?'

'Five pound. She arst ten, but I beat her down.'

'She all right? Safe, I mean? Tart won't come to no harm?'

'My tart didn't.'

'Will you take me along and introduce me so she knows I'm all right?'

'Sure. I'll take you along tomorrow night. What's a matter? Your Elsie in trouble?'

Tommy clenched his fists. If it had not been that he wanted to use Reg he would have promptly swung him a right-hander.

'No, mate,' he said. 'I put a tart in the pudden club. She wants me to marry her, but I reckon I can talk her into having an operation instead.'

'Sure it ain't Elsie? I seen her and your Ernie going up Norland Road together and I thought she looked like she was crying.'

'No, it's just a tart I know.'

Tommy was close on losing his temper. Fred called out from the café to Reg:

'When you quite done jabbering like an old woman, your tea's getting cold.'

'All right, be in in a minute.'

He was eyeing Tommy closely.

'Listen, Tom,' he said. 'I'll have to tell this old dame you and the tart's all right, see? So you might as well give us the tart's monicker.'

'All right,' said Tommy. 'Keep it under your hat though or I'll break your bleeding neck.'

'All right. I won't lollipop.'

'Well, it's Else.'

'Caw, who's the bloke? That cowson?'

'That's him. Well, I got to be going now. Good night. See you on the corner tomorrow night and we'll go up and see this old tart of yours.'

'All right. Good night.'

CHAPTER XIII

Tommy lay on a coconut-fibre mat. He was doing his ground-work. A smell of dust from the gymnasium floor was in his nostrils. His mouth was set in a grim line of determination. The muscles of his stomach and back jumped and quivered with each movement of his feet. He was pedalling an imaginary bicycle.

Harry, one hand balanced against the ring-post, watched him happily.

The kid was coming along good. He was getting such a good coating of muscle round his kitchen that it would take a hell of a belt downstairs to bring him down. He had won every one of ten fights, and had five KOs to his credit.

'OK, Tom,' he said. 'Rest now.'

Tommy lowered his legs to the floor and lay with them stretched out in front of him. He rested his head with his hands.

'You're coming on, Tom boy. We want to bring those calf-muscles of yours up a bit though.'

'Why?'

'Well, it's like this. You seem to lose your speed at the end of a fight. You won't be fighting six-rounders forever. You'll find yourself going ten threes before long. That's half-hour's boxing, not twelve minutes like you're doing now. You got to get more stamina in them pins of yourn.'

'How'm I going to do it?'

'This way.' Harry, the old warhorse, knew most every trick of the trade.

'More skipping, more roadwork ...'

'I hates that bleeding roadwork.'

'Yus, I know. It's a proper bastard, but it's got to be done. You'll be bleeding thankful for it and all at the end of a long hard fight. And then there's a lot of gym-work to be done. You better do twenty deep knee-bends every day with a twenty-eight-pound barbell acrost your shoulders and then do a bit o' heel-raising on one foot, and there's no harm in about fifty to a hundred deep knee-bends starting on one leg and ending on both.'

'That all? Sure you can't think o' no more?' said Tom bitterly.

'Blimey, yes there's plenty more. Hopping on one leg, high kicking won't do no harm, and then you want to develop your old plates of meat a bit. Try this one now. Sit upright. That's right. Now raise your Scotch pegs from the ground. Now clap your feet together as if you was applauding a turn at the Bush Empire. Go on. 'Tain't as easy as it sounds, is it? Go on. That's it. Keep it up.'

'Blimey, you want me to have legs like a weightlifter or an all-in wrestler.'

'No, I want to give you a bit of strength in them Scotches of yours. Go on. Keep it up. I ain't told you to turn it in yet.'

'Won't half slow me down, this caper,' gasped Tommy.

'No it won't, not so's you'd notice it. All right, rest now.'

Thankfully Tommy lowered his feet.

'Spoil me speed, that's what it'll do. Mark my words if it don't.'

'Git on with your bother. Fifteen minutes skipping, hopping on one leg and high kicking'll give you all the speed you want. 'Sides, once you get into better-class boxing and 've got half-hour or more's fighting you don't want all that speed. You'll have plenty of time to do all the work you want.'

'Harry!'

'Yus?'

Harry turned round in response to the shout that had come from the gym door. Sammy Sanders and another man were standing there.

'Jes' a minute. Come over here, will you? I want to chat you.'

'Git on with that bicycling again, Tom. Bring up the old gut muscles.'

Wearily Tommy lifted his legs into the air and went on pedalling away at nothing. Harry walked across the gym. In his canvas shoes he moved lightly for an oldish man. His shoulders were humps beneath his dirty grey sweater. Sammy was as smart as ever. He was wearing a new bowler and smoking a cigar. The man with him wore a dark-brown suit with a thin white line in it. His brown brogues shone with an almost painful brightness.

'How's the kid doin'?' asked Sammy.

'All right, guv'nor. He's picking up wonderful. Building some lovely muscle. I bin trying to give him leg stamina for the longer distance fights.'

'Good. This is the kid's trainer, Percy. An old-time scrapper, knows all there is to know about the fight game, don't you, Harry?'

'Yus, guv'nor,' said Harry bewildered by this unwonted praise.

'Used 'em a bit yourself, haven't you?' asked the stranger.

'Yus guv'nor. I had a few battles in my time. Caw, I fought the best. But it's a hell of a time since I hung up the turtles. Ain't getting no younger, you know.'

'That's right. Where's the kid?'

'Over there, doing that bicycling.'

'Get him over, I want to see him.'

'All right, guv'nor. Here Tom!'

Harry Dunn hardly raised his voice higher than his normal conversational tone, but his years of costermongering had given it, in addition to its husky hoarseness, a phenomenally penetrative power. Tommy stopped bicycling and sat on his haunches like a northern pitman.

'Yerce, watchew want?'

'Come on over here. Gen'lman to see you.'

Tommy got up and sauntered over with an easy grace. Stripped and in a gymnasium, he did not need a flashy cockney swagger. Dressed in a soiled white-cotton sleeveless vest, trunks and boxing boots, and moving with all his muscles co-ordinated, it was clear that he was an athlete trained to the last hair. The stranger eyed him like a farmer eyes cattle at a market.

'Here he is,' said Sammy with a proprietorial wave of his hand, 'nice built kid, ain't he?'

'Looks all right,' said the stranger grudgingly.

Tommy stood looking at each of the three in turn. His face was slightly flushed after the exertion which he had undergone. He was breathing through his nostrils. There was no need for him to keep his lips parted as he breathed. He had not yet taken much punishment about the bugle. A lock of hair tumbled down over his right eye. There was a smudge of dust from the gym floor on his cheek. His feet were astride and his hands hung loosely by his sides.

'Here, Tommy,' said Sammy. 'Here's a gentleman called Mr Percy Naylor. He's interested in your work. He wants to see what you can do.'

Percy Naylor held out a hand. Tommy rubbed his own hands on his boxing trunks before grasping it.

'How'd you do?'

'Pleased to meet you.'

They looked at each other for a moment or two. Tommy was wondering what this Percy Naylor geezer wanted. Percy. There was a name for you. Almost as bad as that Leonard Watts he'd given one to last night. He was dressed smart enough to kill. All done up like a dog's dinner.

'Well,' said Percy Naylor, 'what are we waiting for?'

'How about it, Harry?' asked Sammy.

'How about what, guv'nor?'

'How about showing my friend Mr Naylor here what Tom can do. Let him have the gloves on for a minute or so.'

'Well guv'nor. He won't be at his best. He's had three rounds, three miles roadwork, his top-work and is halfway through his ground-work already. Kid ain't made of bloody iron, you know.'

'Feel like showing what you can do, Tom?' smiled Percy Naylor.

'OK, mister. I'm all right.'

Harry rubbed the back of his palm across his eyes and the bridge of his nose. He was trying to think fast. Was it to Tom's advantage to show him off to his best? Most likely. Show himself off a bit and all he could.

'All right, gentlemen,' he said. 'I'll tell you what I'll do. Let's have a bit of sport. There's life in the old dog yet. I'm good for one three-minute round. And you can't give the kid a better try-out than against an old warhorse like me. I'll have the turtles on with him for three minutes. Right?'

'Right,' said Percy Naylor.

'All right then,' said Sammy. 'Let's get going.'

The four of them walked across the gym floor to the roped square. Tommy in his boxing boots and Harry in his canvas gym shoes walked like athletes. Percy Naylor, in his highly-polished, handmade brown brogues moved easily too, Sammy lumbered along behind them. His shoes squeaked slightly with each movement of his legs, as if his feet were complaining at the undue weight which they had to carry.

From the corner of the ring Harry unhitched two pairs of boxing gloves. He tossed one pair to Tommy who caught them dexterously. Sammy tied Tommy's gloves for him. Before putting gloves on his own hands, Harry peeled off his grey sweater. Naked now, except for his blue serge trousers, Harry looked a fine figure of a man.

His muscles ran heavily from his massive neck to his shoulders where his deltoids bulged ominously. His lumbar muscles rippled on his glistening white back. From his collar-bone to his breast was a thick coating of solid muscle underneath the matted black hair. His stomach was as flat as a board and as hard as iron. On his right forearm were several tattoo marks.

He pulled on his gloves and held out his hands for Sammy to tie them.

'Got a watch?' he asked.

'Yes,' said Naylor.

'Got a second hand on it? I don't want to box more than three minutes.'

'Yes.'

Naylor pulled out of his trousers pocket a gold half-hunter as thin as half a crown.

Harry ducked under the ropes; Tommy followed him.

'All right, then. Give us the wire when to get started.'

As they moved towards the middle of the ring Harry whispered to Tommy.

'All right, kid. Don't be scared. Come in at me two-fisted. Show off what you can do. Don't mind leaving yourself open. I won't take no liberties.'

'Right,' called out Naylor. 'Time.'

There was a quick shuffle of feet on the canvas. Tommy feinted twice with his left, Harry made a slight opening in his guard and Tommy jumped in. He hit his trainer three times about the body and the older man gave ground. As Tommy stepped back he hit him softly on the side of the head.

For three minutes they boxed. Harry called on all his ringcraft to show the bystanders what he and the boy could do. To a casual onlooker, who did not know what the boxers were up to, it would appear that Tommy was all fire and youthful impetuosity, outfighting and outboxing an older man, who, only by making use of his longer experience, was able to keep out of the danger zone. Several of the other boys who were training in the same gym had stopped work to watch the bout. They realised what was happening: they knew that Harry himself was making every opening and that Tommy's sole cleverness consisted in taking advantage of the opportunities offered him. *Esprit de corps* prevented them from saying a word.

Towards the end of the round Tommy began to tire. After all, he was only a six-rounder, accustomed to boxing two-minute heats. Harry realised this and checked his milling on the retreat. He let Tommy tie him up in a knot and hit him at will. Actually, of course, he was covered up in any place that Tommy could hurt him.

'Time!' called Percy Naylor.

Both were breathing heavily. Harry's breath came in snorts. His lips were flecked with snot from his nostrils. Over twenty years ago a right cross had broken his nose. Time had not healed it. Tommy walked with springy steps to the ropes. The vest that he was wearing was stuck to his torso with sweat. It was like a bathing suit as the swimmer comes out of the water for the first time.

Harry picked up his sweater which he had hung across the ropes.

'Well?' he asked.

Percy Naylor thrust his watch back in his trousers pocket. He felt Sammy's small eyes on his face. He became expressionless. He was talking business. He let an aggrieved tone seep into his voice.

'The kid shapes all right,' he admitted. 'Of course I'd like to see him up against a younger man than Harry here. Not that Harry's no good, but he wasn't able to extend him properly.'

Harry, pulling his sweater over his face, smiled. His smile was hidden in its stinking grey woollen folds.

'The deal on?' asked Sammy. 'Remember he'll only be fighting six twos. This try-out was three minutes. The kid might've done bleeding sight better in two twos than in one three.'

Naylor pulled reflectively at his lower lip.

'Ye-es,' he said. 'The deal's on. On my terms. If he does any good and I want him I get an option on him. For two years he fights under my promotion prior to anyone else's. He can fight where you like, but as soon as I want him on one of my bills I can have him. London or Paris, it's all the same.'

'Gor blimey, mister,' expostulated Sammy. 'You bloody thief. What gaol did they let you out of last?'

Percy Naylor shrugged his shoulders.

'Take it, or leave it,' he said. 'It's up to you. The kid's under your management. You're the doctor.'

'That's all right,' said Sammy, hurriedly. He was frightened that all the business details might come out. 'I'll take it. Come on over to my office and we'll have a drink and sign the contract, Tommy!'

'Yes, sir.'

'You're fighting at the Albert Hall on Thursday under Mr Percy Naylor's promotion in a six-round preliminary, see?'

'Yes, sir.'

'Come on, Tommy,' said Harry. 'Get some clothes on before you take cold.'

Tommy dressed slowly and carefully. His mind was full of Dot. She was a smashing bride. All tarts were hell. Look at Else. You never knew how to take a tart. He would go and see Dot. After all it wasn't every bloke had a chance to fight at the Albert Hall, even if it was only as a preliminary boy. There were some right boys who fought in preliminaries there. What about Peter Price? He had fought in an eliminating contest for the Southern Area Lightweight title. If he had beaten Norman Snow he could've boxed Harry Mizler for the title. And if he had beaten Harry Mizler he would've been entitled to meet Kid Berg for the title he had just lost. Snow beat Price and Mizler beat Snow and Mizler beat Berg and Berg beat Mizler and the next fight that Peter Price of Worcester – not many coring mushes came from that part of the country – had fought, had been in a preliminary bout at the Albert Hall under Jeff Dickson's promotion. In his time Peter Price had been among the leading contenders for the lightweight title. He was not ashamed to box at the Albert Hall. What about Daly, the fighting office-boy?

Tommy did his tie.

There was no doubt about it. Dot was a right bramah. Blimey, she could certainly dish it out the way he could take it. That Arthur though was a right cowson. A bloke'd be entitled in letting him have it where it would hurt him most.

Tommy clenched his fists before the dressing-room mirror. He was trained to a hair and, like all men under an unusually heavy emotional strain, was ready to dramatise himself with an unwonted ready facility.

He picked up his jacket and put it on.

He stepped back and surveyed himself. He was looking pretty good. He had bought this new whistle and flute for fifty bob in the Portobello Road. Most of the boys bought their whistles around the Bush. This suit was generously cut. The shoulders were broad. The lapels were broader. They nearly reached the shoulder seams. They were DB lapels. It was a three-button single-breasted jacket, held by the middle button. The pockets were flapless and cut on a slight angle. The trousers had permanent turn-ups, secured by an extra line of machining that held them elegantly in place. They had only one pleat at the waist, but while the crease remained in them they hung beautifully, billowing over the toecapless shoes. He set his snap-brimmed black hat on his head at a dashing angle and put on his new tight-waisted grey flannel overcoat. It was a pity to have to hide such a smashing whistle, but now that the weather was getting a bit sharpish a bloke had to look out after his health a bit.

He settled the overcoat down on his shoulders. It was nicely built up. He smoothed the waist down with his hands and stepped back from the wall-mirror so that he could see more than his hat and face. Yes, he was looking pretty good. Harry came in.

A cigarette was dangling from his misshapen lips. His battered face was broken midway in a grin.

'Well, Tom boy, we certainly fooled 'em, me old cock.'

'Yes?' queried Tommy, with nonchalant weariness.

'That a bit of a break fer you, me cock-sparrer, for strike a light, Albert Hall and all! You'll be among the toffs. Caw, blimey, Tom boy, I think you'll reach the top yet. Stone me blind. I wouldn't be surprised to see you fighting for a title yet. Yes, and winning it. Yes, in a couple of years we'll see the old ref holding up your dexter mitt. "Laa … deesan gentle … men,"' Harry started to intone, '"the wi … nnah! The new lightweight champion of Great Britain!" Caw, strike a light! Lightweights are on the ribs jest now. What's Kid Berg?

He's grown old. Laurie Stevens beat him, didn't he, for the Empire title. What's Walsh worth or Mizler? You'll be a title-holder, Tom boy, and once you've reached it I don't see a bloke as has got what it takes to wallop the champ crown off of that loaf of yourn.'

'Here, listen Harry, what's gwinta happen?'

'What's gwinta happen about what?'

Harry was feeling delighted. Back in his street clothes, without a collar or tie, but with a black-and-white choker about his throat, he did the opening of a step dance as though they were back again once more outside a Notting Dale pub.

'What's going to happen about Thursday night? That's what.'

'Thursday night? Why gor blimey, didn't you hear? You're all set up for a coring match at the old Albert Hall. Where's your ears? Whyn't you wash 'em out? Then you might know what's going on.'

'I know what's going on all right. There's a bleedin' sight too much going on around here if you ask me.'

Tommy in his trim new suit felt aggrieved. He rounded on his benefactor Harry. Yes, benefactor. That's the way they both felt about it, the cowsons. If they both lost their tempers was it all set for a battle or was it?

'How'd you make that out?'

'How'd I make anything out. What'd you think? Caw, I'm s'posed to be a fighting man, eh? We gaw-damned poxy-eyed fighters ain't s'posed to got to have any poncefied lousy brains in our think boxes, are we?'

Dot. Dot. Dot. Arthur the son of a bitch's poncing on Dot. Dot walks Bond Street and Clifford Street every night. I've been to kip with Dot. Dot strips well. STRIPS WELL. That's what I said. There's plenty of tarts what strips well. Who said they did anything more? You dosey son of a Wardour Street bag, speak to me like that again and I'll kick you straight in the teeth. Know where your teeth are? I won't have to reach above your waist to find them. You may have rumpled up a kip with Dot. Let me lay hands on you, you cheap messer around Lisle Street and I'll show you what women are meant for.

'Here, 'old your hosses. What's a matter with you? Done your nut or something?'

'Done my nut. I should bleeding cocoa. Listen, Smarty, you're smart, Sammy's smart. I'm a pore punch-drunk pete what takes the rap. Listen to me, Smarty, an' I'll tell you what's what. And if you don't learn the way to keep off the grass a bit lively, well I'm mistaken. A bloke's entitled to be mistaken ain't it? Who's mistaken? Me or Mr Bleedin' Sanders?'

'Here steady on, Tommy boy. Lay off of that. You're spieling knackers.'

'Knackers to you and all. Here's this. Here's one, here's two, here's three. Up comes Mr Bloody Sammy Sanders. What does he say and do? He dun no more, but he told me I got to fight at the Albert Hall, Thursday. Am I right?'

'You're right, Tom boy. But as God's my judge I don't see what you're bumming your chat about. That's right enough you're fighting at the Albert Hall, Thursday.'

'Yeah? Well, pick this wool out of your chest. Unless I'm mistaken. Of course, I'm only a six-round boxer. I ain't got brains. I'm entitled to be mistaken. Am I right?'

'You're right, Tommy. Only for Christ's sake lay off of the high spots. Cut your cackle and come to the hosses.'

'Well, I'm fighting – we're agreed on that – at the Albert Hall on Thursday. Gawd knows whom I'm fighting, but my boxing shoes'll slip across the resin all the same. Well, believe it or not. Ever read the *Sunday Express*? Here's a Ripley for you. I'm billed and the bleeding godforsaken bills are plastered all over the lousy smoke to be fighting at Shoreditch. I'm reckoned to be fighting a geezer called Young Donnelly.

How'm I going to be at Shoreditch and the Albert Hall at one and the same bleedin' time? That's what I want to know. Harry, you're reckoned to be an old-time scrapper. Have you got it figured out? I'm a millionaire's bastard if I have.'

Harry took two dancing steps forward across the dressing-room floor. He laid his strong heavily-muscled arm across Tom's shoulder. His blunt fingers hung down over the kid fighter's chest. He knew what it was like to be in training. When a geezer had been in training weeks on end, he was entitled to be a bit screwy.

'Listen, Tommy,' he said, 'Sammy's your manager, ain't he?'

'Too true he is, mate.'

'Right. He told you to smack Young Donnelly at Shoreditch, didn't he?'

'He certainly did.'

'He told you to fight at the Albert Hall the very self-same day, didn't he?'

'He done that too and you know it.'

'Well, fer Christ's sake lay off of the hotcha stuff, or I'm the son of a bitch. What's a fighter got a manager for?'

'To fix him the fights, what else?'

'You said it. What else? Sammy's last words are after telling you to fight at the Albert Hall. Am I right?'

'You're right enough.'

'Well, you fight at the Albert Hall. Do I make meself clear?'

'You're clear enough and Dot's a smashing tart.'

'So that's the way the wind blows.'

Tommy grudged a pace and measured Harry with his eyes. Hands were loosely clenched and hung by his sides. Harry eyed him warmly. He doubted he would have to lash the kid ere minutes were an hour.

'Lay off of her, kid,' he beseeched.

'Lay off of me for Christ's sake.'

Tommy swung an arm. Harry ducked it mercifully. His

head was harder than Tommy's badly swung fists. It would have been a hell of a bad mistake to have let the kid connect. Tommy smiled crookedly. He stuck out his right hand.

'Shake!' he demanded.

'Pals!' said Harry grasping the outstretched mitt. For Christ's sake keep the kid quiet. He was a bastard.

'Go to it, kid,' he said. 'Get this bag out of your system. Old bags is poison, see? And when you're in again ask me for advice, I'll help you out. My name's Harry Dunn. I'm your pal, see? Pals, that's what we are.'

CHAPTER XV

Tommy was glad to get out of the gymnasium. He had made a fool of himself and he knew it. It was later than it usually was when he had knocked off work. This Percy Naylor geezer had made him waste his time. That extra round with Harry had been a lot of nonsense.

Harry was not with him now. He had managed to ditch him.

He hopped a bus outside the West London Hospital and rode to Addison Bridge. When the bus passed Cadby Hall he was amazed, as always, at that advertisement of Lyons that changed its wording as you went past.

The bus stopped at the corner of Blythe Road. Tommy did not get down.

He rather prided himself on that.

To hell with Dot. Harry was right. Old bags was poison and no error. If he wanted a tart he could get himself one all right. Most of the girls round the Bush would be glad to go with him. He was getting known. He would ride the bus to the top of Earls Court Road, go up Holland Walk and then down Holland Park Avenue home. He might as well have his full pennorth.

At Addison Bridge the bus was caught in a traffic jam. Tommy got down, and went straight to the block where Dot had her flat. He knew the way this time, but walked less confidently. There was still a smell of metal polish on the third floor as there had been the previous time. He went to ring the bell of the right-hand flat and then drew back. It was a lot of hooey. He looked down over the banisters down the well of the staircase.

'Here goes.'

He just touched the bell. He was scared of ringing it too hard. There was still time to scarper. The same tap tap of Dot's high heels came. The same slither as she stepped on the mat. He held his breath.

Dot opened the door. Again she was wearing a wrapper.

'Why, hullo, Tommy!'

He took off his hat and twisted it in his hands. He did not speak.

'Come along in, don't stand there.'

He stepped on the mat. It slipped a little under his feet. He still did not speak. Dot looked at him with a twinkle in her eyes. She pushed the door to behind him.

'Well, Tommy darling,' she mocked, 'aren't you going to say that you're glad to see me?'

He twisted his hat the harder.

'Yes.'

'That all you're going to do?'

She slid an arm affectionately round his neck. The wrapper fell back. He could feel the soft warmth of her arm against his neck and cheek. She put up her face to be kissed.

Suddenly, he found her irresistible. Her arm goaded him. He caught her fiercely and kissed her. His hat dropped from his hands. Gently Dot disengaged herself. She sighed and patted her hair.

'That's better,' she said. 'At first, I thought you weren't glad to see me. I was wondering why you'd come.'

Tommy laughed. It was on a higher pitch than usual and his voice cracked slightly.

He followed Dot into the sitting-room and sat down in the same chair as he had sat in before. He had the hell of a lot to say, but did not quite know how to get started.

Dot lighted a cigarette and came and perched herself on the arm of his chair. Laughingly, she blew smoke into his face. He shook his head.

'I bin thinking o' you, Dot,' he said.

'Hurrah!' She clapped her hands in mimic childish glee. 'That's good. What you been thinking? Nice things?'

'Ye-es.'

'You don't sound very certain.'

'I ain't very certain, neither.'

'Oh, Tommy, honey, how can you say things like that?'

She rubbed her cheek against his. Automatically, he caressed her face. As always he was amazed at its softness, not realising the hours of torment and hard work that she underwent to keep it that way.

'What's the matter with poor little me that you aren't certain that you've been thinking nice things about me?'

Tommy stirred uneasily. It was bloody hard to explain with her sitting on his knee like this.

'Well,' he said ponderously, 'I ain't at all sure that it's all to the good me seeing you. I can't get you out of my head and I'm fighting at the Albert Hall this week.'

'Who're you fighting?'

'I ain't certain. I reckon I'm substituting for a bloke what can't show up.'

'Well, what's all this got to do with you and me?'

'A bloke's not at his best when he's got a girl on his mind.'

'Well, why have one on your mind then, you great silly darling.'

Playfully she pulled at the slightly flattened lobe of his left ear. This kittenish behaviour, which Dot delighted in and knew how to put over so well, went over big with Tommy. He thought it fine.

'I can't help it. I keep on thinking of you and Arthur, you and other blokes an' all, and I can't keep me mind on what I'm doing. Wisht as I hadn't 've come round here yesterday.'

Dot looked at him with mock seriousness.

'So great big mans is worried by little girl?'

'Yerce. That's about the strength of it.'

She snuggled up more closely against him. He kissed her once absentmindedly and then let more fervour enliven his embraces. She flipped out his tie. He stroked her light head. She undid his shirt and caressed his hairless chest. It was smooth with relaxed muscle. Little beads of sweat clustered in his armpits and trickled chillily down his sides, coasting over his ribs. His kissed Dot again. She let her hand travel down past his breast bone, down to his stomach. Here the muscles, owing to the position in which he was sitting, were contracted. His stomach was as hard as iron. He rested the palm of his left hand behind her crooked knee. The silk of her stocking felt harsh and brittle under his touch. Slowly he slid his hand upwards. It touched the naked flesh where her stocking ended. Her thighs were plumply smooth. His hands were rough and coarse against the tender softness of her skin.

Above the mantelpiece hung a picture in a gilt frame. It represented two fishing vessels, with patched red sails. The sky was lowering and the sea stormy. Dot took her hand from out of his shirt. She could feel his heart thumping against his ribs. It was nice to have a man thinking and feeling this way about her again. Arthur, for all his poise and cleverness, never succeeded in convincing her that he was in love with her. She knew him for what he was. A lay-around. A natural-born ponce.

'Well, this isn't getting us anywhere,' she said.

'No,' agreed reluctant Tommy.

He stopped his caresses.

'What are we going to do?' he asked.

'Frankie said to the Warden: "What are they going to do?" And the Warden said: "Well, Frankie, it's th' electric chair for you,"' sang Dot.

Tommy was silent. Dot rumpled his hair.

'You're a deep one, aren't you, Tommy boy?'

'I'm a mug.'

'How'd you figure that out?'

'If I wasn't a mug I wouldn't of bin here.'

'No? Well, p'raps you'd better go then.'

'Go?'

'If you want to.'

'Want me to?'

'Silly boy.'

Tommy gave it up. Tarts were hell. They were way beyond him. He did not understand what it was all about. Maybe it wasn't about anything. Why hadn't he of picked himself out a nice tart off of his own manor, instead of this flash cow?

Dot looked at him.

'Well, silly boy?'

'Well, what?'

'Well, what are we going to do?'

'Dunno I'm sure.'

'Want to go home?'

'You know I don't, but I s'pose I ought to.'

Suddenly he gripped her arm fiercely. She could sense her flesh bruising beneath his finger clasp. His eyebrows came down. She had seen him look like that in the ring. He had looked like that the first time Arthur and she had watched him fight at the Marlington Hall. Fierce, but a little bewildered. She swung her head back. This was fun.

'Here, Dot,' he said, 'what's up with you? You're making a right mug out of me. Proper monkey. I don't know what to make out o' you. Can't figure you out. Caw, talk about blow hot, blow cold. Regular Miss Weathercock, that's what you are. Why can't you let me alone?'

'Why can't you let me alone?' she riposted. 'You're hurting my arm.'

His fingers slackened. His expression remained the same as it had been.

'Jesus,' he said, 'regular Miss Sharp, ain't you? It's a wonder you don't cut yourself. Trying to take me on, that's what you are. Look, give us a straight answer to a straight question; do us a favour.'

'On one condition.'

'And what's that?'

'That you give me a straight answer to a straight question of mine.'

'All right. That's fair enough. What's yours?'

A smile skirmished with her lips. This kid was easy. It was really unbelievable that one boy should have such a wonderful body and at the same time be such fun. He was really rather sweet.

'Well, here's mine,' Dot said, 'it's a simple enough question in all conscience. Why'd you come and see me this afternoon?'

'Gawd knows.'

'That's not a straight answer.'

'Well,' he wriggled uncomfortably and every movement of his body was communicated to hers through the flimsy silk of her wrapper. 'I dunno. I din't want to come. I made up my mind I wouldn't and then, Gaw blimey, here I am. I dunno. Gawd's trewth I don't. There you are. As true as I'm sitting down here, may I never move from this chair if I'm telling a lie, I don't know why I'm here. That's fair enough answer, ain't it?'

He loosened his collar with his fingertips, shaking his head the while. Dot laughed.

'I s'pose so. Although you haven't told me why you *are* here. Never mind though. Let's hear your question.'

'All right. Now look, I want you to talk straight without fear nor favour, see?'

'Sure,' Dot laughed. 'I promise. Come on, short.'

Tommy looked sideways at her. It was going to be a lot harder for him to frame the question than it would be for Dot to answer it.

'Well,' he said, reddening slightly, 'what's your opinion of me?'

'That's an easy one, Tommy honey. I thought from all the hoohah you were making that you were going to set me a regular teaser. I think you're a sweet kid.'

'That all?'

His heart was thumping furiously. He could feel his tired legs trembling. It was just like he felt when another boxer tied him up in a knot in the corner of the ring.

'That's all, Tommy.'

'Oh.'

The flatness of his tone answered the finality of hers. He looked down into the fire, then up again.

'Well, then,' he said savagely, 'why're you geeing me up?'

'Geeing you up?'

'You heard. Geeing me up, that's what I said. You want to wash your ears out or don't I speak plain enough?'

Dot stiffened. Perhaps she had goaded the kid a little too far. There was no sense in provoking him until either she lost him or he lost his temper. A word might check him.

'Really, Tommy,' she expostulated, 'aren't you forgetting what you're doing? That's not the way to talk, or haven't you any respect for a lady?'

'All right,' said Tommy, 'no offence meant, but still why're you geeing me up? Answer me that one if you can.'

Dot pouted. She knew that, in the dim light, she looked provocative, pouting. She ran her hand over the back of his head, from the long hair on his crown to the loosely cropped part above his shaven neck.

'Honeybunch,' she said, 'do let's stop playing guessing games. Baby's ever so tired of them.'

He shook his head brusquely.

'There you go, you see. Geeing me up again.'

Dot sprang from his knee. Tommy's heart was in his sanded mouth as he caught a fragmentary glimpse of her body when her leap made her wrapper gape open. He lay back in the chair, gazing up at her.

'So that's what you call it when I'm nice to you. Geeing you up, indeed! My God, I ought to be ashamed of myself ...'

'You did and all ...'

'... wasting my time this way with a gutter rat of a kid from the slums like you who can't appreciate a lady. Listen to me, Tommy Mutch, while I tell you something. There are men, real men, not silly little boys like you, and gentlemen, not ragamuffins picked up from the back streets, God alone knows where, who'll pay real money for what you've had for nothing ...'

Tommy leapt from the chair. He was standing beside her, his arms hanging by his sides, the fists loosely clenched.

'... Yes, think of what I done for you. If it hadn't 've been for me liking the sight of you, neither Arthur nor Sammy Sanders would've done the slightest thing for you, and this is all the thanks I get ...'

'Here,' burst in a breathless Tommy, 'you reckon you give me something what most blokes pay for, eh? Proud of it, eh? Well, here's a bit of something what I get paid for, see? And I hopes you enjoy it as well as I did what you give me.'

He swung up his fist. There was a click. It had caught Dot neatly between the edge of the jawbone and the ear. Tommy felt good. Considering the angle at which they had been standing it had been a good blow. It was the first time he had ever sloshed a tart.

Dot's body stiffened to the blow. She rose up on to her toes, then, gradually and by sections, her knees giving way first, she fell to the floor. Her wrapper fell wide open. She was naked, except for her stockings and garters. She began to heave convulsive sobs.

'Tommy, Tommy, why did you do it?'

Tommy looked down at her. It was nice to see her there, to see her body, to know that he had put her down there. That's what janes wanted, a good left-hander every now and then to bring them to their senses.

'Tommy, darling!'

Dot's sobs grew louder. Her whole prostrate body was a token of grief. Abruptly changed Tommy's mood. How easily she had gone down. He had hardly tapped her. Still tarts weren't the same as blokes. There was a mug for you, bashing her like that. Right bastard she must think him. Made her cry and all. He dropped down on his knees beside her.

Covertly Dot watched his move. Had he, she wondered, got her weighed up at last?

Her tears were genuine enough, but they were tears of rage, of rage that she should have been so stupid, so green as not to have known how to handle a kid like this. To have been hit by him. It was unbearable.

Tommy touched her with a timid finger.

'Don't hit me again,' she implored.

That went over swell. He was now all contrition.

'Here, Dot, I'm ever so sorry. I dunno what to say. I must've forgot meself. What you must think of me. I wish I never done it. Straight I do. Have I hurt you bad?'

She guided his hand to her jawbone. It was a little sensitive.

'Here,' she said. 'Kiss it better.'

He stooped and kissed, very tenderly, the spot that he had struck. A savage exultation made Dot shudder. She had won. Frenziedly, she pulled him to her and kissed his lips. The buttons of his suit cut into her naked flesh. His answering kiss was at first timid, then eager. She pushed him away. It was uncomfortable here on the floor.

'Pick baby up, precious,' she begged, 'and carry her into the other room. She wants to lay down for a bit.'

She snuggled against him as he carried her and laid her on the bed. Lying there, she stared up at him with wide, childish eyes, bland with innocence.

He bent down and kissed her gently.

It was an hour before he dressed and left.

CHAPTER XVI

Tea was, that day, a silent meal at 137 Wilsham Street. Elsie sat looking down at her plate. Tommy's mind was so full of thoughts that he did not know what to say. Ernie looked from one to the other. Mrs Mutch, realising that something was the matter, had the sense to say nothing. If they wanted to tell her what the trouble was, they would. If they didn't want to, well, that was their own lookout. She had troubles enough of her own, without trying to borrow other people's. Fred Mutch, perplexed at the silence, thought he was in disgrace for something he had either done or forgotten to do.

He ate his bloater quickly and pushed his chair back. A bloater gave a bloke a thirst that cups of tea weren't no good for. Down at The Norland they sold stuff specially to cure thirsts. Besides, the blokes down there were a bit sociable instead of sitting around like a lot of bleeding dummies.

It was not until his father had his hand on the knob of the kitchen door that Tommy remembered his big news. He set down the cup of tea which he was holding.

'By the bye,' he said, 'I'm fighting at the Albert Hall, Thursday.'

Fred Mutch paused. Here was a bit of news to tell the other blokes. After all, a bloke what had a boxer for his son was entitled to bum his chat a bit. He feigned a complete indifference.

'What, this nex' Thursday as ever is?' asked Mrs Mutch.

'That's right,' said Tommy, 'I'm fighting as a substitute on Percy Naylor's bill. I don't know the name of the other bloke yet.'

'Tha-that's quite a b-big cha-chance fer you, ain't it, Tom?' asked Ernie.

Fred Mutch dropped his cap and picked it up again. He went over to the cracked mirror and retied the scarf round his neck. Anything to waste time and stick around a bit more.

'It certainly is,' said Tommy. 'All the nobs'll be there watching the top-liner. Course, I'll only be scrapping in a preliminary bout. Still, if any of the heads likes the look of me, well, gor blimey, I'm set. Made for life.'

'Don't know who you're fighting yet?' asked Mrs Mutch.

'No, ain't heard. I given you all the details what I know yet.'

Fred Mutch left the mirror and went out. There was no longer any point in staying. He had heard all that there was to hear. And that was plenty to tell down at The Norland. Elsie was still busy taking bones out of her fish and had not looked up.

'Be-be someone g-good, of c-course,' said Ernie.

'Yeah,' boasted Tommy. 'They don't have no punks on there. Not at the Albert Hall. Probably be the hardest contest in me ring career yet it will. Still not that I care if it gets me somewhere.'

He lifted up his teacup again and emptied it in one mouthful. There was no one who could make a good cup of tea, not like mother. Ernie's eyes did not leave his brother's face.

Tommy put down his teacup. It clattered against the spoon in his saucer.

'Ah well,' he said, 'got to be going now. Don't forget, Ernie.'

'Forget what?' asked Mrs Mutch. If Tommy was getting up to any mischief with these rough handfuls he was going with, she didn't want to have her Ernie dragged into it. Tommy knew how to look after himself.

'N-nothin' Mum,' said Ernie. 'Only To-Tom wants me to se-see a be-bloke for him.'

'What bloke?' asked Mrs Mutch, suspiciously.

Elsie looked up at last. Fear clutched her. She was not quite sure that it would not all come out. Tommy shot her a reassuring glance. He hastened to speak. Ernie might be clever all right and good at his job, but he couldn't think quickly, not quick enough to outsmart Mum anyway. Mum was mustard.

'Just a bloke, Mum,' he said. 'You don't know him. Don't s'pose so. I think I'll be able to get a new pair of boxing boots out of him cheap.'

'Well, what I don't see's why Ernie's got to see him instead of you.'

'Well, you see. I said to him last night as I'd see him. This evening, what with the Albert Hall fight and all, I got to go round and see me backers, see? I mean I got to keep in wi' them and I don't want to let this other geezer down, see? So I ask Ern to see him 'stead of me.'

'Aw,' said Mrs Mutch. Her fears were not yet quieted. All this silence meant something. 'Still …'

Before she started picking again at her bloater, Elsie gave Tommy a quickly grateful smile. His back was to his mother. He winked at his sister cheerfully. She bent her head over her plate to cover the flush that she felt spreading up from her neck to her face. Anyway, she was happy now. Tommy and she were friends again.

'Well, good night all,' said Tommy.

He went into the front room and dressed himself carefully. He liked to make a good show in front of the boys.

He slammed the front door behind him and with that action the old turmoil of thought troubled his mind again. The happy feeling of kindliness which the sympathetic piece of lying that he had slipped across for his sister's sake had been shut out with the shutting of the door. Swinging his arms he marched down the dark street.

Underneath the lamppost on the corner, Reg was waiting. He was wearing a new green-and-white check scarf.

'What ho, Tom?' he greeted.

'What ho, me old Reg,' said Tommy dully. 'How's things?'

'Tower Bridge,' said Reg. 'How're they with you?'

'Up and down, same as with you.'

They stood there for a bit in silence. Tommy was enjoying the company of a man. Tarts were hell. Caused more bleeding trouble than they were worth. Look at Dot, look at Elsie, look at Mum even, poking her nose in where it wasn't wanted. Just when he ought to be keeping his mind clear for that Albert Hall fight and all.

'Fag?' asked Reg.

'No thanks,' said Tommy. 'Mustn't break me training. I'm fighting at the Albert Hall Thursday.'

'Blimey, are you and all? Who're you fighting?'

'Dunno,' said Tommy, listlessly. He was getting sick of that question. 'Come on, let's get going.'

'All right,' said Reg. 'This way.'

He threw away the match with which he had been lighting his cigarette. They set off together at an easy pace. At first, their journey was through the slums. Since it was just after teatime and a cold night the streets were almost empty. Afternoons were the time that the kiddies played in the gutters and mothers sat on their doorsteps and gossiped. On one or two of the corners, lads stood and sparred. Tom let his professional eye run the rule over them. He had outgrown that stage now.

'What ho, me old Tom.'

'Whatcher. How're you going on mate?'

Tommy and Reg swung right-handed up the hill. They walked up through a narrow street of shops, leaving the slums behind them.

'Hope we don't see that bleeding bat,' said Reg.

'What's all this about a bat?' asked Tommy. 'All the bleeding boys is talking about bats. I don't know what it's all about. I never seen hair nor hide of one. Not around this way.'

'No? Ain't you heard?'

'I heard a lot, but I never rumbled nuffin.'

They turned left into Clarendon Road and went on steadily northwards.

'Well,' said Reg. 'There's a bleeding bat, see? Lots of blokes round here have seen it. 'Bout this big it is.' He made a vague movement with his hands, indicative of its dimensions. It might have been any size. 'All the kids is scared stiff. Come running home like hell to their mums. Don't half squeak and all.'

'Ever seen it?'

'Well I ain't exactly seen it, but I heard it.'

'Heard it? Doing what? Squeaking?'

'Yerce. Right up be the Merchant Venturers' gaff I heard it and all once. Din't half give me a turn. Made me come over all swimmy in the head like. Attacked an old tart once it did. She's a respectable old dame, lives in Lansdowne Road. She's just come out of the Holland Park rattler and she's turned up Lansdowne Road to go home like. Nothing wrong in that, eh? Well, this here bat's come after her and set about her. Cut her around the clock something terrible. Yerce. The well-known Holland Park bat. Something terrible, that's what it is.'

Tommy shook his head.

'Go on. Djever hear about that ghost in the Avenue?'

'Holland Park Avenue you mean? First house, where nobody's ever bin seen?'

'No, not that one. Real ghost this is. You know them houses down that way as stand back a bit. Most of them's got bits of shopfronts built out in front of them, but there's a few houses what's got gardens in front instead. Shops on the ground floor, know where I mean?'

'Yerce. I know where you mean.'

'Well, there's a ghost there and all in one of them.'

'Go on. You're putting in the gee.'

'Straight up. I ain't a-kidding to you. Bloke told me all about it one night. Give me the creeps he did. This is the story he told me. It seems as there was a couple of nigger students lived there. Egyptians or something they're supposed to be. You know what bastards them nigger students are and all. Well, they've got up to a lot of hanky-panky, you know, worshipping the devil, putting on a lot of dog, and raising the dead and all that caper.'

'Yerce, the cowsons. They don't half get up to tricks. Proper bastards. They's a whole click of them lives in Sinclair Road.'

'Yerce. Well these students scarper, see? I don't properly know the rights of it, but I reckon they got given the gooner. Anyhow they've scarpered, but all them ghosts they've raised and all that's still there. The flat where they've lived's dead empty to this bloody selfsame day. There's nobody'll live there.'

'Yerce? What kind of ghosts are they?'

'Whatsanames. I've forgotten what they call them, but when you go into the room you don't see nothing and you don't hear nothing, then, all of a sudden – bash – something's hit you on the earhole and then, crash, all the plates has fallen on the floor and got smashed to bits or the windows flung open and all the curtains is blowing about or the chairs is overturned. You never know what's going to happen next.'

'Get on with your bother.' Reg made an impatient gesture! 'Expect me to believe all that? Think I'm going into an empty bleeding room and nobody there and all and someone's going to give me one in the earhole? What kind of a mug do you make me out to be fer Christ's sake? Gaw blimey, no one there and all the bleeding plates broke. You know where you can put that.'

'All right. You arst anybody. They'll tell you.'

'Tell me a lot of bloody nonsense. Just because there was a couple of bleeding nigger students there. Go on. You can't tell me that.'

'No? Well it's true all right.'

They had now breasted the slope. Clarendon Road stretched interminably before them.

'Now a proper ghost,' said Reg, 'I could believe in that. Like the one what's in the school I used to go to. When me brother was a spiv he got shut in that school. Got left behind after a club meeting or something and he couldn't make his way out. It didn't half give him a turn I can tell you.'

'How'd he get out?'

'He didn't.'

'Don't talk bloody silly. If he hadn't of got out he'd of still bin there.'

'Well he couldn't bust his way out, the windows was too high and he shouted and yelled. The watchman let him out. Stiff with ghosts that gaff is. They reckon it's built over an old bone orchard.'

'All right. Have it your way. I reckon that ghost in the Avenue's just as likely as any of yourn.'

'Yes, have it your own way. I won't argue.'

They walked along silently for a bit. All this supernatural talk had made them both a little apprehensive. The road was dark and shaded with trees. Reg stopped.

'Here's the gaff,' he said. 'This is where that old tart hangs out.'

'Come on, let's go,' said Tommy.

Reg banged the knocker.

CHAPTER XVII

The two boys stood waiting. Tommy stuck both his hands into his trousers pockets. Through his teeth, he whistled 'The Music Goes Round And Round'. Reg was not to see that he was feeling scared. Reg himself leant against the jamb of the door. He tilted his hat on to the back of his head. He hoped that Tommy was watching him acting the old hand.

The door opened a crack.

'Good evening,' said Reg.

'Watchew want?' It was an old woman's voice.

Tommy could hear the chain bolt being fastened. The old bitch must have seen two blokes standing there and turned scared. Thought they were going to do her or something.

''Member me?' asked Reg. Tommy ceased whistling. He cleared his throat noisily.

'Can't say's I do. I ain't buying nothing tonight if that's what you're after.'

'We ain't selling nothing either,' countered Reg. 'Want you to do us a good turn. That's all.'

'Ain't got no money for no good turns.'

Reg hastily stuck his foot in the door, anticipating the old woman's movement to close it. She must be, he realised, alone in the house. She must have got a bit of money tucked away there and all. He'd have to put the boys on it.

'It ain't money we're after,' he reassured. 'You done me a good turn once. Helped a judy out of trouble.'

'So that's what you're after. Trying to put the black on me. Well, I won't wear it. I don't know what you're talking about.'

'It's all right, ma,' laughed Reg. 'No need to be so bleeding careful. All we want's you to do the same again. That's all, we'll pay you for it. We got the lob.'

The old woman cackled.

'What you bin and got another tart in trouble? Gor blimey. I don't know what's the matter with you young blokes. Straight I don't. Can't control your bleeding selves.'

''Tain't me this time, ma. Once bit twice shy. That's me. It's me mate here. A bloke's gorn and got his sister in the pudden club. He's wanting you to help her. You game?'

'Well,' grumbled the old woman. ''Tain't in me line you know. Not reglar. Still, maybe I won't mind obliging. Not if your mate's prepared to pay me for me trouble. Fair's fair. That's what I says. You help me. I'll help you. Come on in where I can get a look at you.'

She slid the chain off the door. The two boys stepped into the hall. There was a strong musty stench.

'Come on this way into the kitchen.'

The old woman must have had cat's eyes. She walked straight down to the kitchen door. On their way in the darkness the boys stumbled. The walls, beneath their outstretched fingertips, were clammy with moisture. The paper was peeling off. A faint smell of plaster contributed to the general stink. Tommy blundered into a laden perambulator and sent it careering along. Reg banged into the foot of the staircase, and saved himself from falling by clutching hold of the banisters. The woodwork was damp. One or two of the uprights were missing.

'Careful now, careful. Steady does it,' the old woman adjured.

The boys advanced slowly. A faint patch of lessened gloom indicated the position of the opened kitchen door. Their footsteps rang on the uncarpeted floor.

The kitchen itself, when they reached it, was lighted only by a candle, stuck in a battered tin candlestick, which stood on the mantelpiece above the range, casting a very small cone of light. The old woman sat down in a basket chair which creaked beneath her weight.

'Find yourself a chair and sit down,' she commanded. 'Then we can get down to business.'

Tommy moved a pile of newspapers from an old kitchen chair. A cockroach ran out between his fingers as he did so. He sat down. Reg sat on an old deckchair, the canvas of which was frayed.

'Well,' said the old woman, 'as I told you at the door, I don't mind obliging. Not that I do it reglar mind you. So don't keep on coming to me with all the tarts you put in the family way. I don't want to get into no trouble meself, see what I mean? Not that I've lost a case yet. Gawd blimey no. There's lots of mothers round this way what's expecting who'd rather have me in their confinement than any of your hospital doctors. Hospital doctors? Caw, I seen better things in cheese than what they are. Give them away in cigarette packets they do, now that the coupons is done away with. Gawd love a duck, like to have a pound I would for every baby I brought into the world around this way. Be a rich old woman I would, instead o' sitting here mouldering in this here kitchen. Have a bit of money tucked away and houses in the bank.'

She would have rattled on all night if a lean cat had not come into the room, rubbed its scrawny sides against the legs of the table, and then leapt with surprisingly agile grace on to her lap. The old woman checked her chatter and, switching her attention in another direction, began instead to drool and croon over the creature she had made her pet.

Tommy shifted awkwardly on his chair. He spoke the first words that had passed his lips since Reg had rattled the door-knocker.

'Ah well,' he began. 'You see, we come about me sister. She's in trouble.'

'Yerce?' said the old woman, running her fingers over the

cat's indolent fur. 'So yer sister's in trouble. Well, tell her from me it's the cross that women's got to bear. Rich or poor it comes to them all alike. They look at a young feller with a twinkle in the eye and before they know where they are there they are in trouble and wanting someone to help them out. Stories? Blimey, stories. I could tell you some. Stories what'd make your hair curl. What aged tart'd your sister be?'

'Eighteen.'

'Ah, eighteen. The right age fer loving. Ah, when I was eighteen – but blimey I mustn't get talking to you this way. Eighteen's all right, but I won't help out no girls underage. Criminal offence, that's what the bloke's done, and you got to take your chance on that same as what I do every time I obliges, if you see what I mean. How many months she gone?'

'Three.'

'Three? This ought to be an easy matter, not like some as I've handled. Putting 'em off, putting 'em off, taking pills and one thing and another, that's what some couples get up to, and when it's touch and go and not a minute sooner they comes to me and expects me to manage them a miss. Eighteen year old and three months gone, eh? H'm, should be easy enough. Healthy tart and all, is she?'

''S far as I know. Can't remember her having no serious illnesses.'

'That ought to be all right then. How about money? What you thinking of paying?'

'How much d'you want?'

'How much d'I want? As much as I can bleedin' get, me dear. That's all and that's me. Never refuse nothing. That's me motto. I got me living to earn. I'll take whatever you like to give me provided it's reasonable.'

Tommy pulled at the lobe of his ear. This needed some working out. The bigger profit made out of Wattsy the better for all concerned.

'Well, Reg here,' he said, 'did say as you'd do it fer a fiver.'

With a sweet snarl, the old lady swivelled her body round so that she faced Reg. She gripped his knee with her broad fingers. The flickering beam of the candle lighted up her clutching hand. The tendon between her thumb and forefinger stood out and quivered like a live thing. Her nails had been bitten until the quicks were sore.

'Oh you did, did you, Reg me dear,' she snarled, 'trying to cheat an old woman out of a few pounds, just because I'm mug enough to help girls when they're in trouble. Soft-hearted, that's what you think I am. Well, I ain't so soft as that, me dear. There ain't no green in my eye and that's something you got to learn. Risking me liberty for a five pun' note. Not likely. You got another think coming.'

At first Reg had recoiled. Before the old woman had nearly finished all her storm he had recovered. He must not show himself yellow in front of Tommy.

'Here, that's enough of that, ma,' he retorted genially. 'And that's my knee when you're quite finished with it.' Gently he disengaged her fingers and laid her hand back in her lap. 'This is yours, I think.'

'Well, you want to learn your mate to talk sense. That ain't the way to go on. Five pound indeed!'

She sniffed so violently that the cat arched its back in anger. Tommy kept opening and shutting an embarrassed mouth. Reg saw that he would have, reluctantly, to step into the breach again. He had told Tommy the sum he had paid and all. Five pound. The old bitch had asked ten, but he had beaten her down.

'Well, ma,' he began, 'you can't have one price one day and another the next. Five pound I paid you. You arst me ten and I didn't have it. A bloke can't pay money he hasn't got. It just don't make sense.'

'You paid me five, did you?'

'Too true I did. Took me a bit of raising and all.'

'And just because I done you a favour, letting you off light, you tell all your mates I'm easy. Don't think I'm daft, just because I'm a bit silly. You'll be making the biggest mistake in your life as you think that.'

'All right,' said Tom, weakly. 'If you won't take five quid, how much will you take?'

Reg frowned at him, but the significance of the glance was lost in the gloom of the kitchen.

'I told you before it's fer you to say.'

Reg sighed with relief. The danger was past. Tommy was a berk. He didn't know how to talk business. It would do him a world of good to have a barrow for a bit, particularly if he handled his own buying up at the Garden, or did a bit of totting.

'Well you can't talk about what you ain't got. There's no sense in talking big if you haven't the lob. Tommy here ain't got it. He's a working chap same as me and five pun's a terrible lot of money to him. After all, ma, you said yourself that it was going to be an easy job.'

The old woman stroked the cat reflectively.

'Yerce,' she said, dropping her words suddenly out of the silence. 'I reckon it ought to be all right. Five pound. I'll do it. Where's the tart?'

'Bring her along tomorrow night,' said Tommy.

'All right. You live round here?'

'Wilsham Street.'

'That's round Rag Fair way ain't it? Proper neighbourhood and all. Lot of right 'erbs living down them turnings. All putting tarts in the family way. What're you be trade?'

'Boxer,' said Tommy.

'Boxer, eh?' She gave a high-pitched cackle. 'You're a lovely dish and all, I'll lay. You look a well-built sort of a lad. I bet you know what it's for.' She sniggered to the cat. 'You'll be coming to me with your own tart in the pudden club next. You got a pusher you goes with, ain't you?'

'Yerce, but she ain't in the way nor likely to be neither.'

'Blimey. What! Won't she let you have none? You don't want to let her do that to you.'

'Yerce. She gives me plenty of the old Sir Berkeley, but she knows how to look after herself I guess. We won't be troubling you.'

All three laughed.

'Ah well,' said Reg getting up.

Tom rose too. He knew his pal was getting bored.

'So long, ma,' he said, 'be seeing you tomorrow. I'll bring the old skin-and-blister along.'

''Bye,' said Reg.

The old woman laid a hand on Tommy's shoulder.

'Remember this is all on the strict QT,' she adjured. 'Keep this closed. We don't want nobody talking.' She laid the forefinger of her disengaged hand on her flaccid lips.

'That's all right, ma, trust us.'

'Case of have to. That's what it is – see yourselves out.'

The boys groped their way down the mouldering hallway. It was a pleasure to be out in the street again.

'Proper caution,' said Tommy, 'ain't she?'

'Blimey. Don't half give you the horrors. I tell you what, I reckon you ought to drop me a bit of dough, Tommy mate. I must've saved you the best part of five nicker.'

'You did and all; I'll see you all right as soon as I cop from the other bloke.'

'What other bloke?'

'The bloke as has bin messing Else about. He's pestering fer this.'

'That right about your tart or was you only geeing the old mare?'

'It's right enough.'

'Who is she? Local judy?'

'No. You wouldn't know her. I met her boxing.'

'What? They have janes and all in the ring nowadays?'
'No. She's a fight fan.'
'Sounds all right.'
They swung right-handed down the hill.

CHAPTER XVIII

Tommy woke up with a headache. He turned over in bed and lay for a short while on his face. Ernie was dressing. He was in a hurry. The smell of the bedclothes was in Tommy's nostrils. He turned round again and lay uneasily on his back.

Ernie went into the kitchen. He had left open the bedroom door. Tommy could hear and smell his mother cooking breakfast. He did not want to eat. He wanted to go to sleep again. It was hard to sleep at that hour of the morning in a front room in Wilsham Street. The kids were going to school. Most of them went to St James', Norland. They made a hell of a noise.

Dot and Arthur would both be asleep. He knew that. Dot had told him that neither of them got up before the afternoon. At about nine Dot would go out on the batter. She was usually home by four, she said. She never let her clients play a one night stand. Arthur used to muck about in the cafés and clubs of Soho all night, except when he went to watch the fights or had a dog he wanted to back.

Tommy linked his hands behind his head and then unlinked them. He was not feeling so good.

Dot must look pretty good when she was asleep. Arthur was a bastard. He would like to give him one. Arthur and that bloody Wattsy. They were a pair. Wattsy had come across with twelve quid to Ernie. The cowson had made out he couldn't raise no more. A fiver to the old hag, a couple of quid to Reg and there was a buckshee fiver for himself. He had already managed to save six pounds. Six and five made eleven. He rolled over.

Mrs Mutch put her head through the open doorway. Her hair was still in curling papers.

''Ere, Tommy,' she stormed, 'whatsamatter with you? Ain't you getting up? Your breakfast's getting stone cold. You'll be having Harry round in a minute. Gor blimey, ever since you give up going to work you've turned into a reglar stinkabed. I don't know what to make of you I'm sure.'

'All right,' said Tommy wearily.

'It ain't all right,' said Mrs Mutch. 'It's all wrong. It don't do you no good laying there stinking. Proper weakening, that's what it is.'

'All right, Mum. Don't carry on so.'

'It ain't all right. You ought to of bin up long ago. You'll be ruining your health and strength and then where'll you be?'

'Laying in kip.'

'Yerce, laying in kip. That about all you're good for.'

'All right, Mum. I'm getting up now.'

'Mind you do.'

Tommy threw back the bedclothes and sprang out of bed. He pulled on his trousers and then sat down on the edge of the bed and put on his socks and canvas shoes. He then stood up again. His movements had to be careful. If he acted too rapidly his head spun. He fastened the leather belt round his waist and then drew off his shirt.

The effect of his weeks of intensive training were clearly evident in his torso. His back muscles rippled as he stooped to pick up his towel which lay on a chair. His abdominal muscles were a hard casing of steel that held his delicate digestive organs in safety. Ever since his first fight he had concentrated on the development of this particular set of muscles. The other bloke had caught him downstairs with a hard right-hander. The pain at the moment had nearly driven Tommy sick. He had fought on and luckily gained the verdict. It was not until the next day that he had realised the full effects of that damaging blow. On waking he had become immediately aware of a terrible dull ache in his stomach. Practically the whole of that day he had spent at the lavatory. Harry and he, between them, had seen to it that there could be no recurrence of the disaster.

With his rough towel caressing his naked shoulder Tommy sauntered into the kitchen. His father, Ernie and Elsie were all busily eating. His mother, as usual, was busy at the stove.

His father – collarless, unshaven, and with his waistcoat unbuttoned – was putting a piece of bacon into his mouth from the edge of his knife. Ernie was drinking a mouthful of tea. Elsie was scarcely picking at her food. Her eyes were red-rimmed. She looked faded.

'Morning all,' said Tommy and walked over to the sink. One or two plates and cups were piled on the side.

'Want any hot water, Tom?' asked his mother.

'No, I'll wash in cold.'

'You're late,' said his father.

'Just worked that out?' asked Tommy.

'Blimey, if I'd 've spoke to me old man like that he'd 've set about me and give me what for. Strike a light I don't know what's happening nowadays, straight I don't. Nobody's got no respect fer their parents.'

'Who'd you expect to have any respect fer you, you and your pigeons?' put in Mrs Mutch, springing, as usual, to the defence of her children, when they were hard-pressed.

'Who arst you to come sticking your oar in?'

Tommy poured some water into the sink. There was no running water in the kitchen. The only tap was, with the lavatory, in the yard outside. Both the action of the cold water which he splashed at his face and neck and the mere physical act of washing cheered him up. He did not listen to the bickering that was going on. Elsie put down her cup and got up. Tommy picked up the tablet of red soap and, making a lather with his hands, washed his face, neck and shoulders.

'Ain't you going to have no more, Else?' asked Mrs Mutch.

'No, I don't fancy much breakfast.'

She was powdering her nose in front of the mirror which hung on the kitchen door. Ernie cut himself another slice of bread and spread margarine on it. Tommy dried himself vigorously with the rough towel.

'Be ready in a minute, Mum,' he said, moving towards the door. Elsie stood aside, listlessly, to let him pass. He nudged her and silently mouthed the words 'my room' at her.

He went into his room, drew over his head once more the same shirt he had worn in bed, and was just fastening the buttons of his training sweater when Elsie came in.

He laid his finger to his lips and beckoned her over to the window where there was less likelihood of them being overheard through the thin wall which divided them from the kitchen.

''Ere,' he said, 'you ain't doing nothing tonight?'

'No.'

'Good. Well, I fixed it up with that old dame last night. She'll help you out of trouble. Ernie got the money out of that Wattsy of yours last night and all. You come along with me tonight and everything'll be all right.'

Elsie's dull eyes looked grateful.

'All right, Tom. Thanks ever so. I got to go now or I'll be late for work. See you tonight.'

'Sure.'

Tommy was back in the kitchen by the time she had closed the front door behind her. Ernie had lighted a cigarette and had risen from the table. By a nod and a wink Tommy conveyed to him that everything was fixed. Fred Mutch had pushed his plate aside and was now mournfully sucking his teeth over a half-empty cup of tea. Tommy sat down at the table. His mother carried over a plate to him. There were on it three rashers and two fried eggs. His father looked at Tommy's plate and then turned indignantly to his wife.

''Ere. This is a nice state of things I must say.'

'What's a nice state of things?'

Mrs Mutch was collecting the dirty crockery.

'Why should master bleeding Tommy here get more breakfast than what I do? He gets three rashers *and* a couple of eggs while his poor old dad only has a couple of rashers. What's the meaning of this?'

'He's a growing lad and he's got to keep up his health and strength if he wants to fight at the Albert Hall tomorrow night.'

'Yerce, well why can't we all have the same? My health and strength don't matter to you. I suppose that's what it is.'

'Where's the money coming from?'

Mrs Mutch was piling up the dirty crockery in the sink. Arguing with her husband was not important enough to interrupt the household duties. She threw the words over her shoulder.

'There's plenty of money coming into this house,' retorted her husband. 'Ernie and Else are both working, ain't they? Whenever I gets a day's graft I always drops you, don't I, and Tommy here's bringing in good money.'

Mrs Mutch went over to the stove to get a kettle of hot water for the plates.

'That's just about the strength of it. All of the youngsters is bringing in more than what you are what with your pension and all. *Dis*abled Ex-Serviceman you calls yourself, eh?'

Tommy was placidly eating his breakfast. His head did not ache so much now. He put his fork on an egg. The yolk broke and the yellow flooded his plate. He dropped a piece of bread in it.

'That's right, that's right. Throw me disability in me face. Just because I was ready to go and fight for me country during the war and get wounded for me pains you reckon you're entitled to take the mike out of me and starve me to death I s'pose. Well, maybe you're right. P'raps it's all the more bloody fool me fer going and fighting 'stead of taking on a good job in a munition factory.'

He pushed back his chair and got up from the table.

'Got any paper?' he asked.

'Plenty on that chair.'

He helped himself to an old newspaper and went out into the backyard. Tommy drank a cup of milk. While he was in training he had given up using tea for breakfast.

'Old big mouth,' he said.

'Who's an old big mouth?' asked his mother.

'The old chap. Shouting off his mouth that way so early in the morning. What's the matter with him? Mad or something?'

Mrs Mutch came across to the table and collected Tommy's dirty cup and plates.

'That's right now. You start. Can't get a minute's peace in this house what with something or another going on. If you'd 've got up at the proper time 'stead of laying in bed there wouldn't 've bin all this barney. You know your dad's one fer early rising.'

'Him?'

'Yes. Him. You got to have some respect for him. I don't know what's the matter in this house I'm sure. There's young Elsie now. Something's come over her, mark me words. She'll be in trouble before long. If she ain't already the way she's acting queer.'

Tommy bent down to do up his shoes. If he had not made some movement of that sort his face would have given the game away.

'Don't you get worrying about Else, Mum,' he said, 'she can look after herself.'

'There ain't no girls can look after themselves, not with young chaps around. Ah well, I don't know.'

Footsteps sounded in the hall. Harry came into the kitchen. His face was freshly pink from the razor's caress. His eyes were sparkling. The last month or so had made a great difference to him.

'Morning missus,' he said. 'Hallo Tommy. How's things? Ready yet?'

Tommy got up.

'Almost,' he said. 'I ain't bin to the carsey yet.'

'Well, hurry up. We got a lot of work today if you're to fight tomorrow.'

'All right. Keep your wool on.'

Tommy went out into the yard. He rattled at the lavatory door.

'Who's there?' said his father.

'Tommy. Ain't you finished yet?'

'Yerce. I'm finished all right. I'm just sitting here smoking trying to have a bit of peace. Thought this was the only bloody place in the house to get a bit of peace, but it looks as if I was wrong.'

He got up and opened the door. Tommy went in. Fred Mutch stood in the yard looking up at his pigeon cotes. They, at any rate, did not try to take the shine out of him. He went over to the wall at the end where he kept four rabbits in hutches.

CHAPTER XIX

When Tommy left the lavatory he found Harry and his father talking idly. His father was leaning against the wall: Harry was standing with his left hand on his hip, his right loosely clenched and hanging by his side.

'Ready, Tom?'

'Yerce.'

'Come on then, let's get going.'

'What's on this morning?'

'Bit o' roadwork.'

Tommy made a grimace of disgust. Harry took no notice.

Together they set off, running at an easy pace. Both were on their toes – Tommy breathed more easily through his nose than his mentor did. Both held their fists closed and up at breast level while they ran. Their course went through the back streets to St Anne's Road and down through Norland Market into the main road. As they stood, waiting for the traffic to let them cross over into Holland Road, one or two passers-by glanced at them curiously. The two runners ignored them loftily. They were used to the public gaze.

'Keep up on them toes of yours, Tom,' counselled Harry, 'mark time while you're waiting. It don't do to let your muscles get cold and hard.'

They crossed over, went on down the right-hand side of Holland Road and turned right over the Elsham Road bridge that spans the railway line from Addison Road to Uxbridge Road stations. They crossed Sinclair Road and made their way through the back streets in the general direction of Brook Green. Quite a number of people were out, making their way to catch bus or tram or tube to work.

With set faces they were walking, the petit-bourgeois each carrying a newspaper and an attaché case, the workers weighted down with nothing but a kit of tools. Most of the kids had got to school by now and the mothers, for the most part with their hair done up in curl papers, stood at open doorways, shaking mats or scrubbing steps. Those of the men who were not at work were on their way to the labour exchange in Sulgrave Road to sign on. There were, at that early hour, even in the Brook Green Ward of Hammersmith, very few idlers. Rent collectors and tally men went from door to door.

In Rayleigh Road Harry began to feel a tendency to drop back on to his heels. He glanced at Tommy. The boy was still running well, with the short, mincing steps he had been taught to use. There was, however, something the matter with him. His body seemed to lack its usual snap and spring. Tommy's mouth was shut tight. That was all to the good as it made him, perforce, breathe through his nose. But there was something in his expression which made him look more unhappy than a trained athlete should over an easy little training-run.

'Come on, Tom boy,' commanded Harry, 'put a bit of jildy in it.'

Still running, he began to strike blows at imaginary enemies. Tommy followed his example. Viciously he clenched his fists and, without diminishing his speed, carried on a hard-fought battle.

At the end of Rayleigh Road they turned left, then right. In Brook Green there were very few people about.

'Hips firm, knees up!' shouted Harry.

Tommy obeyed the order. He was glad when they swung left-handed into Brook Green Road and resumed a normal run. Harry looked at his charge. He was sweating freely. His hair was tousled and a lock was hanging down over his right eye. His face was flushed and tautly strained. It was clear that he was having difficulty in breathing through his nose and in not dropping back on to his heels.

Something was wrong with the kid.

Harry immediately altered his plan for the day's training. He had intended to run the boy over Hammersmith Bridge on to the towing path and along to Putney. Then a fast walk up Fulham Palace Road had been his intention. They would then have gone into the Hammersmith gym and taken a shower, after which he would have given Tommy a damned good massage and sent him home to his dinner. After dinner he would have brought him back to the gym for some top-work, ground-work and shadow-boxing, ending the day off with a couple of rounds in the ring. That looked like too stiff a bill for the kid in his present shape, particularly as he was due to fight a six-rounder the next day.

In Brook Green Road he said: 'Turn right at the bottom, Tom. We're going straight to the gym.'

Tommy nodded. Personally he didn't give a monkey's where they were going just so long as this damned run ended quick. His head was aching like hell.

They trotted into the gym.

'Strip off and take a shower, kid.'

Tommy obeyed. He dropped his clothes into a heap, and left them lying on the floor. There was no money or anything of value in the pockets and nobody but a fool would want to snitch his old training togs. Harry stripped too. He hung his clothes on a wall peg and then looked critically at Tommy's naked body.

At a first glance the boy looked fine. His skin was smooth and shone; his muscles moved easily beneath it. Possibly he was a little flushed, but so might anybody be after a run in a heavy-training sweater. Harry, however, looked for other things.

To his experienced eye it was clear that the flesh over Tommy's heart and solar plexus was moving a fraction too quickly to be really healthy. His kneecaps twitched a little too.

'Under the shower with you,' he said, 'and get some of that sweat off of you.'

Side by side under the shower they stood, Harry regulating the heat and strength of the downpour. At first it fell on their backs like the gentle warm rain of a summer's evening, ending the day's heat, refreshing the tired earth and washing away the sweat from weary bodies. The shower increased in strength, decreased in temperature. Gradually it became the bitter pitiless rain falling from a leaden November sky, chilling the body, numbing the soul, bouncing back again from the grey pavements, dripping from soaked hat-brims, penetrating flimsy shoe-soles. Harry's regulating hand was still on the chain. The shower was still, and ever, decreasing in temperature, it had become a succession of heavy blows that sent a body reeling and panting to the ropes for succour, ropes that gave no refuge but bounced the bruised fighter back to the blows again.

Gasping, Tommy lurched from under the shower. Harry checked the flow and followed him out. In silence, except for their heavy breathing, the two men towelled their bodies dry. Harry moved over to his clothes.

'Don't dress yet, Tom,' he said, 'I'm going to give you a rubdown. Skip a bit to keep warm.'

With his towel twisted around his waist, Tommy skipped. His body was already in a warm glow from the vigorous towelling and the shower which had preceded it. Harry hurriedly threw on his clothes.

'Right,' he said, 'on to the table you go.'

Tommy lay on his back on the table while Harry worked over him, kneading his arms, chest and torso. Suddenly he slapped him on the stomach with the flat of his hand.

'How's the guts, Tom?' he asked. 'Working all right?'

'Sure,' gasped Tommy. 'I bin to the carsey this morning and all.'

'How many times a day d'you go now?' asked Harry.

'Always once, practically always night and morning.'

'Bin last night?'

'Yerce.'

'That's all right then. Providing you go twice a day reglar you're all right, but it's got to be reglar, see? You don't want to get out of the habit. There's some as says you want to go three times a day, after each meal, while you're in training, but that's weakening to my mind. Stands to reason it can't be good for you. Takes all the strength out of you. S'long as you clean yourself out inside, and twice a day ought to turn the trick, there's no need to do any more, though the old-timers was always taking purges and vomits.'

He pummelled and pushed at Tommy's stomach. A feeling of satisfaction filled him at the hardness of the abdominal muscles. He set to work on his legs. A lot of blokes didn't pay enough attention to their old pins. If a fellow's Scotch pegs didn't hold out in a fight, where was he? Watching his seconds throw the towel in, most likely.

'Something's the matter with you today, Tom. What is it?'

'Dunno. I woke up feeling queer.'

'Yerce?' He gave Tom's ankle a slap. 'All right. Turn over on your face now.' Tommy obeyed. 'I wonder what's up? Where'd you feel queer? In the gut?'

He ran his hands down his charge's back. Tommy gave a little shudder of delight.

'No. I got a bit of headache and I don't feel up to much. Kind of tired out. You know, ain't got no bloody energy. All washed up and everything's too much bleeding trouble.'

Harry worked over Tommy's shoulders.

'Sleeping all right?'

'Yerce. Like a bleeding log.'

'Werl, that's funny then. You know what, if it wasn't the winter I'd say it was the bugs. There's nothing like the old jumpers for making a bloke tired out. He thinks as how he's getting a good night's kip and all the time he's twisting and turning about and scratching his bleeding self and wearing hisself out while he's sleeping. But it can't be that. Not this time of the year. If it was the summer I'd 've said "yes".'

Harry worked on in silence a little while. Worrying over Tommy's indisposition, he massaged a little more strenuously than usual. Tommy's back lost its pleasant glow. It grew to feel hard and sore. He was glad when Harry gave him the order to sit up. He felt like he was on fire.

Harry took hold of Tommy's left hand with his own left hand. He lifted the arm until it stood out almost perpendicularly from the body and then began to massage it.

'You ain't worrying about nothing, are you?' he asked.

'No,' lied Tommy.

'Tell me son, if you are,' Harry almost implored. 'There ain't nothing like worry for making a bloke feel queer. That tart, whatshername, Dot, she ain't getting you down, is she?'

'No,' said Tommy stoutly.

'That's all right then,' said Harry. He had his private doubts, but the wise old man knew better than to badger the highly-strung kid. 'What's it like at home? You ain't having no trouble indoors are you? I mean you're all right with your old man and the old lady?'

'Sure, sure. Why wouldn't I be, for Christ's sake?'

'All right. No need to get the needle. I was only arsting you a question. Free country, ain't it? A bloke can arst another a fair question, can't he? Other arm.' He moved round the table and took hold of Tommy's right arm. 'I was only trying to find out if anything was worrying you so as I could help you. No harm in that, is there?'

'All right, all right, all right, only fer Christ's sake lay off of me. I'm feeling proper browned off. Be flying off the handle, any minute now.'

'That's a silly thing to do,' soothed Harry. 'You wait until you come up against this bloke whatever his bleeding name is at the Albert Hall tomorrow night. Wait till you've got your turtles on. You can do all the battling you want then.'

'Yerce?' said Tommy. 'That's what *you* think. I'll tell you something. I'm getting proper fed up with boxing. All I bleeding do is train and fight and fight and train till I'm sick and tired of the whole bag of tricks, so there.'

Harry dropped Tommy's arm in consternation and stepped back a couple of paces. Horror was on his face. Here was heresy indeed.

'You don't want to talk like that, Tom,' he said. 'You got a big future in front of you. A little more of this here building up and you'll be fighting in eliminating contests for the bleeding title. And then the dough'll begin to roll in.'

'That's what you tell me,' said Tommy. 'I'll never see that dough you're talking about. Sammy'll grab the lot. I'm all tied up with him. Contracts and all.'

'Don't forget we're costing him a lot of money now, Tom boy. Where'd we be if we hadn't of met him?'

'Where'd we be? That's a good 'un. That's a right 'un. Don't make me laugh. I know where *you'd* be right enough. Trying to scratch a living round Shepherds Bush Market. That's where you'd be and that's what you'd be a doing of. I done all the work, ain't I? I'm the bloke what gets his bleeding head knocked off in the ring, ain't I? The rest of you's just poncing on me. Proper lot of ponces that's what you are. Same as that bleeding Arthur and all.'

Harry was standing off a little way, watching Tommy sadly.

'Done your nut, ain't you? Carrying on like that. You ought to be ashamed of yourself you should. Why a little kid going to school'd have more sense than to talk a load of hell like what you're doing.'

'Yerce?' said Tommy.

He swung his legs down. He was now sitting on the massage-table with his feet on the floor. He began to fold his arms. That was too much for Harry. Any other insult or injury he could have borne, but not this.

'Here!' he shouted wildly. 'Don't do that! Don't fold your arms for Christ's sake! You don't know what harm it does you. Blimey. It makes you round-shouldered. It cramps your chest. It spoils your breathing and I don't know what all besides.'

'Hell!' said Tommy. 'A bloke can't even fold his arms now. I'm fed up, fed up. FED UP WITH THE WHOLE BLOODY THING!!!!!! I'm fed up, d'you hear?'

'Couldn't hardly help but hear with all the noise you're making.'

Tommy got up off the massage-table. Harry scratched his poll. Light dawned on him. He had seen tantrums like this before and knew their cause.

'I know what's a matter with you, Tom,' he said.

'What now?' queried Tom, fiercely.

'This. You've gone stale. You've overtrained. That's what it is, son. You bin in training for eight weeks steady now and fighting nearly every week. What you want's a rest.'

'You're telling *me* I want a rest? Do *I* get it? That's the point?'

'You get it all right,' said Harry. 'We don't want you cracking up and going punch-drunk or something. Get dressed and go home now. Take it easy the rest of the day. Go to the pictures in the afternoon or something and get to bed early. After tomorrow's fight I'll see to it you don't have another for about a fortnight. That OK?'

'OK,' said Tommy.

CHAPTER XX

Harry was sitting moodily on a bench, swinging his legs; Tommy was sulkily buttoning up his training sweater when a voice, booming in the gymnasium itself, was heard in the changing-rooms. It was Sammy Sanders bellowing.

'Harry, Tommy! Harry, where the hell are you?'

''Ere we are, guv'nor.'

Sammy heard Harry's voice and, pushing open the door, came along into the changing-room. Tommy's hands left his half-buttoned sweater and fell to his sides. His pupils contracted into pinpoints at the sight of Arthur, who was with Sammy. Both were smoking, and the scent of their cigars was torture in Tommy's tobacco-starved nostrils.

'Bin looking for you two all over the place,' began Sammy.

'Lucky to find us here at all, guv'nor,' said Harry. 'We *had* thought of doing a heavy bit of roadwork this morning, but called it off.'

'Yes?' Sammy was uninterested. He sat heavily on the massage-table.

Arthur leant up against a wall, blowing out a cloud of cigar smoke from his nostrils and lips simultaneously and then following it with his gaze. Tommy glanced furtively at Dot's protector and then dropped his eyes again. He fell to completing the buttoning of his sweater. For Gawd's sake, Arthur was up early.

'Tommy,' said Sammy.

'Yes?'

Tommy looked up. Sammy was smiling at him benignantly.

'I got a couple of things I want you to do for me. Three come to that.'

Harry stood up and moved closer to the big man. Anything that concerned his charge concerned him. He was not going to miss a word.

'Well,' said Sammy, 'ain't you interested in what I want you to do?'

'Of course.'

'Seem bleeding interested I must say. But still.' Sammy exhaled a tolerant wave of cigar smoke into the changing-room air.

'Lad's a bit overtrained,' put in Harry apologetically.

'Yes?' asked Sammy. With an effort he threw one podgy thigh over the other. He was not really comfortable on the massage-table. He began to speak. His tones were full of pompous jollity that seemed to brook no argument. 'First thing, Tommy,' he said, 'I want you to win that little bit of a scrap at the Albert Hall tomorrow night. You will, of course.' He winked heavily at Arthur who winked back. 'I got plenty of lovely money on you and I don't want to lose it, see? It's about time I started getting something back out of all the dough I've sank in you. Still, that's neither here nor there. You will all right. Next, I want you to take a little trip into the country. You fond of country air?'

'Yerce,' said Tommy dubiously. He was playing with the bottom button of his sweater.

'Do the lad a world of good, it will guv'nor,' said Harry eagerly. 'He's a bit overtrained.'

'You said that before,' said Sammy coldly. He was getting a bit sick of Harry, he decided. Better get shut of him as soon as he could find somebody else as good and as cheap. 'Well, Tommy, the LCC may have stopped Sunday boxing in London, but they ain't got no jurisdiction down in the country. That the right word, Arthur?'

'That's right, Sammy old boy. You're coming on. What's the matter with you? Been swallowing a dictionary or something?'

'Something of that sort,' chuckled Sammy. 'Well, as I was saying, down in the country, providing the authorities is willing, there's still Sunday boxing, see? And I've found a place just outside East Ham where it's OK, see? It ain't in the LCC area and it ain't too far from the smoke for the boys to come out to arter their Sunday dinner and an eyeful of the *News Of The World*, see? Well, to cut a long story short, me and another bloke's hired a hall and we're promoting a bill between us and you're going to fight a ten-rounder as the main event, Tom boy. Heading the bill, that's what you'll be doing.'

He shook with laughter. Tommy's face took on an agonised protest. Harry opened his mouth, but before he could speak Sammy was talking again.

'Billed all over the neighbourhood you are, Tom. Biggest bleeding letters on the bloody bill spelling out your name TOMMY MUTCH of Notting Dale. And then in smaller letters underneath it's writ: "The boy who dearly loves a fight. Watch this lad rise to the top of the tree. Straight from his spectacular Albert Hall contest." What d'you think of that?'

Sammy paused and pulled on his cigar. Between the grey of the ash and the brown of the tobacco leaf, a little ruby jewel twinkled, flickered and turned grey. Both Harry and Tommy tried to speak, but Sammy beat them to it again.

'And d'you know who you're billed to fight? No, of course you don't. Frank Franks of Dagenham! You've beat him once before and he's almost a local boy, so we've billed him as dying for a return crack at you. What a laugh!' Sammy shook the massage-table in his mirth. 'And here's where the joke comes in. With the lovely little record you've bin building up fer yourself you'll start a hot favourite. All the money that thinks it's smart'll be on you. You'll be starting at about three-to-one on. Caw! What a giggle! You're going to take a dive and throw the fight and all the smart money will be wrong as usual. I'll clean up.'

'Indeed you won't.'

Tommy surprised even himself with the vehemence of his voice. Harry started and looked across at him surprisedly. Arthur, who had been studying the glowing tip of his cigar, glanced up. Pain shaded Sammy's face.

'What's the matter with you, mad?'

'You've made a mistake, guv'nor, you've picked the wrong bloke in me,' said Tommy. 'To begin with I ain't taking no dives. It ain't bleedin' worth it. I bin buildin' up a nice little record and a few KOs against me would shoot it all to hell. I got meself to study. I wouldn't get no more fights.'

'Leave that worrying to me. *I'm* your manager, ain't I?' Sammy glanced suspiciously at Harry. 'Or has this punch-drunk old pug bin getting bloody fool notions in his own thick skull and passing them on to you?'

Tommy ignored what Sammy had said and went on speaking.

'What's more I ain't even going to fight on your lousy bill. I need a rest and I'm taking it after this Albert Hall contest.'

'Not on your bloody life you don't,' menaced Sammy.

'That's where you're wrong, guv'nor. I'm taking a rest 'cause I feels as I need one, see? You can't make me go into the ring and fight, if I don't want to.'

'Oh can't I? That's where *you're* wrong, son.' Sammy uncrossed his legs and ponderously climbed down on to the floor. He took three paces forward towards Tommy and stood close to him. He thrust his florid face threateningly forward, breathing smoke and stale drink all over the boy. Tommy did not flinch. He had faced up to worse things in the ring. Harry moved unconvincingly towards the pair.

'Ever heard of contracts?' sneered Sammy. 'Never stop to think that in my office safe I got a contract I signed with you? No, you haven't got the brains to 've thought of that. You haven't got the brains to come in out of the rain. Well,

Mr Bloody Stupid, let me tell you this, that there contract says as you've got to fight when and where I stipulate, see? It looks like I got you by the knackers, don't it?'

He swayed his trunk back and thrust two triumphant thumbs into the armholes of his waistcoat. For a few seconds he stood there, teetering from heel to toe, enjoying Tommy's discomfiture. It was Harry who broke the silence.

'You can't make the lad fight, if he don't want to. Never hear of contracts being broke?'

'Never hear of boxers being broke what has broke the contracts?' countered Sammy. 'Never hear of boxers being barred? I can't make you go into that ring Sunday, but I can bring you before the British Boxing Board of Control and have them suspend your licence.'

'Garn,' put in Harry. 'They wouldn't do it. Not for you. You ain't important enough. The stewards would laugh at you. All Tom's got to say is as you wanted him to fight twice in four days and he wouldn't and the stewards would give the case to him.'

'Oh, they would, would they, Mr Knowall,' Sammy was still triumphant in tone. 'So I ain't important enough, eh? Well, maybe Mr Percy Bloody Naylor is important enough for you. And maybe it might interest you to hear that he give me a cheque yesterday fer a hundred and fifty nicker fer a half-share in Tommy. So if I bring Tommy up before the stewards of the BBBC, Percy Naylor is behind me and Tommy Mutch would find he had his nice little licence bloody well took away from him for a bit.'

'He's right, Tom,' said Harry sadly. 'You ain't got a leg to stand on.'

'What did I tell you?' queried Sammy, beaming.

Tommy's eyebrows came down in a straight line. His lowered lip jutted out. He was trying to think.

'All right,' he said, 'I'll fight. It looks like it's a case of got to.'

'That's about the strength and weight of it,' said Arthur.

'You keep your poncefied nose out of this,' said Tommy, taking a step forward in Arthur's direction. 'It ain't got nothing to do with you. You speak when you're bloody well spoken to and not before.'

Arthur fell back with a grieved expression.

'Aye, aye, what's this?' queried Sammy.

'Nothing,' said Tommy. 'Only that poxy cowson don't want to come butting into my affairs. This here's between me 'n' you. I'll fight all right as you seem to have got me by the cobblers, but that don't say I'll take the dive. I can beat that Frank Franks and I'll fight to win, see? When I fight, I fight clean. That's me.'

'Oh yes?' asked Sammy in mock surprise. 'Garn. Don't make me laugh. You kids give me the sick with your bloody innocent airs like a babe unborn. How'd you think you've bin winning all your fights?'

'With these,' said Tommy grimly, holding up his clenched fists.

Sammy gave a bellow.

'Garn, you make me tired. You can't be as innocent as all that. And if you are I'll soon put your bloody mind at rest. Every single one of your fights has been fixed, see? Either the other bloke took the dive, or if that was a bit raw or if we thought we couldn't straighten the other bloke, well we've straightened the ref. We dropped him a bit and let him have a bit of money on same as all the other clever boys. And who did he give the bleeding verdict to? Who but Tommy Mutch of Notting Dale, The Fighter What Never Fought A Fixed Fight.'

Tommy blanched. The successes of which he had been so proud were all phoney then.

'That true, Harry?' he asked dully.

'Not as I know of. They didn't let me into their secrets.' Harry's face was grey.

'Of course we didn't,' said Sammy brutally. 'What'd be the sense in telling a stupid old fool like you what way the fights were fixed. You'd have probably won a bit of dough, got yourself boozed up and then spilled the whole story. But, it's true enough, Tommy. You've gone around swaggering and letting on that compared to you Dempsey was just a good preliminary boy, but ever since you come under my management all your fights have been phoney. And that's flat.'

'Blimey,' said Tommy.

'I don't see what you're arguing about,' said Sammy. 'You bin making lovely money. Bloody sight more than you earned before. Bloody sight more than I could have afforded to pester for straight fights. That's true, ain't it?'

'S'pose so,' said Tommy dispiritedly. A sudden flash of interest quickened him. 'You say that every fight of mine under your management's bin crooked?'

'Well, don't let's say crooked,' smiled Sammy, 'that's a nasty word. Let's call them fixed.'

'Call them what you bleeding like,' said Tommy. 'But they was straight before you took me up, wasn't they? I mean I won them fair and square?'

''Sfar as I know. Of course there's no saying what tricks the local gambling boys had been getting up to, but I should reckon they was all fair and above board. Fact is, you weren't important enough then, Tommy boy, to be fighting phoney fights.'

'Then that first fight you saw me have with Frank Franks was a straight 'un probably? I beat him on the level?'

'You certainly did,' said Sammy. 'I seen the promoter about that and told him I didn't want any phoneys or fast ones pulled. I wanted to see just what you could do that evening.'

'Well, if I beat him fair and square then I can do it again. You've backed the wrong horse, guv'nor. I'll fight on Sunday, but I won't take no dive.'

Sammy Sanders threw out his hands in despair. He had long ago rejected his finished cigar and now had nothing with which to gesticulate.

'All right,' he said, 'have it your own way. But I'll be finished with you. I won't help you no more. You'll draw your wages till the contract's up, but I won't renew it and I won't get you no more fights after Sunday, then when you try to get another manager he'll think there's something fishy about you and won't have nothing to do with you.'

Tommy ran his hand over his forehead, pushing back the lock that had fallen into his eye. He felt like a rat in a trap. He glanced at Harry for help. And help was forthcoming.

CHAPTER XXI

Harry cleared his throat. All this talk was getting them nowhere. The kid was a fighter and would have to go on fighting. That was the long and the short of it. There was no sense in worrying the little bastard with a lot of gup when he was overtrained and all.

'Listen, guv'nor,' he said, 'I been in the fight game longer than what any of you have and I reckon you won't think as I'm taking a liberty when I say as I knows more of the ins and outs of it than all three of you put together. Tommy'll have to fight Sunday and if he's a sensible boy he'll fight under your orders, but that ain't all.'

The three other men in the room looked at Harry inquiringly.

'You've sunk a lot of money in the kid, guv'nor,' the old fighter went on. 'We all know that and we all know that you're entitled to want to get it back, and it seems that the only way to do that is for Tommy to lose on Sunday. Well, there's more ways of throwing a fight than by taking a dive. Taking a dive's a bleeding silly thing to my way of thinking. It's all right, maybe, for an old feller to do it when he's up against a young 'un what the gambling heads is trying to build up, but for a bloke like Tommy to start having KOs in his record against him's stone silly. See what I mean? Besides we don't know how good an actor Tom is. He might be bleeding dreadful at it and give the whole bloody show away and then there'd be an inquiry before the BBBC and Tommy'd lose his licence to fight an' you'd lose your licence to manage and promote, and then where'd we all be?'

'What d'you think's best then, Harry?' asked Sammy

respectfully. The old boy was talking sense. At last somebody was saying something worth listening to instead of the load of bull they had all just been getting off their chests.

'This here, guv'nor. It's billed for a ten-rounder main event, ain't it? Well the boys will be wanting their money's worth or they'll start tearing up the boxing hall, but I don't think Tommy's fit to go ten rounds. He'd last it out all right, but it wouldn't do him no good yet. Let him go all out for eight rounds and give the other bastard hell. That'll get all the fans down that way eager to see what he can do again. Then at the end of the eighth, well what's simpler than Tommy fouling the other bloke, hitting him well downstairs and losing the decision on that count? You needn't have the referee straightened or anything, it's quite simple and it won't do Tom no harm. Losing on a foul won't spoil his record and when in about three weeks time you stage a return bout you'll have all the local fans hopping mad to come and see it. You'll be able to sell every bleeding seat in the house.'

'There's a lot in what you say, Harry,' said Sammy. 'Here, have a cigar?'

He took two cigars out of his waistcoat pocket and handed one to Harry.

'Thank you, guv'nor. I won't say "no", but I'll smoke it later.'

Harry gingerly held the cigar in his fingers. Sammy bit the end off the other, spat a little tobacco on to the floor and lighted up. He blew out a fragrant cloud of smoke. Arthur looked on, jealous that he too had not been offered a smoke.

'Well, Tommy,' said Sammy. 'All this is up to you, you know. What d'you think of what Harry's just bin saying?'

'It sounds all right,' said Tommy. 'I'll do it.'

'That's a good boy,' said Sammy. 'That's what I hoped to hear you say. Gratitood. That's what counts in this world.

Gratitood. I help you, you help me. Stand by your pals. Well, I helped you, didn't I? And now you're helping me. That's what I like to see.'

He laid a podgy hand on Tommy's shoulder. Tommy squirmed.

'What about that other little thing?' asked Arthur.

'Here, Tommy,' said Sammy genially, blowing smoke all over him. 'There's one other little thing me and Arthur'd like you to do. All this here's confidential, so keep it under your hat. That goes for you too, Harry.'

He cleared his throat noisily.

'I don't know exactly where to start,' he apologised.

'Well, you know Dot,' said Arthur.

'Yes,' said Tommy, startled. 'Yes.' He had to say the word twice. The first time, his throat was so full of phlegm that he found difficulty in articulating.

'Well, it's about her,' Arthur went on.

'What about her?' said Tommy truculently. Had she, he wondered, been talking to Sammy and Arthur about him. Perhaps she had told Arthur she had made up her mind to leave him for Tommy. A wild hope ran through him. To hell with them, all of them with their phoney fights, gambling and all.

''Ere,' said Sammy, 'I'll handle this. The boy's got his rag out with you. Gawd knows why. You ain't done him no harm that I knows of, but he's got his rag out all the same. Here, Tom boy, listen to me. This here Dot of Arthur's ain't playing square with him, see ...'

'Who says she ain't?' Tommy was ready to do battle.

'Ne'mind that, boy, not for the minute. She's bin having a bloke round to see her in the afternoons. Some bloke's called the last two afternoons, see?'

Harry pursed up his lips in a soundless whistle. Things were beginning to get a little clearer for him now. There looked like being one hell of a barney getting started any minute. Well, Sammy and this here Arthur ought to be easy enough to take. Him and Tommy'd manage them cushty.

'How'd you get to hear about this?' asked Tommy.

'Well,' said Arthur. 'You see we live in a block of mansions and you know what it's like there. All eyes. The neighbours have told me.'

'Neighbours, eh?' said Tommy. 'Right lot of bastards they must be and all. Shopping an innocent girl like that.'

'Well, that's neither here nor there,' said Arthur, 'the fact remains that someone's been coming to see her in the afternoons.'

'How'd you know it ain't all fair and above board?' put in Harry. 'The geezer might of had a reason for calling. No sense in jumping to things, you know. You don't want to go condemning the tart unheard.'

'That's right,' said Tommy.

Harry, he knew, had tumbled the whole story, but was still sticking to him. Confidence ran through him. They were a match for these cowsons.

'If it had been on the level,' said Arthur, 'Dot would have told me about it. She usually tells me everything. When she starts trying to cover up I know there's something crooked going on.'

'Oh you do, do you?' Tommy's voice, with his regained confidence, had taken on an added truculence. Perhaps his chance of giving this Arthur bastard what he had coming to him was pretty close. 'Well, where do I come in, in this bloody fairy tale?'

'Right here,' said Sammy. 'I bin paying you good money for handling your dukes, ain't I? Now, here's a chance for you to use them for me. I want you to wait this afternoon on the landing above where Dot and Arthur live, see? Hang around up there till you hear somebody coming to the flat and then, if it's a bloke, handle him a bit rough. That's easy enough, ain't it? Gor blimey. I ain't arsting you much.'

Tommy played again for a minute with the bottom button of his training sweater. Harry kept silent. There was nothing he could say or do. In the first place he didn't know how deep the kid was in this mess, in the second place he didn't know how much Sammy and Arthur knew. They might be trying to bluff the boy into giving himself away or it might just be plain chance that they had landed on Tommy to do this job for them. At last Tommy spoke.

'I don't see as how I can do that,' he said. 'Blimey, there's a hell of a lot of things against it. I don't know where Dot and Arthur live. If I start hanging about on that bleeding landing most likely I'll get done. The neighbours'll think I'm a burglar or something and then if I give this bloke one it's a cert I'll get nicked for assault and then where'll I be, and the bloody Albert Hall fight and all?'

Sammy drew on his cigar. Arthur pulled out his cigarette case. He could do with a smoke and it certainly did not look as though Sammy were going to give him another cigar. Lighting his cigarette with a silver-and-leather lighter that most of the girls and all the boys in Soho had admired, he listened to Sammy speaking.

'You don't want to worry about none of that, son,' Sammy was saying. 'Gor blimey it's all simple. Arthur can give you the address. If anybody says "why're you hanging around?" just fanny them along that you're looking for Arthur's flat. He'll say that you're a pal of his and you'll get away with that easy as kiss-me-arm, and if you get nicked for sloshing the other geezer, get the coppers to call me on the blower. I'll come down and spring you on bail and if there's a fine in the morning, well I'll pay that and all. Just trust me, kid. I got money and they say "money talks", or am I wrong?'

'What I don't see,' said Tommy, 'is why you're particular I should have a hand in this. Gawd strike a light. Dot's Arthur's tart, ain't she? Why the bleeding hell can't he look after her himself?'

Sammy laughed. He pointed his cigar at Arthur.

'Look at him,' he said. 'Does he look bloody likely to be able to give a bloke a doing, and all the neighbours is bin saying that this geezer as has bin calling on Dot's a rough-looking fellow, well-built and all. It'll take a bloke like you what's clever with his mauleys to handle the bastard.'

The flattery and compliments got Tommy. He preened himself. Sammy went on talking.

''Nother thing,' he said, 'you handle this little job right and I'll see *you're* all right. How'd you like to come racing with me? I can always use a bloke what's a rough handful and knows how to handle his mitts. You help me out this time and you can just lay back and watch what I do for you.'

Tommy looked first at Sammy, then at Arthur. The thought of these two plotting and planning about Dot drove him wild. He could feel the blood mounting up into his cheeks.

'I'll be bitched if I do it,' he said. ''Sides, I don't see what it's got to do with you, Sammy. If Arthur'd of come and arst me there'd of bin some sense in it. She's his tart, ain't she?'

Sammy looked the picture of elephantine bashfulness. He looked to Arthur for help, but Arthur was examining his fingertips.

'Well,' he began, sweating shyly, 'she is, in a manner of speaking, and then again, she isn't. You see, she's a lovely tart, Dot is, and every now and then I visit her. She's really Arthur's girl, but it's me as pays the rent of that there flat of theirn.'

'Oh, it is, is it?' Tommy was ready to plant Sammy one in his bulging stomach. Harry cautiously sidestepped into a position where he would be able to hold the boy's arms if he tried to start anything. 'Well, you can count me out, then. I'm not going to do a bleeding thing to help you. Not a bleeder. Nothing else but ponces the bleeding crowd of you. Ponces, that's what you are. You want to be bleeding ashamed of your bleeding selves. Poncing on me, poncing on poor old Dot, poncing on the poor bloody mugs who're soft enough to have a bet on with you. Gawd stone me all bloody hurray, I got a good mind to give the pair of you bastards something to bloody well remember me by. So help me if I ain't.'

'Now then, Tommy, now then, steady on. Take it easy. Don't get the needle.' Harry grabbed him by the arm.

'Let go of me for Christ's sake and let me have a go at the bastards!'

Tommy was trying to shake himself free. Sammy had backed away, his face working with indignation at this display of mutiny. Arthur was at a discreet distance.

'You got to remember the boy's a bit overtrained,' said Harry.

'Looks like it and all,' said Arthur.

'Let me get at the bastards. I'll show them,' said Tommy.

'What's the matter, gone mad or something?' said Sammy.

'Blimey, guv'nor, get out of here, for Gawd's sake,' implored Harry still holding the struggling Tommy. 'I can't hold him back much longer and I won't answer for the consequences if he gets loose. He'll do you both in as like as not, so help me Gawd if he don't.'

'He's right,' said Arthur. 'Come on Sammy, let's get out of this bloody madhouse.'

He caught Sammy by the arm and led him away. At the door, Sammy looked back over his shoulder. His coat had come open under Arthur's grasp and his striped tie was blowing about.

'You're a right 'un, you are and all, Tommy Mutch. You'll live to regret this. I'll make you pay for it, so help me, I will.'

The door swung to behind them. Harry released Tommy and sighed. Anyhow he would not have been able to have held the boy much longer.

'Gor blimey,' he said, 'that's about torn it. They'll have it in for you now. You'll have to watch your step now, son.'

Tommy swung round on Harry. His eyes were blazing. His hair had fallen all over his forehead.

'Blimey, Harry mate,' he was saying, 'why din't you let me get at them. I'm the bloke they're after, you know. I'm the bastard they want. It's me what's bin going up and seeing Dot in the afternoons.'

'Yerce,' soothed Harry. 'I know.'

'But them bastards don't. I fooled the cowsons, I'm bitched if I didn't. I fooled them.'

'Yus, mate,' said Harry ruefully. 'You fooled them all right. And for Christ's sake get your hair cut before you go into the ring tomorrow night. The old-timers 'd of bin ashamed to have bin seen with Barnet Fair like what you've got.'

He stooped down and picked something up from the floor.

'Gor blimey. If all the rest wasn't enough for me if I ain't bin and gone and trod on that cigar what Sammy give me, and me with me mind made up to smoke it after the fight tomorrow. Ah well, I can break it up and smoke it in me pipe I s'pose. That's all. Case of have to, I s'pose.'

He slid the crushed cigar into his trousers pocket.

CHAPTER XXII

They were all sitting in the kitchen again, the same old Wilsham Street kitchen, with the same strip of wallpaper hanging at exactly the same angle from the same place above the kitchen stove.

Fred Mutch was sitting sprawled over the table. Something in one of the newspapers spread there had taken his interest. He was reading the item laboriously. Ernie had one foot on a chair and was polishing his shoes. A great chap at polishing his shoes was Ernie. Working in a pawnbroker's, the way he did, had taught him that the more you polished leather the later it cracked. Tommy, who was sitting with his chair tilted up against the wall, was, he knew, feeling fed up about something. What the hell Tommy had got to be fed up about God alone knew. Maybe he was worrying about Else. Well, he had the money and he'd fixed it with the old woman. There didn't seem much sense in worrying.

Mum was, of course, washing up the dirty tea-things. She always left everything straight before she went out evenings. She usually stepped round about nine o'clock to have a glass of stout in The Nelson.

Ernie looked up from his shoe polishing and stole a glance at Elsie. She was pale and looked proper tired out. You couldn't hardly blame her, poor kid. Tommy wasn't treating her right. Help her out of trouble. That was fair enough, but there wasn't no call to be so hard on her. He glanced at Tommy himself.

Leaning back against the wall, he was, whistling through his teeth. 'Smoke Gets In Your Eyes' was the tune he was doing. He didn't look so good himself. Maybe, he was tired and all. His hair had been clipped so closely above his ears that the skin shone through pinkly dull. The top of his head was black and glistening with grease.

'You-you've had you-your hair cut, To-Tom,' he stated.

Tommy stopped whistling. Still perilously balancing he clapped one hand to his head. When he took it away the palm was sticky.

'Gor blimey so I have!' he said. 'It's bloody marvellous ain't it the way people find things out! Blimey, Ern, I'd never 've noticed it if you hadn't told me.'

Ernie bent his head once more to his shoe polishing. His cheeks were crimson. It was not usual for Tom to take him up sharp like that. Mrs Mutch turned round, with a clatter of dishes, from the sink. Her forearms were decked with soap.

'Now then, Tom,' she expostulated. 'There's no need to speak like that. Young Ernie's entitled to make a civil remark same as anybody else.'

Fred Mutch looked up.

'Yus, that's right,' he put in. 'I don't know what the bleedin' hell's come over you, straight I don't. You're getting so sharp it's a bloody wonder you don't cut your bleedin' self.'

Elsie looked up. She had been playing idly with the clasp of her shabby bag. This was something to break the monotony of waiting for the signal to go. What was more, it was somebody beside herself in trouble.

Mrs Mutch was talking to her husband.

'You keep your long nose out of this. Always chipping in. Talk about Tommy cutting hisself. Caw, it's a wonder you ain't caught that long nose of yourn in the door years ago.'

Fred rose with dignity. He straightened the scarf about his scrawny neck and reached for his cap.

'Caw, loveaduck,' he grieved. 'Bloke can't get a moment's peace in this house. I'm going down to The Norland and have one where everyone ain't gone mad and where a bloke gets a bit o' respect.'

Mrs Mutch returned to her washing up.

'Good riddance,' she said.

As soon as the door had slammed behind her husband she rounded on Tommy.

'There you see what you done now? Driven your father out of his own house you have with your sharp ways. You'll have to pull yourself up with a round turn, me lad, or you'll have to be takin' a size larger in hats. That's what you'll be doing.'

She caught sight of Elsie.

'And as fer you, me lady, what's come over you I'd like to know? Sitting there as mum as mum and looking sulky. What's a matter? Has the cat got your tongue or something? Something's wrong with you and you'll be coming to me fer help before you're much older. 'Stead of sitting there moping when you're not out with a feller you ought to be giving me a hand with the work about the house, same as what I used to do fer my pore old mother what's bin dead these last few years. I don't know what your gran would've said if she'd 've seen me working me fingers to the bone for the likes of you. All you can do, all of you's sit around and argy-bargy, 'stead of having a bit of peace in the home. Do you all good to have a hard day's work to do, it would and all. I don't know, I'm sure, why I should of bin cursed with a family like you. Lot of lazy layabouts you all are. Young Ern's the only one what don't start no trouble and now you're all picking on him. Why you want to sort him out? He ain't done none of you no harm ...'

'Coming, Else?'

Tommy had yawned and got off his chair. His mother could, he knew, keep on in that strain for another hour at least. He had to interrupt her.

'Yerce,' said Elsie.

'Where you going?' asked Mrs Mutch sharply.

'Out,' retorted Tommy. 'Together.'

Each word, casually dropped out of the corner of his mouth, was an insult.

'Up to no good, I'll lay.'

'That's as it may be. Come on, Else.'

Elsie rose, powdered her nose before the mirror behind the kitchen door and pulled on her tightly-fitting red beret. Tommy went into the front room and got his hat and overcoat. When they were safely out in the street Elsie laid her arm snugly in Tommy's. This was just like old times before any of these upsets had started.

'Coo, Tom,' she said, 'we got out of that all right.'

'Yerce,' said Tommy, 'we did and all. The old lady's a terror when she gets started. I never known anyone as could lead off the way she can.'

'Proper got the needle tonight, ain't she?'

'Yerce, not that you can really blame her. With all these 'ere arguments going on. Everyone's got the rag out indoors it seems. Me and all.'

'That's right. Which way're we going?'

'Up to Clarendon Road. You ain't scared, are you Else?'

Elsie snuggled up a little more closely to Tommy. His arm was comfortingly hard and muscular, even if he was only her brother. After all, he had gone to a lot of trouble on her behalf.

'Ever so,' she said. 'Well, not really, but you know, you can't help feeling a bit scared, I mean.'

'That's right,' said Tom. 'You'll be all right, though. The old dame says as how she'll be able to do it cushty. She wouldn't be doing it otherwise. You see, if anything was to happen she'd get done fer murder.'

'*Would* she?'

Elsie's eyes were two blue saucers. Murder? Why, that was just like the *News Of The World*!

'Yerce. Illegal operation, you see. Not that anything's going to go wrong, but it just shows you as she's got to be a bit on the careful side taking a risk like that.'

Elsie was silent, visualising a picture of herself in the *News Of The World*. Boxer's sister murder victim, she imagined. Tommy broke into her thoughts.

''Ere, Else,' he was asking, 'what the bleedin' hell made you take up with a bloke like Wattsy, fer Gawd's sake? I'd of thought you could of picked up with a better bloke than him. Yeller, that's what he is. Not that it's none of my business.'

Elsie was quiet. How could she explain to this man, this brother, this stranger, why she had gone out with her Len, why she had given way to him? That he was yellow, that he was a rat, she had known all the time, but she had loved him. At any rate she had thought that ...

Again Tommy broke in on her thoughts.

'Because he was well off, I s'pose. That's what it was. He took you about and spent money on you and so you fell for the bastard. I'd like to break his bleedin' neck.' His own thoughts went travelling off to the matter that they had not been able to drop all day. His voice took on a new tone. 'You know, Else,' he said, 'there's a hell of a lot of bastards in this world: rats, ponces, blokes that oughtn't to be bleeding well alive. Gawd stone me blind I'd like to go raving mad one day, I would, so help me if I wouldn't, and then I'd turn round and kill a lot of these cowsons what didn't ought to be living, what ought to be put out of their bloody misery.'

The bitterness in his voice surprised Elsie.

'Why, what's the matter, Tom?' she asked.

They had breasted the hill and were turning into Clarendon Road.

'What's a matter?' repeated Tommy. 'Don't arst me! I don't know. I'm just a mug, I s'pose. I'm in love, too. That's what the matter is. Yerce, I'm in love, all right. Just another steamer. That's me.'

Elsie let go of her brother's arm in her surprise, and then clutched it again.

Fancy! Tommy in love! There was a new one for you.

'What's she like, Tom?' she asked. 'What's her name? She one of the girls from round our way?'

'No, she ain't one of the locals. Dot, that's what her name is and Dotty that's what mine ought to be. It ought straight.'

'What's she like, Tom? Is she pretty?'

'Ever so, least that's what I think.'

'Does she love you?'

'Gor blimey now you're arsting me something. I don't know and that's what's biting me.'

'Ain't you arst her?'

'*Hev* I arst her?'

'And what's she said?'

'She's laughed at me. She's done no more but she laughed at me.'

'The cat!'

'You leave Dot alone,' said Tommy, 'she's all right. She's got another fellow and all,' he added gloomily.

'There you are! What did I tell you? Cat, that's what she is. Leading you on. Why can't she be content with one fellow instead of messing about. I'd like to scratch her eyes out, so I would.'

'He's a bastard, this other fellow. Poncing on her, that's what he's doing.'

'Why, she ain't ...'

'That's right, she is. On the bash, that's what she is. Yerce, you're right Else, I've bin and fell in love with a brass nail.'

'Ow, Tommy, why'd you want to go and do that?'

'Gawd knows, Else, and he won't tell us. Why'd you want to fall in love with Wattsy?'

'Well, he ain't so bad as all that.'

'No, but he's a right bastard. A proper yellow rat. We're a pair, ain't we, Else? We can certainly pick out the right ones to go and fall in love with.'

They both laughed bitterly. Elsie tightened her hold on Tommy's arm. By her increased pressure she was trying to convey to Tommy the sympathy that she was feeling for him. He realised it and was filled with a warm glow.

'You still in love with old Wattsy?' asked Tommy.

'No,' she said, emphatically. 'Straight I ain't.' The sense of intimacy and Tommy's confidences to her gave her the courage to say words that had been bottled up inside her for nearly forty-eight hours. 'I was in love with him until when you and Ernie came up to him, you know when. I was ever so mad at you then I could've scratched your eyes out, but Len he was so weak and yeller, well I just couldn't love him no more, that's all. If he'd have bin the gentleman he always let on to be he'd 've stood by me in me trouble and have married me.'

'Yerce, the bastard. He ain't no good.'

'Yerce, buying you off the way he's done, that's proper dreadful if you arsts me.'

'That's right,' Tommy sighed heavily. 'Ah well, still it wasn't to be. Me and you's both in trouble together so I reckon that the best that we can do is to stick it out together. What d'you say?'

'Sure.'

Else essayed a weak smile. She was getting really nervous now.

'That why you bin so sharp these last days?' she asked, anxious to say something to take her mind off what was coming to her.

'Yerce. All that and you and boxing and all. I bin a bit overtrained, training too long, fighting too often. I got one fight tomorrow and another Sunday and then I'm going to lay off of it for a bit.'

'Will you take me with you some time, Tom, when you're going boxing? I never seen you fight and all the girls at work are talking about you.'

'Sure. I'll take you.'

Again Elsie clutched Tommy's arm a little more tightly. He responded. They were drawing near the old woman's house now.

'Listen, Else,' said Tommy. 'We're nearly there, now. Keep your chin up and you'll be all right. There ain't nothing for you to go getting scared at, see? She's a queer old bitch, the old dame, and it's a spooky kind of a joint the house she lives in, but don't let it get you down. You'll come out on top, see?'

Elsie clutched a little more tightly still at her brother's arm. It was not sympathy this time, but fear, that impelled her. She caught her trembling lower lip between her teeth.

They stopped at a door.

'This is the gaff,' said Tommy.

He banged the knocker. While he stood there waiting his heart was pounding and his knees trembling. What must the poor kid be feeling? He looked down at Elsie. She looked up at him. There were tears dancing in her blue eyes. She broke down.

'Ow, Tom,' she entreated, 'don't let her hurt me. I'm such a lemon. I'm ever so scared. Ain't there no other way out of this? Oh, please, Tom, can't we find some other way? Oh, ow, ow, I don't want to go into this house, Tom, *darling*, think of something to do.'

'Sorry mate,' said Tommy. 'There ain't no other way out.'

He lifted his hand to bang the knocker again. The door opened as far as the chain would let it.

'Hallo! 'Member me? I'm Tommy. One of the blokes what come and see you last night. I brought me old skin-and-blister along.'

'Oh, yerce, wait a minute.'

CHAPTER XXIII

Waiting at the doorway, Tommy listened for the familiar sound. The door chain was tediously unfastened, the door creaked, and was held open in the old woman's skinny hands. Tommy helped Elsie over the threshold with his hand under her elbow. He could feel her reluctance to move.

'All right,' said the old woman, 'come along into the kitchen. We don't want to stand here gossiping where all the neighbours can see us.'

She pushed the door to. It was pitch black and as smelly as the night before. Tommy struck a match. He knew what it was like walking down that hallway. He had had some. He didn't want to have Elsie frightened out of her life.

The match-flame was a little island of light in the stinking place. The old woman led the way. Tommy pushed the trembling Elsie along. The match went out. It had burnt his fingers.

'Here, Else,' he said, 'half a minute. Let's get another light struck.'

He struck another match and held it aloft with his left hand; with his right he impelled Elsie. They safely negotiated the perambulator and the staircase. Again the match flickered and went out. The old woman was already in the kitchen. Tommy steered Elsie through the door and then stood there, with one arm thrown protectingly around her shoulders.

'Well?' asked the old woman. 'This the tart you two young fellows was talking about last night?'

'That's right,' said Tommy. 'This is the tart all right. And how about a little more light on the subject, ma? It's too dark in here to hear yourself think.'

'Well,' said the old woman grudgingly. 'If you got a penny to spare for the gas, I'll see what can be done.'

Elsie began to fumble in her bag, but Tommy forestalled her. He dived down into his trousers pocket and brought out a penny.

''Ere y'are, ma,' he said. 'See what you can do with this.'

'Some of you people seem to have got plenty of money to chuck around,' she grumbled, as she took the coin.

Tommy could hear her fumbling with the meter which seemed to be set high up in the wall.

'Where's the gas, ma?' he asked. 'I'll light it, while you're getting that penny put in.'

'Over there on the wall by the stove.'

Tommy left Elsie standing for a moment by herself in the middle of the room. He went over to the wall. By the dim light of the candle he could just see the gas jet. There was no mantel. He waited until he heard the coin drop into the meter and the handle turned, with its grating sound. His fingers twisted the gas-tap. There was a hissing sound. He struck a match and held it to the jet. There was a roar. A flame about nine inches long shot out. Tommy jumped back. The old woman cackled. Tommy sprang forward again and adjusted the gas-tap until the jet was burning with an even blue-and-yellow flame.

He immediately went back to the middle of the room and put his arm round Elsie again. He looked at the room. He had never seen it in a proper light before.

It was just an ordinary kitchen in a working-class home. Maybe a little dirtier than usual, maybe a little smellier, maybe a little less homelike, but there was nothing sinister, nothing romantic about it. Tommy was glad for Elsie's sake that the gas had been lighted.

The old woman was sitting in her basket chair.

'Well,' she said, 'so this is the tart what's got herself put in the family way. Was he nice, me dear? Did he love you proper? Did you thrill when you felt him taking your cherry?'

Tommy felt Elsie stiffen and shudder. He held her the more tightly.

'Gawd bless you, me dear,' the old woman went on saying. 'You don't want to be frightened of an old woman like me. If I can't do you no good I won't do you no harm. So you're in trouble, eh, me dear. You're in trouble and you come to me to get you out. Very nice, I'm sure, very nice. Werl, it comes to you all, I've said so a thousand times before and I'll say so a thousand times again. You have your moment's pleasure and then you have to come to me. When you're enjoying yourself with your young chaps you don't think of us old women, sitting at home, all alone in the dark, do you? But when you're in trouble, why then you come flying to us. Ah well, it's the way of the world, I s'pose, the way of the world.'

She stared fiercely at Elsie.

'What aged tart are you?' she asked suddenly.

'I told you last night. She's eighteen,' said Tommy.

'All right, young man, all right. There's no need to get airyated. No need at all. So you're eighteen are you, me dear. Eighteen and all the young chaps is winking at you, I'll be bound, and before you know where you are you've landed yourself into trouble. Ah well, I'll oblige again, I suppose, same as I've obliged before. How many months are you gorn?'

'Three,' whispered Elsie.

'Three months gorn. Three months, eh, since he had his way with you. Was he the first?'

'Yes,' whispered Elsie.

'How many times has he had you?'

'I dunno,' whispered Elsie.

'So many times you can't remember, eh? Ah, love and young blood. They will get up to their tricks. They will get up to their tricks. He's had you, of course, since you've clicked?'

'Yes,' whispered Elsie.

''Ere,' Tommy felt it was time to thrust himself into this controversy, ''ere. There ain't no need to arst all these questions. Keeping on at the poor kid like that. Can't you see you've got her frit to death?'

The old woman's voice rose delicately in high-pitched disdain.

'You leave me alone, young man. I know what I'm a-doing of.'

Tommy relapsed, muttering angrily, into silence. The old woman spoke to Elsie again.

'And you've taken pills, me dear, and one thing and another, ain't you, me dear?'

'Yes,' whispered Elsie.

'And when everything else had gorn wrong, you've come to see the pore old woman, ain't you, me dear?'

'Yes,' whispered Elsie.

'You couldn't be in better hands, me dear. You couldn't be in better hands. Not though I says it as shouldn't. Ah well, it'll cost five pound. Five pounds and a lot of pain's what you got to pay for your pleasure. You got five pounds, me dear? It was the price me and your brother agreed on last night.'

'Yerce,' said Tommy. 'I got it here.' He tapped his pocket.

'Let's see it, young man, let's see it.'

Tommy disengaged his arm from Elsie and came over to the old woman. The few steps that he had to take across the floor towards her filled him with shyness. He handed her five one-pound notes. She took them, felt them, counted them.

'Five pound,' she said, 'five lovely pounds, all fer a pore old woman fer helping a young tart out of trouble. That's what it's for, isn't it, me dear?'

'Yes,' whispered Elsie.

The old woman laid her hands on the arms of her basket

chair. She groaned, the chair creaked. With an effort she was on her feet. She went over to the dresser and from a drawer took out a bag into which she put the notes. Slowly she moved towards the middle of the room. Both Elsie and Tommy were motionless. They were too frightened to be anything else. The old lady laid her hand on Elsie's shoulder. Elsie shrank from it.

'So you don't want to be a member of the pudden club, no more, eh, me dear? Well, the poor old woman'll help you. Come over here into the light where I can get a good look at you.'

Trembling, Elsie allowed herself to be led nearer the gas-jet. The old woman peered at her.

'A healthy-looking tart,' she mused with a professional air. 'Yes, a healthy-looking tart. Only eighteen and only three months gorn. There shouldn't be much trouble with you. A pretty-looking tart you are and all. A pretty-looking tart. You made a good rattle I'll be bound. You gave your young chap a lot of pleasure, didn't you, me dear?'

''Ere,' said Tommy, 'a little less o' that, if you please.'

'You keep quiet, young man. Well, me dear, he's had the pleasure and now you've got to suffer for it. We shan't be long. You go away, young man. You're not wanted.'

Elsie looked imploringly at Tommy.

''Ere, ma,' he said, 'can't I stay and see she's all right. I can stay in a different room. But I don't like leaving her. She's my sister and she's a bit scared, see? You let me stay, ma. I won't give you no trouble.'

'No young man, you can't stay. This is a woman's job, not a man's. A man gets young tarts into trouble, and an old woman gets them out. That's the way of the world, me dear. Come back in an hour's time, young man, if you like and take your sister home. The job won't take long, but she must lay down for a bit after it. Now be off with you. The sooner you've gone, the sooner everything will be over.'

'Don't go, Tommy, don't go. Don't leave me.'

'You be quiet, me dear. This ain't nothing to do with you. Off you go now.'

Tommy looked at Elsie despairingly.

'There ain't nothing I can do, Else mate,' he said. 'If she says I got to go, go I must.'

'There's a sensible young chap.'

'So long, Else,' said Tommy, 'keep your chin up. You'll be all right. I'll be back in an hour's time and take you out of this.'

With his head turned away from her he pressed her hand and then hurried off. If he had stuck around much longer he would have broken down himself. He hurried down the hallway to the front door. Having left the kitchen door open it was quite light and he could see what he was doing. It cost him quite a pang to slam the front door behind him. It looked like he was a bit of a bastard to leave Elsie all alone like this to that ghastly old bitch, but then, blimey, what else could a bloke do?

For a couple of minutes he stood around in Clarendon Road, not quite sure how to fill the hour in. Oh, go for a walk, it was the only thing to do. He set off eastwards.

Proper bastard life was and no mistake. Everything was in a hell of a tangle. Here was he wandering about all night and he had to be fighting at the Albert Hall next night. He ought to be getting a proper night's rest in. It didn't do a fighter any good to go getting all upset like this. He would probably go and lose that bleeding fight. Not that it mattered if he did. He didn't give a monkey's about boxing any more. Proper carve-up it was. Everything was a carve-up. Dot and Arthur and Sammy and Harry and Elsie and Reg and his bleeding self, they were all carving each other up, all poncing on each other. Here he was with seven pound Ern had given him from Wattsy to get Elsie out of trouble. Bloody ponce himself, that's what he was. What was he doing, if not poncing on Elsie? Caw, strike a light, it was a tangle. There didn't seem to be no way out of it.

In Ladbroke Grove he had swung southwards, right-handed. There was a coffee-bar down the road on the way to the Royalty Cinema. He went in. About a quarter of an hour had gone by.

'Tea, please.'

He banged a penny and a ha'penny down on the counter. A boy in a belted overcoat and a check silk scarf was looking him up and down. His nose was thickened. He looked a tough enough boy. Well, let him be tough.

'Know me again, mate, won't you?' said Tommy.

'Know you already, me old pal. Tommy Mutch, ain't you?'

'Yerce. That's me all right. Can't say as I can place you though.'

'Freddie Carson.'

'Gor blimey, not the Freddie Carson of King's Cross? The bloke I boxed last Saturday week?'

'That's right, mate. Fighting at the Albert Hall tomorrow ain't you, Tom boy?'

'Yerce.'

'Watchew doing out this time o' night then, breaking training?'

'Having a cup of tea, mate. Can't yew see?'

Tommy poured some of his tea into his saucer and blew on it. He wanted to drink it up quickly and get out. The hell with hanging around and chatting this half-bake punch-drunk.

'Doing all right fer yourself now, ain't you, Tom boy?'

'I should bleeding cocoa.'

'How'd you come to get yourself an Albert Hall fight?'

Tommy tilted his saucerful of tea back into the cup. Slowly, he drank a mouthful and turned on the other.

'How'd I come to get meself an Albert Hall fight? Because Mr Percy Naylor thought as I was a good enough fighter to box on one of his bills, see?'

He picked up his teacup again.

'Alls bay. You can't tell me that. Dropsy's done it. The fight game's all cop and no drop from the promoter's angle. Garn with you. You must of got a good manager.'

'As a manager, he's all right.'

'There, what was I telling you.' Freddie Carson looked triumphantly at the counterman. 'What did I say? Bleeding carve-up, that's what it all is. Bloke gets the big money behind him and he gets Albert Hall fights. There's lots of fighters good as you, Tom, and they don't get a bleeding look in. Carve-up, that's what it is from top to bottom. I reckon the bleeding fight's fixed already for the gamblers, ain't it? Who's throwing the fight, Tom? You or the other boy?'

Tommy put down his cup.

''Ere,' he said, 'if you can't learn to speak in turn you'll be getting something what you don't like. There'll be a bleeding fight right now let alone the Albert Hall and – what's more – I won't be throwing it, neither. I fight straight, see?'

Freddie Carson threw back his head and laughed.

'You fight straight, eh? Caw stone me blind all bloody hurray. That's a right one. Don't make me laugh!'

'I'll be making you bloody cry in a minute.'

Freddie hung on to the counter in affected mirth.

'Think you can beat me, eh?'

'Now then boys, now then. Have a bit of sense. Don't get starting anything in here or you'll drop me in for it. I'm the bloke that'll have to take the can back.'

The counterman was getting agitated.

CHAPTER XXIV

Tommy swung round. He was in no mood for argument.

'I'll tell you something, mug,' he said. 'I beat you before. I'll beat you again.'

Freddie let go of the counter and squared his shoulders.

'I'll tell you something and all. You never beat me before. The money was on you, that's all. They give me half-a-quid to throw that fight. *And* you know it.'

'That's a bloody lie. You take that back.'

'Take that back my bloody arm. It's the Gawd's truth, so it is. Half-a-quid, that's what the manager give me.'

'I'll knock your teeth down your bloody throat!'

Tommy sprang forward. The counterman vaulted over. He was between Tommy and Freddie.

'Now then, pal. You keep off of that,' he begged. 'I got me living to think of. I'm only a working feller same as you.'

Tommy tried to brush him aside.

'The lying bastard. Let me get at him!'

'Who's a bastard!'

'You are.'

''Ere, mate, scarper for Christ's sake. I can't hold this bloody idiot much longer.'

''E called me a lying bastard.'

'And so he is. Let me at him. I'll knock his bloody head off. So help me Christ if I don't. Get out of my way or I'll give you one and all.'

A man put a timid foot on the threshold. He saw the makings of a fight, stepped forward eagerly, hesitated, then stepped back again. The counterman looked at him despairingly.

'Get a copper for Gawd's sake. Hurry.'

'Copper, eh? Here's one for you, you bastard and all.'

Tommy hit the counterman flush on the jaw with a half-arm right swing. The man was too close to him to be hit hard, but he sat down heavily, holding his face. Across his head, Freddie swung at Tommy, who, swaying back, nearly lost his balance. The other fellow ran. Freddie jumped forward and collided with the counterman getting up. Tommy recovered his balance and jumped in. He hit Freddie on the nose with his left and brought up his right to the counterman's stomach. The counterman sat down again. Freddie caught Tommy a nice left-hander on the ear as he jumped back. His hat fell off.

''Ere, what's all this?' A policeman was at the doorway.

The two boxers froze in their positions. The counterman got up for the second time. He put one hand to his stomach and another to the wall.

'These blokes were having a bit of a bundle,' he said.

'He called me a lying bastard,' said Freddie.

'So he is,' said Tommy.

'Less of that.' The policeman came forward. 'What was you doing on the floor?'

'One of them hit me.'

'Hurt bad?'

'No.'

'You got a swelling on the jaw.'

'That ain't nothing.'

'You wait, I'll get you yet.'

'Shut up you, want me to take you in charge? Whose hat's that?'

'Mine.'

'Well, pick it up and go on home.'

Tommy stooped to pick it up. The policeman caught hold of Freddie.

'You and all, outside. Now, off with you.'

'I ain't done nothing. Bloke ain't even allowed to protect himself now.'

'Come on, outside.'

Tommy shrugged and walked out.

He started to wander aimlessly around the streets. There was not much fun in anything. What was Dot doing? She must be doing something. She was probably out on the batter, weighing up blokes, going up to them, putting her head on one side and smiling the way she did. The blokes would walk on and take no notice of her. Maybe she had lumbered one back by now; maybe he was undressing her; her clothes would be falling to the ground with a rustle and then she would step out of them, her white body and her smooth shoulders gleaming. The old steamer she had picked up would be gloating at her, knowing that in a couple of minutes he would be feeling the softness of her against his flesh, knowing that in a couple of minutes his body would be joined to hers. What the hell.

'Just a minute, you!'

A big broad-shouldered man wearing a mackintosh and a bowler hat was talking to him. Tommy halted.

'Talking to me?'

'Yes, I'm talking to you all right. I want you to give an account of your movements for the last half hour.'

'You want me to give an account of my movements? What the hell's up? Who d'you think you are for Gawd's sake? Come off it.'

The big man was talking wearily. He was repeating a well-worn formula.

'I am a police officer and have reason to suppose you are a suspected person, loitering with intent to commit a felony. Before taking you into custody I want to verify my suspicions.'

'Blimey, mister, you got me all wrong. It's like this. I got to go to Clarendon Road in a little while, and I bin hanging about waiting to fill the time in sort of. No harm in that, is there? Bloke's entitled to stand around in the streets, ain't he?'

'What've you got to go to Clarendon Road for?'

'Well, it's like this, mister,' Tommy was trying to think quickly. 'I got to go to Clarendon Road to take me sister home.'

'Where's home?'

'Wilsham Street, Notting Dale.'

'You live in Wilsham Street? There's a lot of bad characters around that way. You ever bin in trouble?'

'No, guv'nor. Straight up I haven't.'

'You sure of that? I think I recognise you.'

'You got me mixed up. I never bin in trouble.'

'Well, we can soon find that out down at the station. What's your name?'

'Tommy Mutch. Honest, I ain't done nothing. There's no call to take me down to the station.'

'We'll see about that. How old's your sister?'

'Eighteen. Come on, guv'nor, be a pal, let us go. I'll be late.'

'If your sister's eighteen, why can't she see herself home? It's not far from Clarendon Road to Wilsham Street.'

'She's queer.'

'Oh, she's queer, is she? What's a matter with her?'

Tommy scratched his head. This was a facer. It was all very well. He was talking to a slop. A slop would have your guts for garters. How was he to tell him that Elsie was in the pudden club and that some old tart was helping her out of trouble? It would only make plenty of grief for all of them.

'What's usually a matter with tarts when they're queer?'

'You mean she's in the spud line?'

'I don't mean nothing. She may be, she may not. I don't know.'

'Then what's she doing around Clarendon Road? Why'nt she go and see a doctor?'

'She's going up to see him tomorrow.'

'Pretty thin kind of a yarn you're telling. Where've you bin this evening?'

'Where I bin? Nowhere much. I just been down to that caff you know, near the Royalty, had a cup of tea and then started to have a bit of a walk round to fill in the time.'

'Yes? Well, I reckon the best thing you can do is to step down to the station with me and I'll just check up on your statements.'

'When'll I be able to get away?'

'After the magistrate at the West London's dealt with you tomorrow morning – if you're innocent.'

'Here, listen mister. Be a pal. I can't stick around all that time. I got to get a proper night's rest in. I'm supposed to be fighting at the Albert Hall tomorrow night.'

'Who're you supposed to be?'

'Ain't you heard of me, mister? I'm Tommy Mutch, the fighter. I'm supposed to be having a go in a six-round preliminary tomorrow night and that's stone ginger. You can go back to that caff and arst them if you don't believe me. What's more they'll identify me there. It ain't likely I'd be out on the knock-off tonight, is it now?'

'Maybe it isn't likely all right, but all you blokes are screwy anyway. Come on, we'll go down Ladbroke Grove to the station.'

'Just a minute, guv'nor. My manager's got a bit of influence. Sammy Sanders. He won't half kick up a shine. I suppose I'll be able to get him on the blower and get him to bail me?'

'You'll be allowed to communicate with your friends – if you want to. An officer will be sent down to any address. Come on now.'

The detective caught Tommy by the arm. They started to walk down in the direction of Notting Hill Police Station. Tommy was silent. He had a reason to be silent. There seemed to be no way of talking this guy out of things. He certainly seemed to be one hard nut to crack. It was the detective who broke the silence.

'So you're supposed to be a fighter?'

'Yes, guv'nor. That's right.'

'Well, if you're such a tough guy, whyn't you try and cut and run for it?'

'What's the difference? You got my name. You'll be able to come around and lift me any time you feel like it. I'd only be making it all the worse for my bleeding self if I started anything.'

'You're right there son. It's a long walk over the hill down to the station.'

'It certainly is.'

'Maybe we're wasting time going there.'

'Maybe we are, but it's your time you're wasting, guv'nor, as well as mine.'

'Look here, son. It looks like you're on the level. Beat it. But don't let me catch you hanging around no more.'

The detective let go of Tommy's arm. Tommy stood for a moment, looking at him. Suddenly, he realised he was free to go.

'Thanks, guv'nor. You're a sport. Good luck to you.'

He turned quickly to the right. It was a whole lot longer than an hour since he had been at the old woman's place. Else must be through by now. He walked along as rapidly as he could, without looking as though he were hurrying. It would be a silly thing to do to get knocked off again.

He did not have to wait long at the Clarendon Road house this time before the old lady opened the door to him.

'Taken your time, haven't you?' she grumbled. 'The young tart's ready and waiting for you. Come on, girlie.'

Elsie came to the door. She looked pale and kind of shaky. There were circles under her eyes.

'Don't forget what I told you, me dear,' said the old lady. 'And drop round again tomorrow night. G'night, me dear.'

Elsie stepped out into the street. The old lady closed the door. Elsie took Tommy's arm.

'Ow, Tom,' she said.

'Was it as bad as all that?' he asked.

'Worse.'

He pressed her arm against his body. A current of sympathy passed from one to the other. They were just a couple of kids from the slums. A few years back they had been playing hopscotch on the chalked pavements, and collecting pennies for the Guy, starting halfway in October. It was a hell of a life whichever way you looked at it.

CHAPTER XXV

The Albert Hall was a funny place to be fighting in. Even if you were only a six-round preliminary boy, it was a funny enough place. It was a Percy Naylor promotion and that certainly meant something. Yes, it meant among other things that prices were sky-high. And if prices were sky-high, what happened? The gallery boys weren't there, and the blokes who usually sat in the ringside seats at the local hall were sitting up in the gods and the ringside seats were filled with geezers in evening clothes and a whole lot of flash janes. All that put quite a fresh complexion on everything. It meant that the real wide boys were sitting too far away to be seeing the finer points of the game and it meant that those who could see the finer points of the game from where they were sitting didn't give a damn for them. It meant you had got to show action and plenty of it. Yes, it was a Percy Naylor promotion.

Tommy was fighting on a Percy Naylor promotion. He was fighting under the management of Sammy Sanders and he knew what that meant. Yes, Tommy had finally got around to being wide-oh. Tommy had been a mug long enough. He was wised up now. Why, he even knew who was going to win. As he walked through the crowd from his dressing-room to the ring, shouldering his way along the uninterested aisle he knew he was going to win. Before he had always hoped he was going to win. If Harry had kidded him enough he had been sure he was going to win. Tonight, he knew. It was in the bag.

Harry walked along behind him. He was carrying a bucket, a bottle and a sponge. There were a couple of towels slung over his shoulder. He was wearing a clean white sweater. The spectators were clapping. Not everybody had come in yet. You didn't come in early when you paid a couple or more guineas for a seat. It was the boys who paid nine-pence at a local hall who came in early. Try to prise them loose from a single round of boxing and see what happened. It was a lot different when you had paid big money.

Particularly if you had brought along a dame with powdered, naked shoulders. You had to buy her a big dinner first and she didn't want to leave it for a couple of punch-drunk kids fighting a fixed six-rounder. She wanted to see sparks fly. That was the way it went – feed her well, take her along and show her a couple of real men knocking the hell out of each other and then, oh boy, was she good when you tumbled her?

They were clapping a little as Harry and Tommy went along to the ring. They always clapped to show that they were true British sportsmen. Of course, they had to turn to each other and explain a little shamefacedly why they were clapping.

'Often put up a rattling good show these preliminary boys, don't you know?'

'Yes, real clean fighting. Proper toe-to-toe hitting. None of this hugging you see in the big fights so often nowadays.'

'Yes, and there's one satisfaction. You know it's straight. There's no fixing of these small bouts. Both boys are always out to win.'

They were clapping a little. Not too hard, though, because these clean preliminary fights, with both boys out to win, were not so exciting. Besides, nobody ever betted very heavily on them. It was when you betted heavily that you really cheered a clean, straight boy.

Harry held up the ropes and Tommy climbed through. Harry climbed through after him. He was getting a bit stiff. Tommy was glad he had brought a flash dressing-gown. There were a lot of janes in the crowd. His hair was plastered flat with brilliantine.

The other boy was coming through the crowd. The crowd was clapping him. He was another clean, straight boy out to win. He had worked in a pit down in South Wales till he lost his job. Now, he lived in Kilburn and did odd jobs. Sammy had given him twenty-five shillings to throw the fight. He climbed through the ropes.

The referee called them to the centre of the ring and gave them the usual instructions. Tommy did not listen. There was no need for those usual instructions. He knew he was going to win.

There was clean white canvas on the boards. The ring posts were freshly padded and the ropes a glistening white. There were no bloodstains. Patrons of a Percy Naylor promotion did not like to see bloodstains about the ring before the fights started.

The boys went to their corners. The MC came into the ring for a couple of minutes and introduced them. He did not take long. These fights had to go off to a scheduled timetable. The main event was to be broadcast. Percy Naylor and the BBC were like two sticks.

The MC got out of the ring. The first gong sounded. The seconds left the ring. Tommy was not feeling his customary excitement. He knew he was going to win. He was not frightened. He was not elated. He was just earning himself some money.

The second gong sounded.

The next sound was a slither of boxing boots on the clean canvas as the two straight boys advanced towards each other. They touched each other's gloves in simulated handshake, a token to all patrons that it was a clean fight and they were both out to win. Tommy stepped back. The Welsh boy followed him up. Tommy's guard was low. There was no sense in tiring his arms unnecessarily. He was going to win this fight. Suddenly his head was jerked back. He had taken a nasty left to the chin. His guard came up automatically. He felt the right hand hit him hard on the ribs. He sidestepped.

Hi! What was going on? Of all the carve-ups. This fight was supposed to be fixed. The Welshman was on him again. He sidestepped once more. Once more his opponent followed him up. They were chasing each other round the ring. The crowd was getting restive. This was not the way that clean, straight boys were expected to behave. It was as bad as a heavyweight title contest.

The Welshman came in close. He hit Tommy three times downstairs. Tommy lost his temper. The dirty double-crosser. He'd show him. His blood was up.

His opponent's head was low. Tommy jabbed at it with his, purposely missing, and equally purposely drawing the back of his glove across the other's eyes. As the Welshman tried to jerk his head back out of Tommy's reach, he found himself uppercut on the chin. His head was knocked sideways. Tommy caught him in the eye with the heel of his left glove.

The Welshman ducked into a clinch, his head low, his arms round Tommy's waist. He was, he knew, quite invulnerable as long as the referee allowed him to remain in that position. The fight was now quite up to the Albert Hall traditions.

The referee called out to them to break. Tommy wrestled himself free. His opponent straightened up. For a second they feinted and weaved, then both jumped in. Tommy's left fist caught the other boy downstairs, and bringing up his left shoulder he gave him a nasty one on the eyebrow. The Welshman hit him four or five times hard on the ribs. Tommy went into a clinch, getting his left fist caught up under his opponent's right shoulder.

'Break!'

The referee was again taking a hand.

The Welshman tried to push Tommy clear, but the fist under his shoulder brought him off his balance. Tommy hooked him hard over the left eye. This was the third time he had taken punishment there. A little trickle of blood appeared. The gong went.

Harry was mad. When Tommy was back in his corner the elder man stormed at him like a pickpocket.

'Gor blimey can't you do no better than that? Fust you let him chase you all round the ring like you was a couple of schoolkids playing "last across" and then you bring off every kind of dirty trick you know. Stone me blind if I'd 've known you was wanting to 've carried on like this I'd 've taught you a couple or so more but I thought as how you was supposed to be going on fer being a boxer. Caw I don't know what's come over you, straight I don't. 'Ere, whyn't you try kicking him next round?'

Sammy had a word to say. He took his cigar from his lips.

'Here you, Tommy,' he said, 'you're supposed to be winning this fight, see? Winning, understand? If you carry on this way you'll never get another fight on a Percy Naylor promotion. Action, fire, life, colour, and clean sport, that's what the public want to see. Go in now and give it to them. I've sunk a lot of lovely money in you and I want to get it back.'

'Have a go at that left eye of his, Tom,' advised Harry. 'You had it opened up at the end of last round. Open it up again and you'll get through.'

He whipped away the stool as the gong went. The two boys shaped up to each other. There was no necessity for the mockery of a handshake this round. Both boys had got the needle. The Welshman did not like losing to a man he felt he could beat. He did not enjoy being fouled. It was a Percy Naylor promotion.

The Welshman feinted with his left, Tommy's head moved to his left. At the same time he brought his fist out smartly to the other's ribs. The Welshman blocked it. Tommy crowded in and tried to rush him off his feet, but he would give no ground.

For almost half a minute they stood there, swapping punches. Both had their rag out, both hit each other about the head with a fine disregard for the rule that says blows should be delivered with the knuckle part of the glove only. Tommy was trying desperately to get at his opponent's left eye. The spectators were cheering ecstatically. This was just the kind of fight they enjoyed watching and just the kind they expected to see put up by a couple of clean, straight, preliminary boys.

At last a right swing of Tommy's missed badly. The other jumped in, hit him three times in the face and once in the stomach. Tommy had to give ground. He was dizzy. The Welshman came after him. Tommy sidestepped in order to avoid being crowded on to the ropes. The Welshman hit him again just above the jaw. An angry flush sprang out on Tommy's cheekbone. Tommy tried to cover up.

His mind was in a whirl. If his opponent was being paid to throw this fight, he was concealing it very cleverly. He could feel the other's gloves thudding about his protecting arms. He had to do something quickly. If he could think what to do, it would be easier. How could a man think when someone else was pounding away at him? He'd bet a pound that that cowson Arthur was watching, too. Maybe Dot and all.

He shook his head trying to get it clear.

The precious seconds of the round were slipping away. Unless he got in soon and hit the other bloke hard about his eye it would probably be too late. It would be difficult to hit him hard enough later on.

The thudding of the Welshman's gloves on his forearms ceased. Tommy opened up and, with his head down, came forward. He hit his opponent twice in the stomach and then something caught him on the chin. It was a right uppercut.

For a flash it hurt him more than anything had ever hurt him before. There were two distinct areas of pain: his chin and the base of his skull. He stumbled and fell. The canvas was gritty against his cheek. Far away, like the tide coming in on Brighton beach, he could hear the crowd roaring. He was being counted out.

'One!'

It was pretty nice lying here. It was like being in some kind of a hole. Nobody could hit you. It was like when you were a little spiv and people turned nasty with you and you wanted to …

'Two!'

… talk to your mother and ask her was it all right. It was a pity they made this canvas so damned gritty. It didn't give you a chance to rest. The base of his skull hurt like hell.

'Three!'

Sleep was coming over him in great waves. It was nice, but he had to fight it off. Down it came, down and round and then down.

'Four!'

He drew up his knees. He put his palms on the canvas. It was still thudding down on him. Sleep, the Welshman's gloves, the old lady in Clarendon Road, the red-faced copper, Dot was on the batter, Arthur was a ponce.

'Five!'

He struggled. He was on his hands and knees. He shook his head. It was clearing. He was going to win this fight. It had been fixed that way. It was a Percy Naylor promotion.

'Six!'

He fought off the sleep. His head was clearing. Four more seconds and he would be fighting again. Money. That's what it was. All money. Money-spinning game the fight racket. Swell idea if you didn't have to do the fighting yourself.

'Seven!'

One more second and he would get up. He could see the Welshman leaning against the ropes. He was a clever boy and packed a wallop. There could not be much of this round left. If this was what it meant to fight a contest you were fixed to win he would hate like hell to be tangled up in one he had to throw. That came next Sunday.

'Eight!'

Slowly he climbed to his feet. The Welshman rushed him. Tommy blocked a left-hander and ducked a right. The Welshman swung again. Tommy ducked again. Ducking didn't do his spinning head much good. How much longer was this round going to last?

The Welshman jabbed him viciously with a couple of lefts. Tommy felt himself slipping. He managed to clamber into a clinch. The referee called to them to break. Tommy could feel the other bloke trying to push him away.

The gong went.

He flopped back to his corner.

Before Harry could start work on him Sammy had to put his oar in.

'Gor blimey, what's a matter with you? Gawd stone me dead. You're supposed to be winning this fight. Winning it, d'you hear? Crimey, you know what you look like? Just like a cripple with paralysis. You're letting that there kid knock the daylight out of you. I ought to have known better. Taking up with a piece of cheese like you. I want my brains tested. That's what I want.'

He paused for lack of breath. Harry was at work on Tommy's face.

'Want me to throw the towel in, kid?' he asked.

Tommy shook his aching head. He had to go through with it. The precious minute slipped past. The gong went. The second gong went. He had to go out and face it again.

He was in the middle of the ring. The Welshman feinted and Tommy slipped into a clinch. He could feel the warm flesh of his opponent's body against him. He could smell his hot breath. The Welshman was whispering in his ear.

'All right, kid. I've had a go. I'll let you take me. Give me a couple of good 'uns and I'll take a dive.'

Tommy pushed the other clear, and rushed in with a straight left. The Welshman's sidestep was a fraction too slow. He took a nasty one on the clock that put him off his balance. Tommy was in. He was battering at the other boy's gate. He saw him slip to the floor beneath his relentless fists.

CHAPTER XXVI

Tommy sat in the dressing-room, holding his head in the palm of his hands. There was no doubt about it. He had been given a proper pasting. The guy had let him have it no mistake.

He was sitting on a bench, wearing trousers and socks. His shoes were unlaced, his torso bare. Harry had been working over him, but still he felt bad.

'Not feeling right, yet?' asked Harry.

'Feeling right? Blimey, that's a stroke to be coming out with. I feel like hell right now.'

The door swung open; the Welsh boy came in. Harry turned on him.

'What you want?'

Dressed, the Welsh boy looked even bulkier than he had stripped. He was wearing a loudly-striped suit, a shirt with a loose low collar and a black-and-white-striped tie. His shoes were brown with bits of black patent leather let into them. On his head was a cap of grey, so pale it was almost white.

'What's that to you, old 'un?' His voice had a rising pitch. 'I want to chat to Tommy here.'

Tommy looked up.

'What's a matter, mate?'

'Nothing's the matter at all. I was going to say would you like to come up to the West End with me and celebrate your victory? There's not much sense in staying to watch the other fights. You won't learn nothing from them.'

'He's going home,' said Harry. 'Can't you see he's not feeling right. A good lay-down's what he needs.'

'Don't come sticking your oar in,' said Tommy irritably.

'Well, are you coming, pal?' asked the Welsh boy.

'Don't forget you're fighting Sunday,' said Harry. 'You want another rest before then.'

'Aw, what does that matter? It will do him good to get out, enjoying himself.'

'Yerce, a bit of fun won't do me no harm. You know that I'm getting kind of stale.'

Harry stood up. He opened his hands in a gesture of despair.

'I don't know what's come over you, Tom. You don't seem to be doing yourself no good. Ain't you interested in what you're doing no more? Gawd strike a light, you was just getting ahead nicely in the fight game and you go on as if you was wanting to sling it all in …'

The Welsh boy took a couple of paces farther into the dressing-room. He was now standing in the centre of the floor.

'Are you going to listen to this all night, Tom boy?' he asked. 'Leave this old woman alone and come on out and have some fun.'

'Here. Gimme me shirt.'

Absently Harry handed it to him. Tommy drew it over his head. He walked over to the mirror. Both Harry and the Welsh boy followed him with their eyes. Tommy fixed his collar and tied his tie. Harry spoke. His voice sounded quite uninterested. He was just asking a question.

'You going out, Tom?'

Without turning round, Tommy nodded. The two pairs of eyes were still watching him.

'That's the boy.'

The Welshman handed him his jacket and waistcoat. Tommy put them on. Harry sat down again. Tommy walked across the room, took his overcoat from a peg, put it on, and carrying his hat in his hand walked back to the mirror. He carefully adjusted his hat on the side of his head and knotted his spotted scarf. He had plenty to do to compete with the Welsh boy's flashiness. Ready. He gave a glance to Harry.

'Ah well, so long. Be seeing you tomorrow.'

'Yerce. S'pose so.'

The door swung open: Sammy came in. He took in the three of them with a glance.

'Going, Tom lad?'

'He is coming out with me up West,' said the Welsh boy.

'That's right. Enjoy yourself while you're young. Splendid fight tonight. They ate it up. That's what the public likes, just what they likes. Plenty of fireworks. I'll see if I can't fix up a return for you two boys. The promoters ought to jump at it.'

Tommy moved to the door. He neither looked at Sammy nor answered him. His head was hurting: he felt resentful. The Welsh boy looked around, shrugged his shoulders and followed Tommy. Sammy took his cigar out of his mouth. He did not quite understand what was going on. After all he had given everybody a square deal. If there had been any carve-ups, well it wasn't his fault, and now everyone looked at him like he was some kind of a bastard. It just showed you. With heavy and forced geniality, he spoke.

'Have a good time while you're up in the old jacket and vest, but leave the Sir Berkeley alone. Won't do you no good.'

The door swung to behind the two boys.

The Welsh boy turned to Tommy in the passage.

'Is that guy your manager?'

'That's right.'

'Looks a twisting kind of a bastard.'

'It ain't only looks, mate. He *is* a twisting kind of a bastard.'

'Come along. Let's get going.'

They left the Albert Hall and crossed over the road. The first bus that came along was a number 73, the next 173, but the third was a number 9. They boarded it before it had halted, each showing off to each other more than a little. They climbed to the upper deck and sat down.

'We might as well ride straight to Piccadilly Circus,' said the Welsh boy.

'Sure,' said Tommy.

The conductor came upstairs. Tommy paid the fares. There were only two other people riding on the top deck. At Hyde Park Corner three more got on. A clock in Piccadilly showed the time to be a quarter to ten. Tommy and the Welsh boy were talking.

'There will be plenty of time,' said the Welsh boy. 'The boozers don't close down till eleven. We can have a mooch round first.'

'Yerce, have a look in at the Sports Garden and all. Nothing like seeing life.'

At the Circus they got off. For a moment they both stood still on the pavement outside Swan & Edgar's. The suppressed excitement of a West End night filled Tommy. Although it was the lull before the theatres broke he was stimulated by the crowd and the lights to forget his aches and pains. The humiliation of only just having scraped home in a crooked fight had slipped his mind altogether.

'Come on,' he said, for the first time dominating the other. 'Don't let's stand around gawping. How about taking a ball of chalk round the Sports Garden?'

'Ay, come on, we might as well.'

They both set off, diagonally, through the traffic of the Circus. Each was equally anxious to impress the other with his own complete sang-froid. Each earned his living as a tough guy.

They went into the Sports Garden with a swagger. Both were flash. Both were prepared. If anyone wanted trouble they were ready to dish it out. That was what they were paid for.

There was no trouble. Just a few punters playing the automatic machines and a few couples riding on the racing cars. There was a smell like a third-rate gaol. Tommy looked at the blokes who had girls with them. It must be, he thought, swell to have a girl of your own. One you could take around with you. A nice blonde would do. One with curly hair, that could sing all the popular tunes and get the other blokes looking and whistling after her. That was the stuff. He wished he was one of those who could crack a joke and knew when to say 'so what' and 'you're telling me'. Reg was the guy for that.

The Welsh boy broke in on his thoughts.

'Come on, let's get out of here. Gives me the jitters does this place.'

They walked up and took a stroll along Coventry Street. There were some right-looking brides outside the Corner House. They swung up into Shaftesbury Avenue.

'What about a wet?'

'Yerce, might's well,' said Tommy.

The Welsh boy pushed open the door of a saloon bar. Tommy hung back diffidently.

'No, mate, don't let's go in there. Let's go into the public.'

'What, ashamed are you to mix with the nobs in the balloon?'

'No,' answered Tommy, who was.

'What then? You are frightened of wasting your money? You want to go in the cheaper bar?'

'No. It ain't that.'

'Well, we're as good as they are. We're men, aren't we? And good men too, if you ask me.'

They went in. Their defensive swagger became more pronounced. Tommy determined to get a suit like his companion's. There was no sense in having a fine pair of shoulders if you would not show them off.

'What are you having, palsy-walsy?'

'Oh just a glass of ale.'

'Don't show your ignorance. You can't get no ale in here. Have you never been in a saloon bar before?'

'Hundreds of times,' lied Tommy. 'I'll take a drop of Scotch.'

Maybe this place was so flash you could not drink beer of any sort.

The Welshman ordered two whiskies. Actually, he would have preferred a glass of bitter, but he saw no sense in ordering Scotch for someone else and a cheaper drink for himself.

They drank up. Tommy bought a drink. The Welsh boy bought another. Tommy bought the fourth. They lingered over that. Both were feeling pretty good. Their talk wandered on to the technicalities of their profession.

'There is not much sense,' said the Welsh boy, 'of boxing straight unless you stand a chance of getting to the championship class. Why are you in boxing at all? Tell me that.'

'To earn dough,' said Tommy.

'Yes, that's the way it comes. Well, look at it this way, man. You have a few fights. You can tell the way it's coming. Maybe you reach the top of the tree. That's fine and dandy. You start earning money. Maybe you won't. You can soon tell. Me and you, Tommy boy. We're both novices. We won't never reach the top, see? You can tell that. We'll both be just good fighters, plodding along. Maybe we'll one day be earning twenty or thirty pound for a fight. We'll never be earning no more ...'

'Yerce, just plodding along. That's right. Plodding along ...' An expression of sagacity came over Tommy's face. He was acting hard to register that he was a real wide boy.

'You see the way it is, man. Why shouldn't we pick up a bit of money, acting crooked? Everybody acts crooked in the fight game. They're all poncing on the fighters, I tell you man. Take me tonight. I gets twenty-five bob for fighting you. They came to me. They say, "Dai boy, you're going to lose this fight. It is worth to you an extra twenty-five bob." Fifty bob that makes. I bet my fifty bob on you. All they give is even money. Still, that's a certain five pound for me, see? I put up a good fight. I let you win. Everybody's satisfied.

Two real game boys fighting, they say. What is nicer than that? Let's see them fight again. You heard what your manager said. They fix a return. I win. The money's on me. Your money, my money. One day we will have saved enough to buy us a nice little boozer apiece.'

'That's right.'

'Too damn true it's right. Let's have a little whisky.'

He ordered two more drinks. He was dry after all that talking. They sank it pretty quick. Tommy ordered two more. The Welshman's voice grew more highly-pitched than ever.

'Come along,' he said. 'Let us get out of here and take a stroll. We might pick up a judy. They like fighters.'

He winked and nudged Tommy.

CHAPTER XXVII

Tommy spluttered and coughed as he followed Dai's example and tried to put his whisky down in one. But a bloke had to show how tough he was and that he knew how to take his liquor – even if he didn't.

They both went out into Shaftesbury Avenue. Tommy felt it was time to assert himself. This Welshman was too cocky by half. After all, London wasn't his town.

'Come on, let's go down this way. Let's have a look at the old brasses down in Lisle Street.'

'Go on, man. What do you want to be bothering your head with them for? They're no good. Just ordinary judies. You come with me along the other side of the Dilly and have a look at the real ones, along Sackville Street and Burlington Gardens.'

They walked down the Avenue and took a short cut through Denman Street.

'Let's have a dekko at the Glasshouse Street girls, while we're here,' said Tommy making one last effort to preserve at least a show of independence.

'Glasshouse Street. Any girls there, are there?'

'Any girls in Glasshouse Street? Gaw blimey, mate. Use your loaf. There's a ton of them.'

'What're they like?'

'Lousy. Still we might's well look 'em over. They're not so well dressed as the janes around Sackville Street and Bond Street, but they're a lot better than the Lisle Street push.'

'Yes? Well come on, man.'

They walked up Glasshouse Street in silence. Although both were excited at the sight of the prostitutes, neither was willing to admit it. Both affected an air of nonchalance. The Welshman began to boast again.

'There's a couple of pushers gets around Baker Street,' he said. 'I'm like this with them.' He held up two fingers close together. 'I'm always all right for a bit from them, whenever I feel like it.'

Tommy laughed. This was like taking toffee apples from a schoolkid.

'Blimey, mate. That's nothing. There's a jane I know hawks her greens in Bond Street. Right flash bramah she is and all. I drop around her flat whenever I want to.'

'Dan, man, you don't say. Will she be out on the bash now?'

Tommy swaggered a little. He wasn't going to let this Welsh bastard know that this was like a knife straight in his heart.

'Yerce, she'll be there all right. Unless of course she's got a client.'

'Do you ponce on her, mate?' There was an added respect in his interlocutor's tone. Tommy turned on him savagely. His annoyance was not altogether feigned.

'Do I look as if I was a ponce? There's a hell of a lot of difference between poncing and having a bit off of a girl, ain't there?'

'All right, man. All right. Keep your shirt on. There's no need to get so wild. Let's go and take a look and see if she's there now.'

'Right.'

They cut across Regent Street and down Vigo Street. At the top of Sackville Street the girls began. Tommy was wishing he was not there. He would hate like hell to see Dot out on the batter. The girls glanced at the two boys and summed them up, for what they were. Two leary kids from the slums taking a look round at goods that were a whole lot too expensive for them. Just by the telephone kiosk in Burlington Gardens

Tommy caught a flash of Dot. He squared his shoulders. She was talking to a bloke. He nudged Dai.

'There she is. That girl there.'

Dai looked. Both boys were wildly excited.

'What are you going to do to the bloke, bash him?'

'How can I do that, dopey? Bloke's probably a steamer. You can't interfere with her. She's got her living to earn same as you and I have.'

'All the same, I wouldn't have no blokes talking to my girl.'

As they drew level, the man, who was well-dressed, raised his hat and walked off.

'Hallo, me old Dot,' said Tom.

'Why, Tommy, what're you doing here?'

'Oh just taking a ball of chalk. This is a friend of mine.'

'Pleased to meet you, lady.'

There was an awkward silence. Dai looked from one to the other. With elephantine tact he touched the peak of his cap.

'Ah well,' he said, 'I'll be moving along. Good night all. Be seeing you, Tommy.'

'Leary-looking bastard,' said Dot. 'Who is he for Christ's sake?'

'Oh, just a fighter,' said Tommy. 'Him and me's bin boxing at the Albert Hall.'

'Oh yes, Arthur was telling me about it. It was fixed for you to win, wasn't it?'

'What you know about that?' said Tommy, sickened.

'Oh, Arthur tells me what's going on. Well, don't stand around here chatting. I got to earn the rent tonight. Take a penn'orth out of it, Tommy boy. You won't do yourself any good hanging around this place. A clean boy like you ought to be in kip.'

All Tommy's resentment, aided by the whisky, flared up.

'Nice clean boy. That's a hot one. Nice clean bloody mug

that's what you mean. Nice clean boy. Yerce, you might of called me that before I got wised up to meself. Stone me blind. Here's me, fighting dirty crooked fights, going with a girl what's on the bash and me not man enough to tell her ponce to clear off, me sister in the pudden club and I go and get an old woman to make her drop her load. Yerce, that's right, nice clean boy.'

'Don't make such a noise, Tommy, you'll get me knocked off.'

'Bloody good job too.'

He stood there, irresolutely.

'Well, if that's the way you feel about it ...'

Dot moved off with a flounce of her buttocks. Tommy followed her up.

''Ere Dot. What we going to do?'

'I know what I'm going to do. I'm going to find a steamer who's got a bit of money to spend on a naughty girl who'll give him a good time, and the sooner you clear to hell out of it the better I'll be pleased.'

'Don't you bloody well talk to me like that.'

'I'll talk to you any bloody way I please. Who the hell are you, anyway? Just a kid from a back street who thinks that because he's brutal enough to let himself be knocked about for money he's an important bloke. You give me a pain.'

'Oh, I give you a pain, do I?'

'Go on. Get out of it. Take a penn'orth. Gimme the sick you do. Let me get on with me bloody job.'

They were standing now at the corner of Bond Street. Tommy stuck one hand in his overcoat pocket. He did not know what to do. He was obstinately determined not to go away. Dot looked at him.

'Go on now, you bleeding little nuisance.'

'I ain't going. I'm entitled to stand here if I want to.'

'You get out of it.'

'No bleeding fear. I ain't going to have you picking up with no fat old steamers.'

Dot looked at him in despair. There seemed to be no getting rid of him. If she did not watch her step, Ginger George or some other lousy flatty would be along in a minute and before she knew where she was, the pair of them would get lifted. Swear your life away, the bastards would if they got half a chance. An idea came to her.

'Got any money on you, Tom?'

'Whaffor? I ain't going to pay you for a bit of under if that's what you mean.'

'No, I mean, have you got enough for a taxi fare?'

'Where to?'

'My flat.'

'What? All the bleeding way to the Olympia? Gaw blimey, let's take a camerer cuss.'

'No, just round the corner. I got some kind of business premises around there, where I lumber my clients.'

'Yerce, I s'pose so.'

'OK. Let's bump this one.'

She hailed a cab. They got in. Dot pulled down the occasional seat in front and put her feet up. Tommy sat forward, gingerly, on the edge of the seat. He was not used to riding around in taxis. Dot, however, was always glad of a chance of resting her legs.

They went round a couple of corners and drew up. They got out. There was nine-pence on the clock.

'Give the bloke a tanner tip, dear,' whispered Dot. 'We girls always like to stand in well with the drivers.'

As Tommy paid off the driver, Dot put her key in the front door. They went up a narrow set of stairs, past two landings to the top floor. Dot opened another door: they went into the hallway of a flat.

'Go along into there, dear.'

Dot pointed towards the front room. Tommy walked in. It

was, he thought, pretty flash. Dot must be making plenty on the batter to have a flat like this, besides the one she lived in.

Actually, of course, she shared it with a couple of other girls.

Dot threw open a door leading into another room. Three blokes were sitting there playing cards. One of them was Arthur. They all looked poncefied bastards.

Arthur half rose from the chair.

'What's up Dot,' he asked, 'bit of trouble?'

'Yeah, this bloke's cutting up nasty.'

The three men left the card-table and walked into the front room. One of them went straight to the door and put his back against it, turning the key in the lock. Arthur, coming forward, recognised Tommy.

'Well, if it's not the punk fighter,' he said. 'Look out, fellows, this kid knows how to handle his bunch of fives. What seems to be the trouble?'

'Little bastard got bothering me in the street, wouldn't leave me alone, so I reckoned the best thing was to bring him here for the boys to take care of.'

'You said it. We'll give him one.'

Tommy made a dash for the door. The bloke who had been guarding it leapt out of the way, the key in his pocket. Tommy rattled at the handle. He knew what was coming to him. He had seen more than one bloke get done round Shepherds Bush.

While his back was still turned to the room, somebody clouted him behind the ear, while another guy kicked his legs from underneath him. As he fell, Tommy got hold of one of them and brought him down with a crash. He kicked him in the face and got up again. Arthur dodged out of the way. Tommy would have liked to have had a go at him, but thought it better to get his back to the door. The man on the floor made a grab at Tommy's ankle, but got his hand trodden on nastily.

Dot was standing over in a corner. Her eyes were glistening. She liked to see somebody get a good kicking.

'Come on, boys,' she called out, 'make it snappy. One of the other girls may be bringing a client back any moment now, and don't bust the bloody joint up.'

The three ponces hung back. None was particularly anxious to come to grips, face to face.

'Come on, you bastards, have a go.'

Tommy's taunt stung them. The three made a concerted rush. He brought his knee up, with the greatest pleasure, in Arthur's groin and swung him a nasty right in the eye. The others closed in on him, pinioning his flailing arms to his sides. He bit one of them hard in the ear and lashed out violently with his feet. Arthur, keeping clear, aimed a blow at his face and knocked his head back. It hit the door with a hell of a crash. Tommy felt his teeth rattle. He brought his knee up in the stomach of one of his captors. He gasped and let go of the kid's right arm. Tommy jabbed his other captor hard over the left eye with an overarm swing, at the same time shaking himself free. He rushed at Arthur with a savage yell. He was on him.

He drove him back with a series of pile-driving lefts and rights to the face. Arthur's guard was like paper. Every time Tommy struck, his fist connected with soft flesh which squelched and spurted blood beneath his hammer blows. Arthur fell to the floor. Tommy jumped on his face and ground an iron-shod heel on his nose. He could feel the bone crack. It was a happy feeling.

Now he was ready for the other two ponces. He'd give them a lesson. The bastards thought they could fight. They'd got another think coming. He sprang forward between them; the blood and mucus on his shoe heel made him slip; he fell to the ground; falling, his hands clutched one of his adversaries, his fingers fastening and twisting round his vitals.

The two lay locked on the floor. Tommy bit the other guy

savagely in the throat. It tasted kind of salt. Dot was sobbing. This was a lovely fight, she'd never seen a better. Arthur was coming to. He was breathing in heavy spurts. His mouth was open and his crushed nostrils quivered with pulped bone and jellified mucus.

Tommy jerked himself free from the recumbent ponce. The third bloke ran into the back room and hid, locking the door behind him. Tommy kicked the ponce on the floor. One boot caught him in the jaw, the other in the abdomen. He grunted, heaved, and lay still.

Arthur could have his undivided attention. Tommy jumped at him and jerked him to his feet. He stood there, blubbering and slobbering. With his left hand clutching the back of Arthur's neck Tommy hit six times hard into the blood-bespattered mask. His knuckles were sore. Arthur's eyes were closed now.

'Stop!' shouted Dot. 'You're killing him.'

'Bleeding good job too. Poncefied son of a bitch. This'll teach him to ponce on girls and fix fights. I'm fighting bloody straight now.'

He let go of Arthur. He slumped to the floor. Tommy kicked him in the face and jumped at Dot. Give her one and all, just for good measure. He sloshed her on the side of the head. She crumpled up.

There was nobody else to clean up. He went, happily, to the door. It was still locked. He burst it open and went downstairs. In the street there was a taxi. He hailed it.

'Drive us to 137 Wilsham Street, mate?' he asked.

The driver looked at Tommy. His hat was gone: his hair was standing on end: his overcoat was nearly off his back: his collar had sprung open: his face and hands were bloody.

'Where the hell's that?'

'Notting Dale.'

'Got any money?'

Tommy showed him a note.

'All right. Hop in.'

In the cab Tommy dozed off. It had been a swell scrap, but after the towsing he had taken in the ring, earlier that evening, he was tired out. He was one mass of pains. He did not wake up till they were in Holland Park Avenue. The driver had opened the door and was shouting at him.

'Which way, mate?'

'Up Penzance Place and bear round Rag Fair.'

Tommy sat forward and watched the familiar turnings. They would all think he had gone nuts or something, coming home in a jam-jar. Still, what the hell.

There was a hell of a crowd in the street still. It looked like there had been a fire or maybe someone had been knocked off. When the coppers came to try to take any of the Notting Dale boys there was always a proper turn-out.

He stopped the cab and paid it off. One of the bystanders, attracted by the sound of the cab, had turned his head.

'Here comes Tommy Mutch now.'

Tommy elbowed his way along to 137. The crowd gave way for him. They were silent. None commented on his appearance.

'What's a matter, fer Christ's sake?' he asked.

An old woman answered him.

'It's your sister.'

'What, our Else, what's a matter wiv her?'

'What's a matter? She's died.'

Tommy ran up the rest of the street and burst into the house. His father, his mother, Ernie, and a stranger were in the kitchen.

'What's a matter, Mum?'

Mrs Mutch threw her apron over her head.

'Ow, Tom.'

She was sobbing bitterly.

CHAPTER XXVIII

Tommy sat in the ring, waiting for the third round to come up. All his money was on the other boy. When he lost he would pull in about seventeen nicker. He was not having to throw the fight. It was pretty simple to lose it. He had been boxing badly.

Everyone was against him. Sammy had heard about the turn-out at Dot's. Harry was mad at him. His shoulders and body ached from the belting he had had. Else was dead. There was going to be an inquest. He might get knocked off.

The gong went. He moved like an automaton towards the centre of the ring.

'Come on, let's see a fight this bloody time.'

It was a bum fight and the patrons were certainly not getting their money's worth. For a top-liner it was terrible. Frankie Franks kept on trying to bore in, but Tommy always kept him off till the Dagenham boy was in a fury. A straight left would send him back on his heels, or if he tried to come in, head down and arms flailing, he found that a stinging right uppercut stopped his rush. Full of their Sunday dinners, the spectators were in a mood to be entertained.

Entertainment was lacking. They grew vocal. Franks feinted, shifted his feet, and tried to come in once more. Tommy sent him back with a crash and then failed to follow up.

'Come on, come on, have a go!'

Frankie Franks tried again. Tommy's left drove him back. He tried to duck under the guard and was caught on the side of his head with a right. Tommy stood off and let him recover. He was facing Harry and could see the signals that were being made at him.

Yes, maybe, that was best. Jump in, make a fight for it for the end of the round and then foul Franks. That would put a stop to this bloody misery anyway.

He dropped his guard a fraction. Like a flash Franks led with his left, straight into the trap. Tommy caught him with a hard right-hander and then followed up. Left, right, left, right. He slammed Franks round the ring.

The spectators cheered. They thought their encouragement had started this battle.

Franks retreated. He was up against the ropes. Now was Tommy's chance. A few hard ones, and then one just a little too far downstairs.

Franks had covered up. Tommy banged him about the ribs until he had to protect his body. Into the gap Tommy thrust his left.

Franks' head jerked sideways. The ropes were supporting him. Tommy's boxing blood was up. The other kid was in a tangle. He was a helpless victim. For a change it was not Tommy who was the victim. Everything was right instead of wrong.

He drove his fist hard in Franks' stomach. The Dagenham boy's head came down. There was only one thing to do. Tommy did it. He brought his right fist up in an uppercut. The arc was short. There was a neat click.

Franks slipped to his knees. One hand held the ropes. Tommy went back into the corner. The count was on. One by one Franks' fingers relaxed. At three he had let go of the ropes. At four he was on his face. At eight he was on his knees again, shaking his head and struggling to gain his feet. At the tenth second, he was still struggling. He had been counted out. The referee ran lightly across the ring and held up Tommy's arm.

'The winner!' he yelled.

There was a storm of cheering. Tommy hung his head.

Winner me arm. Seventeen nicker had gone down the drain.

THERE MUST BE JUSTICE

The following three articles by James Curtis
appeared in *The Spectator* magazine
in the months leading up to the release of
There Ain't No Justice.

THE DOOM OF THE COSTER

The shocking proposal to close the Caledonian Market and erect blocks of flats in its place is being bitterly received in all the poorer quarters of London. It is just another example of a tendency which is growing too pronounced, and which may result in the final extinction of that typical Londoner – the stall-merchant.

Modern conditions make it increasingly difficult for a man to earn a living; unskilled labour will soon find its only outlet in illegal transactions of some sort or another. It almost seems as if the various authorities that control the London of today have decided to get together and make things as difficult as they can for those who, with no trade at their fingers' ends, have found a livelihood as street-traders and barrow-merchants.

The first blow fell, of course, when Rag Fair was closed down: Rag Fair, Notting Dale, had been, for the past eighty years at any rate, the outlet for all the waste-paper and rag-and-bone trade in London. Many fortunes have been founded in Notting Dale, and a humble barrow has been the basis of not a few flourishing businesses. Certain abuses had no doubt grown up, and the houses of the adjoining streets had fallen into a grotesque state of disrepair while their inhabitants had earned a lurid reputation as roughs and toughs. Bangor Street had won a name for ferocity only equalled by that of Nile Street, Hoxton, and so the LCC and the Royal Borough Of Kensington made, several years back, a concerted drive on the market. The occupants put up a fight for it, but authority won. The stalls have all gone and the goods are sold today from the doorsteps instead. Rag

Fair is but a shadow of its former self, and the 'totting' trade has received a staggering blow. Business is increasingly passing into the hands of big firms; the small barrow-merchant, calling from house to house, seems to be doomed.

All over London the same thing has been going on. Little street-markets have been closed down, and sometimes, as at Fulham and Euston, enormous market-halls have been built in their place. The result is, of course, that trade is cut in half, for who would bother to go into one of these gloomy, echoing, cavernous vaults when the bright lights and breezy back-chat of the streets are open to them? In some places the markets have vanished and not even a covered hall has been built to replace them. Bad though the halls are, they at least provide a locale where the trader is allowed to work in peace.

The street-trader proper, the costermonger, has been finding that each year makes his lot a little harder than before. Regulations get more and more severe. An appreciable proportion of his exiguous profits have to go towards paying fines for 'obstruction', and the police are becoming progressively stricter in their interpretation of the word. A technique has, therefore, been developed by which a man can serve from a barrow which his mate is still pushing. Stories are told of a man appearing three times in the same day – paying a fine, going out to earn some money to replace it, and being promptly rearrested. Each appearance was due to the same alleged offence – obstruction – and the penalties were strictly in accordance with the laws of geometrical progression. The usual amount of the fine varies, and has been known to swallow up a month's profits.

The recent edict from the Ministry Of Transport closes to the costermonger all the principal West End streets – naturally his most profitable selling centre. Ostensibly this is merely a step towards the straightening out of London's practically inextricable traffic tangle, but in many a humble home it is a ukase received with consternation, mingled with bitterness and suspicion. It would almost seem – as is the very prevalent belief – that the authorities, both national and local, are anxious to drive street-traders out of business altogether in favour of the larger stores in which their members are often directly or indirectly interested. However this may be, that is the effect their actions have.

For the banned, selling balloons or toys in the gutter is the only alternative. That may sound feasible enough, but all the best pitches have long ago been annexed, and it is a hard experience to change from being a small, independent trader into something very similar to a beggar.

Most street-traders, in fact practically all, have been brought up in the street-trading tradition. Their fathers and elder brothers have either pushed barrows or sold from stalls. Everybody in their district has made his living that way from time immemorial. So a coster or a 'totter' has never bothered to learn a trade. Increasing supervision and interference have already made him regard the policeman as his enemy. He considers he is not getting a square deal and has a grudge against authority. He has an active brain and a traditionally nimble wit; it will be small wonder if wholesale recruiting into the army of crime does take place.

The Islington Borough Council, the LCC and the whole body politic would have far more reason to be proud of themselves if, instead of closing down Caledonian Market, which amuses the bourgeois as much as it benefits humbler citizens, they pulled down the neighbouring gaol at Pentonville and built their flats on that site. Better housing and ample facilities for a poor, but enterprising, man to earn an honest living are signs of a healthy social system – which will make the reduction of London's prison accommodation perfectly practical.

October 1st, 1936

THE CRIME CALENDAR

Nowadays, evenings are dark: the flat-racing season is over and the crooks are getting ready for their winter's work. They are prospecting houses in Hampstead, planning out the way to climb into Belgravia's mansions from some quiet mews, and buying their tools from barrows and stalls in markets where no questions are asked and faces easily forgotten.

Every year the crime calendar runs the same course. Even the police would agree that April and the opening of the flat-racing season invariably sees a drop of about a third in the weekly total of jobs done, and that November and the Manchester Handicap herald a corresponding rise. Now that the number of nights on which dog racing is permissible has been restricted, more and more of the boys will be thumbing the catches of their electric torches and wondering.

Summertime is, of course, easy going. The better-class crook either manages to spend the season holiday-making on the profits he earned during the months when night fell early or else goes to work in some capacity for a bookmaker. For the confidence man summer is harvest time. To London come the visitors with money to spend and with time on their hands. The task for the crook is to get the money and none of the time, and so back from continental resorts and transatlantic liners come the tricksters, trotting out the same old gags, dropping the same rosaries, flashing the same Bank Of Engraving notes. Every year they reap their unfailing harvest. The cheaper kind of crook, however, has but lean pickings. He keeps alive by stealing from unattended motorcars, by playing tricks on unsuspecting shopkeepers and householders in the suburbs, or even has to get a job of sorts and go straight.

During August, naturally, money can be picked up in various ways. It is not for nothing that the month has been called the 'silly season'. A petty crook will find it easy enough to swindle seaside landladies out of small sums: 'professionals' of a higher class can pick up appreciable amounts from hotels and their visitors, and even the unfortunate man who finds it difficult to get away from town can still turn a dishonest penny. Householders, going on their holidays, may perhaps have been wise and put their valuables in a bank or safe deposit. Still, they usually leave their electric-light fittings and the linen and blankets on their beds, all of which can be sold for money that helps to keep the pot boiling. But with the fall in the price of base metals, it is no longer profitable to steal brass taps from bathrooms and lead pipes and gutters from roofs; thus the world depression helps to make life hard for businessman and criminal alike.

Fogs, of course, bring good thieving weather. During December, with strange and unaccustomed alacrity, artists of the profession leap from their beds in Notting Dale, round Nile Street, Hoxton, and the Elephant And Castle. The sky is clear, or maybe it is going to drizzle. Back to bed they will go, for there is no sense in standing around the cold, empty streets or sitting about in cafés. If fog or mist is hanging about they are up like larks. Work is to be done, and good pickings are for the bold and fleet of foot. Scotland Yard is inquisitive enough to keep statistics about most ways of dodging work, so it probably has figures dealing with the number of jewellers' shop windows broken, the number of parcels lifted from the back of delivery vans, and the larcenies in general that take place in December and November fogs. Their total must be pretty considerable.

An election night, when everybody is out, is a burglar's paradise. It seems a great pity that the Quinquennial Act and durability of British governments should combine to make this such a rare event. In compensation, however, a charitable lady of title gives a servants' ball at the Albert Hall every winter. Mayfair and Belgravia, with no one to cook their dinner and no one to serve it, have to dine out, and when they dine out the burglar takes occasion to drop in.

Christmas, with its share-out clubs, brings crime of all sorts. The defaulting secretary manages to get away with the funds. A good thief should have nothing but contempt for him, since he is only an amateur, suffers remorse and is nearly always caught. But then, at this season, practically everybody has some money at home, and the lesser house-breakers, who dare not face a climb up a stack pipe or the burglar alarms of a millionaire's mansion, will find it quite simple to break in and loot the little homes in badly-lighted, under-patrolled back streets.

Somehow, indeed, Christmas seems to be the peak. Although January and February are just as dark as December and November, out-and-out burglary begins then to yield pride of place to shop- and warehouse-breaking. A few desperate characters do go 'drumming' in the suburbs, ringing front-door bells and effecting an entrance if there is no answer; but this is a practice disapproved in the best circles. The rewards are usually small and the risks disproportionately great. The big houses of the West End and the isolated mansions of the country seem, after Christmas, to become relatively immune.

So the year goes on, till the Lincolnshire and lighter evenings drive the housebreaker out of business and put the trickster to work in his place.

One day will arise a genius, the 'Mastermind Of Crime', fit to be ranked with crooks of fiction like Professor Moriarty, Arsène Lupin and Jimmy Valentine. Like every genius, he will be just a trifle eccentric, and so will startle the world – and baffle the Yard – by doing everything the wrong way round, by burgling country houses in June and robbing

232

seaside hotels in February. Until that day criminals will stick to their own humdrum round and have a code quite as rigid as that of the sportsman or hunter with regard to what is, and what is not, in season.

December 4th, 1936

CRIME AND CLASSIFICATION

Classification, so the experts tell us, will solve the intricate problem of how to reform our prisons and, incidentally, our prisoners. Sex, naturally, must be separated from sex, and hardened sinner from youthful first offender. And so, different types of imprisonment are arranged all over the country. At Wormwood Scrubs the criminal whose sins have been found out only once is given a chance of expiation under conditions far less rigorous than those which are in vogue at Pentonville. Penal stations at Maidstone, Chelmsford, Parkhurst and Dartmoor have, each of them, differing regulations for treating long-term convicts with varying degrees of severity and of experiment. 'Stars', 'spots', 'stripes', first offenders, special class, intermediate class, recidivist, juvenile adult, young prisoner, lodger – the terms multiply until Bill Sikes himself begins to wonder what he is and how the authorities will decorate his arm. Borstal institutes rightly exist in such numbers that the young criminal can be dealt with in the way most suitable to his upbringing, environment and acquired characteristics. Yet an impartial observer is forced to ask himself whether in spite of it all the problem is tackled at the right end.

In the last century it was left to the courts to say roughly to what sort of prison a convicted man should be sent. In modern times it has been found very much better to reserve the task of classification and allocation to the prison authorities, who have far more knowledge of each individual and of the opportunities of each establishment than can be expected from the court, which only sees the offender in the dock and never sees the establishment. It might be expected, therefore, that the prison commissioners would lavish a little more care and devote a little more of their classifying energy than they do to the unconvicted prisoner. Their reports contain, it is true, interesting tables of figures giving the total number of men – presumed by the theory of English law to be innocent – who waited trial in the many local prisons up and down the country and were subsequently found to be guiltless of any crime. But no figures can tell us the total number of innocent men who, remanded in custody and subsequently acquitted, have had their mentality and outlook on life warped by contact with ruffians and scoundrels of all types. Yet a little more of that panacea – classification – might have saved them.

Brixton Gaol is the only prison in the whole of England specially reserved for adults awaiting trial. Even there, debtors and a few convicted men, who carry on the essential housekeeping tasks of prison life, help to complicate matters. Still, an effort is made for the establishment to fulfil the purpose for which it is intended. Debtors are kept separate from remand prisoners and convicted men from both. There is a hall set apart for the cells of those men who have never previously been in the hands of the police. But that is all. No attempt is made by doctor or psychologist to probe into the wretched man's past, unless the court has called for a special medical report. Prisoners may be kept there any time up to six weeks or two months, a fact which, it might have been supposed, would have provided an excellent opportunity for something of this sort. A confidential report could easily be made on the mentality, past life and future prospects of everyone charged with indictable crime, and this report should lie on the judge's or magistrate's table at the subsequent trial. After conviction efforts are frequently made along these lines, so that it would seem sensible to say that the scientist should be at the disposal of the court as much as of the prison.

Still worse is the lot of the man whose alleged crime has not been committed in the area served by Brixton. A small local prison, such as frowns over many a country town, usually has a mixed bag within its walls. There are convicted men doing short sentences of imprisonment, there are convicts sentenced to penal servitude and doing their 'separates' before going away to a 'lagging centre' or convict station, there are debtors, there are young prisoners and borstal boys awaiting removal to their appropriate establishments, there are remand prisoners, there is frequently even a women's wing. The governor, whose space is limited and whose salary as the ruler of such a small, if miscellaneous community, is proportionately exiguous, cannot be expected to devote much time to the study of his unfortunate charges' warped minds. His chief preoccupations are, naturally, the security of his bolts and bars, the proper discipline of his staff and the prospects of his promotion to a larger prison and increased emoluments. The chaplain and the medical officer are, as a rule, only in part-time employment, and even within the walls have enough to do to heal the spiritual and physical ills of the various classes of convicted prisoners. The wretched remand man practically never has any attention paid to him.

If the country were divided into, say, five large areas and, in each of these areas, one small prison, already existing, were converted into a sort of local Brixton with a resident medical officer, who was also a trained psychologist, the state of affairs would be very different. In the first place the pressure on the other local gaols would be relaxed. The governor and his staff would find administration far easier in the absence of unconvicted prisoners, all with rights and privileges in excess of his other wards. Jealousy, strife and 'trafficking' would without doubt diminish substantially and discipline would be much simpler. Then, in the new remand prisons, the man – innocent or guilty, but awaiting trial – could receive far fairer treatment.

If classification at any cost is such a desirable achievement, a man could be classified by hall, by landing and by cell block even before he received his sentence. Remand prisoners with a long criminal record could be kept on landings far distant from those experiencing their first taste of incarceration. There would be no need for the old man whose first offence was still sub judice to be contaminated by association with the juvenile, but hardened, rascal, just because the crime of neither had been proved to be more than a policeman's guess. And the psychologist, the psychiatrist, even the anthropometrist could, if necessary, ply their trades uninterrupted. Judges and magistrates would find their tasks considerably lightened by the advice of helpful reports, and the man whose folly or bad luck had led his stumbling steps into a criminal career could be more certain that imprisonment was going to be not merely society's retribution, but possibly a means by which he could rehabilitate himself in the eyes of the world.

For, if classification does not lead to the possible reformation of the reclaimable prisoner by means of appropriate punishment, treatment and instruction, it is a valueless piece of extravagance and a waste of time and effort. There is no sense in starting to classify once the work of contamination has been done. The 'slogan', therefore, of the prison service should be: 'Classify him as soon as caught.'

January 15th, 1937

237

LONDON BOOKS

FLYING THE FLAG FOR
FREE-THINKING LITERATURE

www.london-books.co.uk

PLEASE VISIT OUR WEBSITE FOR

- Current and forthcoming books
  - Author and title profiles
    - Events and news
  - Secure on-line bookshop
  - Recommendations and links
- An alternative view of London literature

London Classics